Responsible Revenge

by Amari Amson

Triggers: emotional abuse, physical abuse, killing

Content warnings: frequent swearing, hospitalisation, instances of sexism

ISBN-13: 978-0-6488751-1-6

This book is dedicated to my friends, without whom it would not exist. Thank you for all your support and encouragement over the years, everyone. And yes, I mean *you*.

If you're interested in seeing more of my content, please subscribe to my newsletter emails at http://www.amariamson.com.

You'll get the latest updates on my novels, including preorder/release dates and discounts. You will not ever receive spam, and you can unsubscribe at any time.

Thanks so much for your support!

CHAPTER ONE

Respect

I wouldn't call my life an adventure even on a good day.

Today, unfortunately, is already far from a good day. We're at a board meeting on the thirteenth floor of a nondescript office building in San Francisco. The room is empty of any decorations, any minor hints of perspective or humanity. Even the large windows on the wall only offer a view of another building — not the city skyline, not a park, nothing green or vibrant. Work is the only thing you're supposed to think about when you're in here.

There are six old white men sitting at the conference table, two white women, and a number of people networked in on a video call. I'm standing in the corner near the door, watching. No one's gaze flickers my way. No one is making eye contact with anyone else at the table, largely because of the uncomfortable argument brewing between the CEO and the one person brave enough to challenge his bad ideas.

"There's no reason *not* to," the woman insists.

"No reason!?" the man sitting at the head of the table says before she even finishes her sentence. "*You* might be happy for your salary to drop that low, but I'm here to maximise profits, not to *pander* to *minorities*."

"My mistake," the woman answers, more calmly than I would have. "I meant to say there's no *valid* reason not to."

There's a sharp inhale down the other end of the table, barely perceptible. I watch the man's expression with detached interest as it goes from shock to confusion to anger. Everyone else in the room is tense, waiting for his reaction; for my part, I'm looking for anything, *anything*, that indicates he might be a good person who treats all his employees with respect, someone just having a very bad day. So far, I see nothing.

"Please explain to me," he says,

dangerously quiet, his face working to keep his anger in check, "how giving in to these demands benefits any of us in *any* way."

"Of course," says the woman. "Happy workers make better games, and better games earn us more money."

"And, in the process, we don't meet our deadlines, we don't keep our promises, we waste *more* of that money, and all our customers jump ship to the companies producing content every week."

"It's not a waste of money to pay people what they're worth! If you would just look at —"

"No, I'm done. Does anyone else have an actual realistic idea?"

He dismisses her easily, like she's not even there. If I were a pessimistic person, I'd bet that he'll invent an excuse to fire her before tomorrow. He'll go home at a reasonable hour tonight, too, while the people who work at his company pull the eighth all-nighter they've had in two weeks to try and have a video game released on time, and he'll sleep easily while his employees worry about how they're going to pay next month's bills.

I *am* pessimistic. I'm just not sure I qualify

as a person.

My head is starting to hurt, and I've seen nothing to convince me there's any reason to resist my compulsion this time. I walk toward the conference table and smile at the woman who spoke up, now staring dimly down at her laptop.

"Keep it up," I tell her. "Everything's going to be okay. If you play your cards right, you could even be running this company next week."

She doesn't answer, or give any indication that she heard me. No one ever does. I walk by the back of the man's chair, brush my fingers across his shoulder, and leave the conference room.

There's a swell of panicked shouts behind me as I approach the elevator. I wait until the elevator doors open and a small group of first aid officers pour out, then I slip in behind them and ride the elevator back down to ground level. There's two ambulances and a fire engine there as I walk out onto the street. Honestly, a *fire engine*. A rich white man has a heart attack, and they send in the cavalry. It almost makes me laugh.

Within a few minutes, they're carrying the

man's lifeless body out the front doors and rushing it into the ambulance. I know exactly what's going to happen, but I wander over to the ambulance anyway to listen as they try to resuscitate him. The paramedic uses the paddles once, twice, three times. The man's heart does not miraculously start beating again.

They call it. Time of death, 3:15 pm. No one gives me a second glance as I leave the scene.

~~

I've been waiting for some sort of explanation for as long as I can remember. Every time someone's gaze coincidentally falls on mine, I half-expect time to freeze so they can walk over, introduce themselves, and apologise for not doing so sooner. Like a scene right out of some fantasy coming-of-age movie, where the mentor appears out of nowhere and finally provides the protagonist some answers.

Obviously, that's never happened. I don't know what I am. I've been left to figure it all out completely on my own, and the only conclusion I can come to is that I'm some kind of invisible monster. Or, at the very least, a monumental jackass.

Ten years ago, I woke up in the middle of Times Square in New York City lying flat on my back staring up at searing summer sunshine. I'd never had a drink in my life — or at least, I was pretty damn sure I hadn't — but it felt a little like how people describe waking up with a hangover. I felt heavy. My head didn't feel right. My thoughts didn't want to work. It took me nearly an hour just to sit up, and when I did, I realised I couldn't remember how I got there, and I couldn't remember who I was. A lady pushing a stroller walked right through me, and if you've never experienced what that's like, let me be the first to tell you that I would choose the hangover any day of the week.

I barely remember anything about that time now. I don't remember what I did after I stood up, or how I spent the following weeks. I might have just wandered aimlessly in a haze of confusion. I vaguely remember not understanding how things like credit card transactions worked, but it didn't take long to learn. I also remember getting on a boat, and I remember knowing someone onboard needed to die, and the next thing I knew I was in New Jersey, surrounded by

chaos and news crews and paramedics
because some young famous man had
suffered a fatal heart attack.

I knew that was because of me. I couldn't
touch anything, not tables, not food, not
even walls, but I could touch him. I brushed
him on the shoulder, and twenty minutes
later he was convulsing on the ground.

I don't think I *felt* anything about it, back
then. I didn't feel regret, or remorse, or even
confusion. It was weird, sure, but that was
it, as far as I was concerned. Mostly, I was
just happy to be out of New York, with its
constant crowds and bustle and *noise*
assaulting me from all sides. In comparison,
New Jersey was peaceful. It felt like I could
finally *think* again, and if killing someone
was the price to pay for that, then —
whatever, he probably had it coming.

The news didn't think he had it coming.
There were candlelight vigils, memorials,
tons of people saying it was a huge loss for
the world. I'd *like* to say that was when I
first felt something, but if I remember right,
I think all I felt was annoyance.

It's one guy, I thought. *He did bad things.
The world can **easily** move on without him.*

In those early months, I felt compelled to

follow people I came across in the street, people I didn't know and had never seen before, to make sure they met their untimely end. In those early months, I never once felt the need to resist that compulsion. I knew, in my core, that they all had it coming, even if I couldn't tell you *how* I knew, and that was good enough for me. It was a pretty easy way to live, actually. I could travel wherever I wanted, do and see whatever I wanted, and sometimes I would touch someone on the shoulder, and then I would keep travelling wherever I wanted, doing and seeing whatever I wanted, without a second thought.

For as hazy as those early memories are, though, I can tell you the *exact* date when all that changed and my memory became painfully sharp.

I'd just killed a woman. Not young, but not old, wearing a wedding ring, doing some grocery shopping. I'd followed her into the supermarket, obeying that compulsive pull, and now she lay dead on the tiled floor in the cereal aisle by herself, unnoticed, completely alone.

That's what struck me first, I remember. She was the first person I killed who didn't have crowds of people around her trying to help from the moment she collapsed. She died alone, and scared, with no fanfare and nothing to mark her passing. And that felt *wrong*. She had a wedding ring on. She wasn't supposed to die alone.

It took a good ten minutes for someone to turn down the aisle, freeze, and then run off to get help.

Why? I remember wondering. *What did she do to deserve that?*

And, predictably, nothing answered me. No spirit came down from on high to explain exactly what her sins were. No mysterious knowledge planted itself in my mind. It was just me, and the dead woman, and all her hopes and dreams lying shattered on the floor.

From that moment on, I did three things.

First, I made absolutely sure no one I touched ever died alone. Even when it hurt me, even when their sins were obvious, even when I was certain no one would ever mourn their passing, I always made sure we were in a crowd, somewhere with other people around. I always delayed as long as it took to make sure no one died alone and scared.

Second, I started paying a *lot* more attention to who I was killing, what they were like, how they spoke and how they acted.

Third, I began resisting those compulsions.

It's been ten years since my very first memory, and I've never been able to ignore a compulsion completely. It feels like my head rips itself apart if I resist for too long. But I've trained it, like working out a muscle. I've increased the amount of time I can resist for, both so I can learn more about my victim and what they're like, and out of pure, vindictive spite. The longer I've done this, the more it's felt like something else is controlling my actions and my decisions, and whenever my empathy or compassion is low on the ground, the bitter unfairness of being *controlled* by something is what carries me through the day. If I'm going to choose to kill someone, it better be *me* making that decision.

The company suit in the conference room on the thirteenth floor of the office building felt more like my choice than anything else had in a very long time. I didn't mourn him, and I suspected no one else would either. I

don't have guaranteed access to news —
mostly I rely on people reading magazines,
or newspapers, or turning on a news
channel — but I like to think that woman *did*
take over the company. Wishful thinking,
maybe, but I'll take my happy endings
where I can get them. I've ended too many
stories before they had a chance to be happy.

CHAPTER TWO

Redacted

Five years ago, I tried contacting a psychic.

This went about as well as you might expect. People who advertise, I found out, are usually frauds — or, if not frauds, then just as incapable of perceiving *me* as everyone else. People who don't advertise are extremely hard to find, and usually a disappointment when I do find them. One elderly lady swore to everyone she knew that she could see and speak to her dead husband, and since she *hated* her late husband, she wanted it to stop. I thought, for a while, that she could see me, because her gaze kept flickering over to wherever I was in the room. But she certainly couldn't

14

hear me, no matter how many times I clapped right in front of her face or how many hours I spent rambling endlessly about whatever topic came to mind, and in the end, I had to give up on her as well.

I'd almost decided it was impossible, until I met Lady Arabetta.

Lady Arabetta is a practising medium who doesn't advertise. She's not in any phone book, and not on any website. She relies entirely on word of mouth, and since she's the real deal, that works out well for her. In spite of her occupation, she's the most down-to-earth person I've ever met, which clashes in weird and interesting ways with her aggressively occult aesthetic and living space. She likes to say she does that on purpose, because she doesn't want to waste her time with sceptical idiots.

I've known her for a few years now, and more than New York City, more than *anywhere*, she feels like home. So, with no new compulsions to follow, I decide to pay her a visit.

One flight across the continental United States, and another flight across the Atlantic Ocean — which came dangerously close to crashing, as I found out while eavesdropping in the cockpit, and not a single passenger on that plane will ever know. Then, one moderately short train ride to Surrey later, I find myself standing outside of Lady Arabetta's modest apartment. Most days, there's a small flea market on the lawn beside her building. Today, they've long since packed up by the time I arrive, and the lawn is bathed in the soft warm glow of a setting sun.

Another advantage of being mostly incorporeal is that I don't get tired, which is really handy for when I need to go *up*. I can't use elevators if no one else is using them, and sometimes not even then, so stairs are my best friend. And when you have to climb over twenty flights, it helps that your legs won't be screaming at you by the time you make it to the top.

Ara's building, fortunately, is only three stories high. In no time at all, I'm approaching her door, and I stand in front of it for a moment staring at the peeling wood. There's a bead curtain just on the other side of it. This side of the door, apart from a plaque with 207 written on it, is bare. Also in dire need of maintenance.

She's not the only one inside her flat. I can

tell because I'm starting to feel that murderous compulsion again, drawing me inside, and I know it's not for her.

I take a deep breath and step through the door. The bead curtain doesn't make a sound. Ara's lobby is empty of people, but unabashedly filled with all the tricks and tools of her trade — crystal balls, broomsticks mounted on the walls, Oriental curtains, framed tarot cards. They're all things she says she knows for a fact don't work. Personally, I've been waiting for the day one of her customers proves her wrong.

I can hear dim voices on the other side of one of the curtained doorways, and my heart sinks. Customers. It's one of Ara's customers. There's nothing else for it, so I step through the curtain, and Ara's muffled voice instantly becomes clear as a bell.

"You understand," she says crisply, "that I can't actually talk to the dead. Wherever your mother is now, I have no idea. She could have turned into a bloody tea cosy for all the difference it makes to me. What I do is take snippets of her from while she was still alive — her emotions, her feelings, her thoughts — and I relay them to you. Whatever they mean belongs to you and you alone."

The woman sitting across from Ara — no, not a woman, a teenager, 15 years old at most — nods. "I understand," she says.

"Good," says Ara. "And *you* -" She glares in my general direction. " — no interrupting. I'll have time for you after this. Now, let's get started."

The girl twists in her chair, but her gaze passes right over me without seeing. "Who are you talking to?" she asks, both excited and nervous.

The boy sitting next to her scoffs.

"*Sam.*"

"What? It's a *trick*. This is the kind of thing they do to —"

He falls silent under the withering glare of Lady Arabetta. "For your information," she says, "and in case you didn't hear it the first time because you're either deaf in one ear or stupid, *I don't talk to the dead*. That there's Roy — that's what I call it. I don't know what it is. It's never told me. It's the only thing I talk to that I can't see, but it's as real as you or me, so show it some damn respect."

Sam doesn't say another word, and despite myself, I can't help laughing.

"Good," says Ara. "Now." She sighs, closes her eyes, and leans back in her armchair.

"Do you need to me to do anything?" the girl asks. "Do we need to hold hands, or...? Should I turn out the lights?"

"Here's what I need you to do," says Ara, eyes still closed. "Shut up. I won't find anything if I'm distracted."

"Oh! Okay."

The girl shuts up. I stay quiet in the corner of the room. Several silent minutes pass during which Ara doesn't move a muscle, and the girl begins shifting impatiently in her chair, pulling her legs up under her. Sam passes the time by staring in my general direction, angry and suspicious.

Then Ara opens her eyes and smiles sadly. "Cancer, huh?"

The girl starts, then nods.

"I'm so sorry, honey." Ara unfolds herself and leans forward. "I couldn't get very much, I'm afraid. That happens sometimes, if it's been a while, or if there aren't all that many feelings by the end. But I'll tell you what I did get. I got some bitterness, which is pretty standard with cancer. Who the hell deserves cancer, right? I got some

melancholy and depression in there. I also
got — and this is the important one — I got
love. So much love. It's hard to explain to
living people, the feeling you get when
you're near the end if you're emotionally
reconciled. It's like… peace. It's like when
you're getting into a hot bath with sore
muscles. It's just pure, gentle, easy peace,
and certainty, and love for you, and love for
your brother. And she had a… knowledge, I
guess. A knowledge of passing time. Things
end, things start, and it's the parts in
between that matter. She knew that. She
wanted you all to go on to live the parts that
matter."

The girl's tearing up, but stubbornly
refusing to let the tears fall. Sam is openly
staring.

"Now, underneath *that*, I got a word, but
that's it, I'm afraid. Just a word."

The girl sniffs and clears her throat.
"What word?"

"Down."

"Down?"

"Down."

"What's that mean?"

"I don't know. I'm the messenger, not the
translator. I thought you'd know, sweetie."

"I don't know anything about *down*."

"I might have misheard. I've been known to do that."

"It — it doesn't mean, like, *hell*, does it?"

Ara scoffs. "No. No such thing as hell. Like I said, it's a piece of what she was thinking when she was alive. *Down*. Your mother ever have a safe, or a secret room, or an agonising riddle she never told you the answer to?"

"I — I don't think so."

Ara shrugs. "Then I'm sorry, but I got nothing. Just that word. Down."

There's silence after that. It's half thoughtful, half depressing. Ara looks completely at home in it, and doesn't make any move to try and break it, but neither do either of the two customers sitting across from her. Not even Sam the sceptic. I want to follow their example, but I'm all too aware of a painful pounding in the back of my head.

Ara grunts and rubs her neck. "Ow."

The girl looks up immediately. "Are you okay?"

"Fine, fine." Ara waves a dismissive hand. "Just a headache. Too much incense, maybe. Who knows."

21

"There's incense?"

Ara hesitates. "Actually, no, not today."

"Do you usually get headaches after —?"

"Now that you mention it, no." Ara looks in my general direction. "Roy? You okay?"

I give her an exasperated look. What am I supposed to do, use smoke signals?

The girl looks nervously over at my corner, following Ara's gaze. Sam stubbornly *doesn't* look at my corner. Instead, he pulls his wallet roughly out of his back pocket, drops a few bills on the table, and pulls the girl to her feet. "Come on, Melanie," he says. "We're going to be late."

"Late? Kim's not expecting us for like an hour."

"I know, but — she might need help setting up."

"She literally hired a —"

"Shit, will you just *listen* to me for once? Let's go, come *on*."

He heads for the door, and Melanie gives Ara a light smile. "Thanks," she says. "And — sorry about Sam, he's…"

"… been through a lot," Ara smoothly finishes the thought. "I had a feeling. It's fine, really. So long as no one's coming at me with a knife, I can handle anything. Don't you worry about me."

Melanie picks up her bag, and it's now or never. Here, where I know Ara will take good care of things, where I know no one's going to have to die alone. Here, where it's warm and safe, out of the light drizzle I can hear starting outside. I step forward and brush Melanie on the shoulder.

Her breathing becomes sharp with pain as soon as she approaches the door. "Sam —"

"What?"

"I can't — stop, wait, *please* —"

Her face is ashen, all the blood drained from it, her legs shaking. Sam reaches for her just as her strength gives out and she falls to the floor like a boneless rag doll.

"*Melanie!*" Sam swears and pulls out his mobile, then swears again and shoves it into his pocket. His eyes snap to Ara. "You have a phone? Call 999!"

Ara vanishes back into her kitchen. I turn and leave the room, leave the flat, leave the *building*, and walk angrily up and down the streets of Surrey.

~~

It's past midnight by the time I've calmed down enough to go back to Ara's flat. Even

23

if I didn't know the way by heart, I would
have known exactly where it is tonight; a
siren is blaring, flashing red and blue lights
of a police car visible against brick walls
before I even turn the corner. I hesitate, then
skirt around the vehicle, go inside, and
climb the stairs.

With my anger gone, all that's left is a
growing sense of fearful dread. I didn't even
try to resist the compulsion. I know my
justification in the moment — it's always
more important that someone die where
they're not alone and they'll have all the help
they need. That may even be valid. But all I
can think about right now is that Ara knows
exactly what happened and she knows to be
afraid of me and I've lost my only friend in
the world because I didn't bother to take the
time to *think*.

Part of me wants to turn and run and
never look back, but the idea of how
crushingly lonely that would be keeps me
walking until I reach Ara's door.

"Look," I hear Ara say explosively as I
step through. "I don't know why you're even
here. What is this, terrorise the black lady?
She's into voodoo crap, she must have done
it? *They* came to *me* because *they* wanted *my*

services."

"And that service is...?" asks the police officer in her apartment. He's standing by the door with a little notebook and pen out. Ara is, stubbornly, sitting cross-legged on her sofa.

She groans, and then says, with a touch of unadvised melodramatics: "Psychic readings."

"So you told them you can talk to the dead?"

"Holy fuckin' *no, I did not. I can't talk to the bloody dead.* I told them all I can do for 'em is —"

She stops, and her gaze flickers in my direction.

"Ms Yeboah?"

"Sorry. Thought I saw — sorry." She shakes her head. "Officer, am I being charged with a crime, or are you under the mistaken impression that my services cover fornication?"

"Excuse me?"

"It's late. I'm tired. You said you don't want tea. You actually *took* all my tea and my teacups for your crime lab folks. So charge me with attempted murder, or kindly vacate my premises, please and thank you."

The officer looks at Ara with the same expression many people do, where they haven't quite figured out yet how seriously to take her. He taps his notebook thoughtfully a couple of times, and then shakes his head. "No, ma'am, you aren't being charged with anything tonight. You have a good rest, and I'll talk to you tomorrow."

He sees himself out. Ara waits until the door clicks shut before scoffing loudly: "*Sure you will.*"

An awkward silence falls, one I'm not sure I would break even if it was possible for me to do so. Ara stares sightlessly at the floor for several seconds that stretch into eternity.

Then she sighs. "Roy? That you?"

I sit down next to her on the sofa. Her elbow twitches away from me, and she sighs again, deeper this time.

"Roy, I want to ask you something. I don't know how in the name of everything holy you'll *answer* me, but I'm sure you'll think of something. Are you an angel?"

I stare at her. "*What!?*"

"I ain't religious," she says quickly. "I never cared. But you — that girl — Melanie.

26

She could *die*. No one's sure... I mean, if she hadn't been here where I could call them right away, she *would* be dead. They said that. They told me that. She only has a fightin' chance because whatever happened, happened right here, 'cause her brother's phone has no battery, and *he* swore up and down there was never anything wrong with her — you know, right before he accused me of..."

She trails off into silence. I shift uncomfortably on the sofa. I've never understood why I can sit on furniture, but walk through walls. I gave up ever figuring it out a long time ago. Right now, though, it seems like a better thing to contemplate than the terrible idea that I might be some sort of murderous *angel*.

"I know it was you," Ara goes on, startling me. "And I just want — I *need*, I need reassurance that it's... I don't know, kosher. That you're good. That you can choose who lives and who dies 'cause you're *meant* to, not because..."

She trails off again, like she's waiting for me to answer. I can't. After a few seconds, she puts both hands down flat on the table. "Well," she says cheerfully, "I'm having one hell of an existential crisis. I hope you're happy. I'm gonna go boil some eggs."

She stands up and goes to the kitchen, presumably to boil some eggs.

It occurs to me, as I stand in the corner of the kitchen and watch her cook, that her existential crisis is about whether or not I'm a good person. That wouldn't be possible unless some part of her still believes that I am, right? For some reason, it's difficult to hold on to that thought. I've never had anyone struggle to tell me that they believe in me. I don't know what to do with the silence; half of me wishes I could pick up the glass sitting on the table and smash it.

I even try it, just to be sure, but naturally my hand passes right through.

Ara is, in ten years, the closest thing I've ever had to a friend. She's never seen me, never heard me, never even touched me; she doesn't know anything about me or the things I'm compelled to do. But she knows when I'm there. She knows when I visit her. She calls me 'Roy'. She's home.

She's seen me kill someone, and she still wants me to be family.

"I know the tarot cards didn't work," Ara says once her boiled eggs are deshelled and

sitting untouched on a plate in front of her.
"Or the crystal balls, or… anything, really.
But what do you say we give it another try?
Maybe one of us just wasn't feeling great.
Maybe I was hungry. I'm not hungry now. I
dunno why I boiled these eggs, actually.
Guess I just needed something to do."

"Nothing you have is going to work," I
say, not for the first time.

"We could — well, I could… I could hold
my nose and pick up a fucking Ouija board."

"That's not going to work either," I
mutter. "I can't move the pointer."

Neither of us speak for a short while.

"The thing is," Ara says abruptly, "the
only thing we *know* works is you bein' here."
She lights up. "So I got an idea. What about
this? Stay here for yes. Leave for no. That
sound like something you could do?"

I perk up. "Sure."

Ara waits a beat, then nods. "We probably
oughta test it first. So just go out into the
living room, then come back. Go."

I step out into the living room, wait two
beats, and return to the kitchen. Ara's smile
grows.

"I felt that!" she says. "You did it! You can
understand me! I mean, obviously I always

knew you could, but now I *know* know, you
know? God, what a trip. Okay. I don't know
why we didn't think of this years ago, but
then again, I ain't never seen you hurt
anyone before." She hesitates. "I'm gonna
ask the questions now. You good?"

I smile, and stay where I am.

"Perfect. So first up — what happened to
Melanie. Was it you?"

I don't move.

"Was it deliberate? Purposeful? Not just
you bein' here or anything?"

I don't move.

"Did you mean to?"

I don't move.

"*Why?* Wait, no, hold on." Ara purses her
lips in thought, then shakes her head.
"Screw it. You an angel?"

I step out into the living room, then come
back.

Ara stares down at the floor. When she
speaks again, her voice is a lot softer. "Did
you *want* to?"

No, I answer again. Not with Melanie.
Not with the cruel corporate man in
California. Not with the old lady in the
grocery store. Not with *anyone*.

Ara looks relieved this time. All the

tension leaves her face. I should be glad, and I think I am, but more than that I find myself growing frustrated. Why does she believe me? I could be lying. I could be putting her in direct danger. All she knows for sure is that I killed someone — why is she giving me the benefit of the doubt? What does she need the friendship of some spirit of vengeance for? When is the other shoe going to drop? Why isn't she *furious* with me? I know how to process fury. I don't have the first idea how you handle someone's trust.

"Okay," Ara says down at the floor. "Glad to hear that, but I'm a little lost now. Is someone forcing you?"

Yes.

"So there's others like you?"

No. Not that I know of. Not that I've ever seen.

"So who's forcing you?" She waits, then scoffs at herself. "Shit. Sorry. Do you die if you refuse? Or vanish, or… whatever things like you do?"

No. Not that I know of.

"Then how is someone forcing you? Does it hurt if you don't?"

I'm startled, and a little suspicious. *Yes.*

"Do you know why you had to hurt Melanie?"

No.

Ara blows out a breath, scoops her boiled eggs into a tupperware container, and sticks it in the fridge. "Roy, you are just about the loneliest soul I've ever met, ain't you?"

I stay where I am. *Yes* and *no* are too simple, but *yes* is the default, so that's the answer I give her. I guess it's true, but being lonely means missing someone's company, and you can't miss what you've never had. I want to ask Ara what she means by *lonely*. I want to ask her if she considers me a friend. I want to tell her about what happened in California, because I don't know how to reconcile not wanting to murder with how there are bad, selfish people in the world who crush others under their heel. I want to get her advice, because she grew up in a community of people and knows how morality works. But I don't know how I'll ever be able to do that, if the only way we can communicate is through *yes* and *no* - and it took us five years just to learn how to do that.

I miss Ara, even when she's right here.

Yeah. I guess I *am* lonely.

CHAPTER THREE

Request

Believe it or not, in spite of everything about her, Ara doesn't enjoy talking to thin air. She hates what she calls 'spiritual stereotypes' — like people thinking she can talk to the dead — and talking to thin air does absolutely nothing to help her convince people she can't. I still remember the first time I sought her out; it took hours for her to acknowledge I was even there, and when she did, it was explosive.

'Will you stop hangin' around and bugging me every minute of the livelong day!?' I remember her screaming in my direction while she put together dinner, making me jump up into the ceiling corner. *'Making a lady question her own sanity. Your parents raise*

you in a barn, or what?'

So unless Ara has something she specifically wants to tell me, she usually keeps quiet. Most of the time, I don't mind. She does little things here and there, like getting a second chair for her kitchen table. If I'm around when she's cooking, she'll even set a second place at the table, even though I can't use it. Little considerate things. I usually find it touching.

Right now, though, it's stifling. She doesn't say another word to me after our one-sided conversation in the kitchen, and I get the feeling that maybe she wants space to sort her own feelings out. So I leave at the end of the next day, get back on the train to London, and I'm forced to stand at the end of a carriage so I don't accidentally sit or stand inside anyone.

I form a loose sort of plan, dependent on not having any compulsions for the foreseeable future. Overnight, when no boats are running, I'm going to spend the time wandering through a slumbering London. I play a little game with myself whenever I do this; I have to touch every single floor in a tall office building without coming across anyone working late, and if I do, then I have to try another tall office building. I win if I find a completely empty building by the time the sun rises.

The best part is, when someone is working alone in a cubicle in the semi-dark, I could almost *swear* they know I'm there. They'll look up, startled, when I make a noise. They'll stand up suddenly if I linger behind their chair. When I'm in a bad mood, that can be very empowering, knowing I have *some* effect on the world around me, and one that doesn't involve murder.

Then, when the morning comes, I'm going to get on a boat to Ireland. Ireland's pretty close, compared to Japan or South Africa, and when you lose yourself in the rural countryside, you can almost believe you're not lost at all. I can lie on the grass in a forest clearing, then get up again to see I've actually left an imprint in the ground, flattened grass blades in the shape of my body. I've never even seen my reflection, so to have real, incontrovertible proof that I *exist* and I have *form* is one of the best therapeutic things I can do for myself.

I've wandered through three different office buildings by the time I reach *Oath Holdings, Inc.*, near enough to the M25 that I

can hear the quiet roar of speeding cars
when I'm standing on the pavement outside.
Sixteen stories, I count, so chances are it's
not going to be empty either, but what the
hell. I have several more hours to win, and I
don't think I've ever been inside this one
before.

I start at the top. Touch the executive
office — empty. Down the stairs. Nothing
but empty offices. Down the stairs again. A
bullpen of empty cubicles in the middle of
the floor —

— and raised voices coming from one of
the closed offices on the far end.

I roll my eyes, annoyed at losing my own
game, and walk over to eavesdrop. I might
as well get *something* out of all this, after all.

"You can't prove it!"

"Buddy, I don't have to. They've been
looking for an excuse to turn you down, and
an excuse to start an investigation, and I can
hand them both of those on a silver platter.
What are you still doing here, anyway? Go
home, get some rest. Start looking for other
jobs. You know how this is going to turn
out."

"No one else is going to hire me if it comes
out that — he's going to *kill* me, Andrea, he

36

— god, do you even hear yourself? Don't you care about how many lives you're going to ruin, you corporate *bitch*?"

"Frankly, no, I don't. You can write 'references on request', if you want. Hopefully by the time anyone asks for them, you'll already be offered the job, and you can start scamming them just as easily as you and your brother tried to scam everyone here."

"*Don't —!*"

"Good *night*, Louis."

"*Don't you dare —!*"

There's a crash and a muffled scream. It takes me almost a minute to react, frozen to the spot out of shock and confusion. I force my legs to move and I reach the door and sail easily inside —

T h u n k

A woman in a smart pinstripe suit sinks against the desk, fumbling for something on top to hold on to, then crumples to the ground. A man in a dishevelled vest stands over her, tall and terrified, wielding something ornate and sharp. The only sound in the office is his heavy breathing.

Blood soaks into the carpet from the woman's chest.

I have never, in my entire semi-existence, been faced with a murder I didn't commit. My whole mind seems to have shut down. Time moves far too slowly. The man puts his weapon down on the desk where it stands on its own, then runs out of the room, his sleeve over his face.

He leaves the dying woman completely on her own.

No one should ever die alone.

I sink to my knees and crawl over to where the woman lies crumpled on the ground. She's still breathing, but barely. Her eyes are unfocused, her eyelids keep fluttering. I put my hand as near her shoulder as I can without touching it. "You're not alone," I tell her desperately. "I'm here. I know you can't tell, but — I'm here, and I'm not going to move until someone else is here, I *promise*."

Her gaze flicks over to me, her eyes right on mine. "Louis...?"

I can't answer. Her eyes are *right on mine*. She can see me. *She can see me.*

I can tell the moment she's gone, the moment the light leaves her eyes and she's just a still husk. But I still don't move. I think I might be crying, something I don't think I've ever done before, but I don't know how to tell and I don't care. I feel like if I move even an inch, no one will ever see me properly again. If Louis comes back into the room at all, I don't notice, and don't care. What I *do* notice is the sun rising, faint pink light filtering in through the window — which means it's been all night.

No sound of sirens. No ambulances. No emergency services. He never told anyone. No one came to help her.

~~

It's not until one of the dead woman's colleagues enters and screams that I manage to stumble to my feet. Within two moments, the office is packed with people, and I have to endure the feeling of walking right through them — ice-cold, hooks in your gut, like when you miss a stair, or like when someone you love doesn't come home. The sparsely furnished open office space is a mercy, the stairs are heavenly, and by the time I reach street level I've put myself together enough to be able to dodge my way over to the train station.

Ara, I think to myself. *I have to see Ara.*

And then, the very next second, I'm in Ara's kitchen.

She spins with a shriek, and drops a mug of tea that shatters on the floor at her feet. I jump up to hover somewhere near the ceiling, confused and petrified.

Neither of us move for several seconds.

"You can't just —!" Ara steps away from the shattered mug in her bare feet, pulling her dressing gown tighter around herself. "You *can't* — ! Jesus H. *Christ*, Roy, how the hell did you do that!?" She stares at the wall in my direction, and then her gaze slowly travels up. "Are you — are you on the ceiling again?"

The moment I realise the answer to that question is 'Yes', I go crashing down to the floor.

"Okay," says Ara, in that frazzled way she has when she doesn't have the first clue what to do next. "Okay. Okay. I'll tell you what. *I* am gonna go put some clothes on. I wasn't expecting company, even company of the invisible variety." She folds her arms tightly over her dressing gown. "Then I'm gonna come back, and we're gonna talk about boundaries, and also my ceiling. Sound good? Good. Hold tight."

She vanishes into her bedroom.

I don't usually feel physical pain; about

the closest I've ever gotten is when I'm
walking through a lot of people at once.
Falling from the ceiling almost does it,
though. I'm definitely *stunned*. It takes me a
while to process what Ara said, and then it
takes me even longer to stand up and stare
suspiciously up at the ceiling like I'm
expecting it to suck me back up any second
now.

Then I stop and ponder how the *hell* I
made it to Ara's apartment in *no time flat*.

Am I a ghost? I've wondered that before,
because it's the most obvious explanation for
pretty much everything. But I can't be the
only ghost in the world, can I? So no. A
spirit, or an elemental, or a poltergeist, or, I
guess, a goddamn *angel* — but none of those
answers make sense either. More than once,
I've completely forgotten I'm not actually
human, sitting at Ara's kitchen table at the
place she set out for me and watching her
cook herself some dinner. More than once,
I've been surprised when she doesn't put
some lasagna in front of me, or when she
doesn't answer a question I ask. I've always
had this odd idea that I *am* human, if
invisible and intangible.

But the woman who died in London last

night saw me. She *locked eyes* with me. Could she always do that? If I'd walked into the office during the fight with Louis, would she have demanded to know what I was doing there? Or was it something that only happened because she was dying?

Could I have saved her life if I walked in earlier?

Ara walks back out into the kitchen, fully dressed in her no-nonsense ensemble, with a draped shawl the only indication she dips into the macabre. "Okay," she says again, like no time has passed. She carefully sidesteps the shards of the mug on the floor and sits down at her table. "So. Leave the room and come back if you're okay to keep doing our yes-no system."

That's easy enough. I do it. I don't bother to sidestep the shards of mug on the floor, and they don't bother to cut into my feet.

Ara nods. "Good. Is something *wrong*, Roy? You've never just *been* there before, all of a sudden, without coming through my door first." She hesitates. "Wait — leave for no, stay for yes. There. Is something wrong?"

Yes.

"Can I help?"

Yes.

Ara laughs. "This is going to be the most annoying game of Whodunnit I will ever play, huh? Okay, let's do this. How can I help, how can I help... do I need to call someone?"

No.

"Do I need to go somewhere?"

Yes.

"Shit. Is this important?"

Yes.

"Is someone's life at stake?"

No.

"Is it urgent?"

Yes.

"Like, right-now urgent?"

Yes.

"Do I have to leave my neighbourhood?"

Yes.

"Do I have to leave the country?"

No.

"Do I have to get on a train?"

Yes.

Ara pauses, thinking. Then she abruptly gets up and goes into the living room. When I follow her out, she's rummaging through a trunk and pulling out several atlases. She spreads one out on the floor showing the whole of southern England.

"In here?" she asks, tapping the page.

Yes.

"In London?"

Yes.

Ara flips through several pages until she finds more detailed maps of London. "Do you know *exactly* where? Like a street address?"

Yes.

"We're gonna have to do this page by page, then."

And we do. It takes half an hour of narrowing down the map area, going page by page, answering *Yes* or *No*, before Ara finally finds the right street. She stares at it for a moment, her fingers resting on the street name on the map, and then she stands up.

"If I go there," she says, "can you come with me?"

Yes.

"When we get there, can you lead me to wherever it is?"

Yes.

Ara nods. "Great. Give me a minute to grab my things, and then we'll go."

CHAPTER FOUR

Reluctance

The *Oath Holdings, Inc.* building is roped off on street level with bright yellow CAUTION tape. There's a small group of scattered bystanders craning their necks to try and catch a glimpse of what's going on. There's an ambulance parked by the kerb, sitting completely unused, and two police cars with their lights still flashing.

I stand at the tape next to Ara, who's staring up at the top of the building with guilt, exasperation, and fear warring on her face.

"Be great if you could answer some questions *now* for me," she mutters. We tried her system again on the train, but neither of us were willing to put too much distance

45

between us, and Ara can't tell if I'm standing on her right side or her left — just that I'm nearby. All the people around in public seems to mess up the connection a little. Just another reason for me to hate crowds.

Ara takes a deep breath, and flags down one of the officers milling around. "Excuse me! Sir?"

It takes a while for anyone to acknowledge her, and when someone finally does, they take their sweet time walking over. I wait impatiently, grumpy that Ara can't just walk through the tape and into the building, and grumpy that I can't put the name *Louis* into anyone's mind.

"Yes?" says the officer who answers Ara. He sounds friendly, but his face is completely expressionless. "How can I help you?"

"What happened here? There some kind of accident?"

The officer shakes his head. "I can't comment on an ongoing investigation, I'm sorry."

"I'm not a reporter, sir, I don't give a damn what the investigation is. I just want to know what happened, you know, as a concerned citizen. Do I need to be worried? Is there a serial killer on the loose?"

"No, ma'am, there isn't a serial killer on the loose."

"So no one's dead, then?"

The officer hesitates.

Ara's eyes widen. "Someone's *dead*?"

"Ma'am —"

"Someone's dead, and you can *guarantee* that there ain't a serial killer on the loose?"

"Ma'am, I can't confirm or deny anything for you, but I can promise you that you're not in any danger, alright? Why don't you go on home."

He gives her a smile, and then walks back over to the group at the building's doors.

"Let me guess," Ara murmurs. "You know who the killer is."

"It's someone called Louis," I say. "I'll know him when I see him. I think he works here, or — or at least he *used* to work here. "

Ara doesn't answer, because she can't hear me. She looks back up at the top of the building, and closes her eyes with a sigh. "Let me get this straight," she says slowly. "You want me to walk into the police department, put on my whole supernatural act, tell them I'm a psychic medium and I know who the killer is, and demand to get a list of all the suspects? That's what you're expecting me to do? You're expecting me to be a goddamn psychic-for-hire?"

"I know you hate that, but — I have to make sure he doesn't get away with it, Ara. I have to know more about who she was. *Please.*"

Ara grumbles something inaudible and turns away from the tape. "Fine," she says. "Might as well start by getting a cheap hotel room. Something tells me this is gonna take a *while.*"

~~

It's a lot easier to communicate in the relative peace and quiet of the ground-floor motel room. It takes a while to come up with the best plan of attack, and I feel largely useless during the discussion, given that all I can contribute is *yes* and *no*, and Ara keeps having to pause for several minutes to get her breathing back under control.

But finally, hours later, we're on our way to the local police department. Neither of us know how jurisdiction works, so we take Ara's best guess based on a brief internet search, but something about the flurry of activity outside the station tells us we're on the right track. As Ara would say, you can't kill a rich person and expect to get away with it. Unless you're me, but last I checked, no one is, least of all *Louis*.

Ara walks straight into the station without stopping, head held high, one of her hands clenched mostly hidden at her side. She stops at the front desk and smiles. "I need to talk to an officer of the law," she says, direct and confident. "Please."

The man behind the desk looks up at her. "Concerning?"

"I understand that someone was murdered last night in an office downtown. I believe I have some information about the identity of the killer."

There's a brief pause in which the uniformed officer looks surprised, and then he nods and stands up. "Please take a seat, I'll be right back."

Ara sits very, very still, and apart from making one joke about how waiting would be easier if she had someone she could make conversation with, she might as well be a statue. I pace up and down the waiting area, debating the wisdom of heading in on my own to see what I can find out — but what if someone comes to see Ara while I'm gone? It's hard enough to prove my existence when I'm *there*.

Finally, someone comes out — and Ara and I are both startled to see it's the same man who spoke to Ara at the CAUTION tape outside of the building earlier. He's not wearing a uniform, apart from a badge at his waist, and he has the general tired expression of someone who's about to retire in a couple of weeks — except he can't be, because he's way too young. He doesn't look a day over 35. He just looks tired.

He seems startled to see Ara as well, but he recovers quicker than either of us do. "Okay," he says slowly, "ma'am, I'm only going to ask you this once. Is this genuine information?"

Being offended is, bar none, the quickest way to get Ara to stop being self-conscious. "E*xcuse* me?"

"I mean no offense, I'm sorry. I just need to be sure. Usually, when someone's gawking at the crime scene and they come in to the station a few hours later, it's because they're thrill-seekers. So — is this genuine information?"

"*Yes*," says Ara, flatly and firmly, in a tone

that invites no argument.

"Good. If you'll just follow me, then."

He leads us back into the bullpen, where there are a lot of desks, a lot of detectives, and a lot of people milling around in uncomfortably tight quarters. Ara takes one look at the open desk the officer is leading her towards, and she stops in the middle of the floor. "Nope," she says. "Nuh-uh. I need somewhere a lot more private than *this*."

"Why?"

"'Cause I'm about to make a goddamn fool of myself, that's why, and I'd rather do that with as few people around to *gawk* at me as I can."

He openly studies her, some of the tiredness in his face replaced by curiosity. "Okay then," he says with a small shrug. "I'll go see if we've got an interrogation room free."

They do. Within five minutes, we're standing in one, and Ara is eyeing off the chair at the table. The detective opts to stand, hands in his pockets, so Ara does the same thing. I smile when I see her idly trying to put her hands in her pockets before she realises she doesn't *have* any pockets.

"I'm Detective-Inspector Casey

Lavinder," the officer says, "now that we're meeting properly."

Ara smiles. "Lavender? Like the herb?"

"Yes, but spelled differently. I, instead of E. Can I get your name for the record?"

"Lady Arabetta Yeboah."

Lavinder pauses. "I'm gonna need to write that down and have you spell it for me."

"Yeah, most people do. I go by Ara when I'm not working."

"Ara. Tell me, what information do you have about my victim?"

Ara looks at the corner where I'm standing. She can't see me, but I flash her a quick thumbs-up anyway.

"Well," she says, "you see, I'm a psychic."

The expression on Lavinder's face grows fixed. "I'm sorry?"

"I'm a psychic. A medium, more accurately. I have a moderately profitable business where I can give people slices of the thoughts and feelings of their loved ones from when they were alive. Now — no, don't you dare interrupt me, Casey, I'm on a roll here and I'm gonna lose the nerve to talk if you cut me off. Gotta respect your elders, for chrissakes. Now, a few years back, I ran into some kind of spirit thing, and now it hangs around like a bad penny, and I *think* it saw your murder go down, and, for some reason known only to God, it thinks *I'm* the best person for telling you lovely folks, even though it can't talk, or I can't listen, or however the hell it works. We've got a system for *Yes* and *No,* but that's it. I can't give you a name, but I *can* tell you which of your suspects it is, if you give me a list to choose from. That's what I have to offer, right there. Take it or leave it."

Lavinder's expression is oddly hard to read. Disbelieving, definitely, but not in the immediately dismissive way that many people who meet Ara greet her with. Considering? Thoughtful? He looks like he sees more than he lets on.

"There's no reward," he says.

Ara blinks. "Excuse me?"

"There's no reward. If whatever you tell me leads to us arresting the right person, you're not going to get anything for it."

"Good. I can get some peace and quiet for a change."

"There won't be any publicity, either."

"*Good.*" Ara perks up. "Actually, can you keep my name out of it completely? 'Police

Reluctantly Consult An Angry Psychic'. The last thing I need is for idiots to show up at my door wanting to know who killed their poor dead relatives."

Lavinder goes quiet again, with that same soft, studious expression. No one says anything for what feels like an eternity, stretching around all of us like a stifling blanket.

"*Yes* and *no,*" Lavinder finally says.

"What the hell does that mean? You want me to *half*-help?"

"That system you said you had, for communicating *yes* and *no*. What is it?"

"Now, not for nothing, Inspector, but I'm not in the business of revealing all my trade secrets at the drop of a hat. Are you asking because you want to know more about how I can help, or are you asking for shits and giggles because you're curious? 'Cause if it's the latter, I ain't helping you, and I'll just go ahead and get out of your hair right away."

Lavinder almost smiles. The slight pull of his mouth is hypnotic. "I'm asking because I figure your help can't hurt."

"That's not an answer."

"I'm asking because I can't just give you a list of suspects and ask you which one did it.

We can't give out details about an ongoing investigation, even and especially to well-meaning members of the public. If you really want to help, humour me. What's the system?"

Ara lets out a long, dramatic, woe-is-me sigh. "I can feel when the spirit's there," she explains. "Right now, for example, it's in that corner right there. So I ask a yes-or-no question, and if the answer is yes, it stays. If the answer is no, it leaves for a few seconds and comes back."

Lavinder nods thoughtfully. "Okay. Could you have it spell out the name of the killer?"

Ara frowns. "How?"

"Start with A. Yes or no. Then B, then C, and so on."

Ara stares at Lavinder for a moment, then blinks rapidly, then laughs and puts both her hands over her face. "Why in the *hell* didn't either of us think of that?" she says. "No, wait — why didn't *I* think of that? Roy might have thought of it. Roy, are you looking at me like I'm an idiot right about now? I sure wouldn't blame you."

I'm not. I didn't think of it either. I'd been too busy with the shining novelty of being able to communicate at *all*.

"What did you call it?" asks Lavinder, his head tilted quizzically to the side.

Ara takes a second to recover. "Roy. It's just a nickname. I had to call it *something*, and it was the first thing to come to mind, that's all. Roy, you good with spelling out the name like that?"

I stay where I am. For the first time in months, I'm practically vibrating with excitement. I'll be able to influence the world, change how things happen, and I'll be doing all of that in pursuit of justice for a woman who didn't deserve to die alone in her fourteenth-floor office — I can't think of anything *better*. Except for no one to be dead, obviously, but I'll take my victories wherever I can get them.

"Roy says yep." Ara takes a deep breath. "It'll probably take a while. Hey, Roy, how many letters —? Wait, that's dumb. Look, Inspector, why don't you just leave me here for a while?"

Lavinder raises his brow skeptically.

"Lock me in, for all I care. I just think it'd be mighty awkward for us both to be here while some ghost spirit thing picks out letters for me one at a time."

Lavinder *actually* smiles this time, and I can feel excited joy ballooning inside me. "Fine," he says. "Knock on the door if you need anything."

And, true to his word, we hear the lock of the door snap into place once he's closed it behind him.

CHAPTER FIVE

Rejection

It doesn't take nearly as long as I dread, because Ara is quick on her feet and the best thing that's ever happened to me.

The first two letters puncture my excitement because of the tedious wait. Ara can't just go 'A, B, C, D'; she has to wait a little in between each one to make sure my response isn't changing. 'U' takes forever, for obvious reasons, and I'm full of nervous energy by the time I confirm the letter, trying so very hard to move in the exact same patterns for Ara's benefit. I'm resigning myself to the next one when Ara says: "L, O, U. Lou. Is it Lou? ... No. Is it Louis?"

I could have hugged her. I almost do.

Louis, I silently confirm for her. No, I don't know the last name. No, I don't know any other names. Yes, he's white. Ara thinks for a minute, then asks about the colour of his hair. I confirm when she guesses it was black. She asks if I know anything else she can try to guess at. I have to be honest: no. How do you guess at what a nose looks like?

While Ara gets up to knock on the door, I sail out into the bullpen, looking for Lavinder. He's sitting at his desk on the other end, watching his computer screen with his chin in one hand. When I go over to investigate, he glances up, looks right through me, and then returns his attention to the screen.

I pause. Did someone behind me make a noise? I've never seen a reaction quite like that before, like he thought he saw someone out of the corner of his eye. It must have been a noise I didn't notice.

It turns out he's looking at police reports. I read what's on the screen over his shoulder. It's a little frustrating, like it always is, because no matter how hard I try I can't focus long enough to read the whole thing. Some words blur out, snaking

through the holes in my concentration;
others repeat over and over until I have to
look away.

But one thing I can't miss is a photo of
Ara's driver's licence.

My first thought is *Great, he figured out
how to spell her name!* My second thought,
less immediate but no less clear, is *Why do
the police have a picture of Ara's licence?*

I squint at the words. *Suspected poisoning,*
I can make out. *Melanie. Hospitalised.*

I remember someone was questioning Ara
about that when I went back home after my
walkabout. The police don't really think *she*
killed Melanie, do they? They can't, or Ara
wouldn't be walking around free right now.
Still, something cold settles in my gut at the
thought, because I have no idea how I
would clear Ara's name — and is *this* why
Lavinder locked her in the interrogation
room?

Lavinder makes an annoyed grunting
noise and spins around in his swivel chair.
"Look, I told you —"

He cuts off when he doesn't see anyone
there.

For several seconds, neither of us move.

"You say something, Casey?" asks an

officer walking up the aisle of desks.

Lavinder blinks, and his gaze slides away. "Nope."

"Frankie said you've got a civilian report about the Relshaw murder. Anything useful?"

"Not sure yet."

"What do you mean? You haven't taken a statement yet?"

"You could say that." Lavinder leans back and taps his computer screen. "She's a psychic."

"She's a *what*?"

"A psychic."

"Oh, for cryin' out loud. Cut her loose then."

"She's a really convincing psychic."

"You're not buying into all of that crap, are you?"

"Like I said, I'm not sure yet. There's a report from yesterday — she got questioned when someone visiting her had a heart attack in her flat."

"So?"

"A teenager. A *teenager* had a heart attack in her flat."

"Oh, man, that's weird." The other officer — older than Lavinder, close-cropped hair, casual and fluid — leans over to see Lavinder's monitor. "Do they think your psychic had anything to do with that?"

"Not in the end, no."

"How's the teenager?"

"Stable. They're keeping her a few days for observation, but the report says she's going to be fine."

"They're — *what*!?" I cut in, out loud, stunned.

"The report says she's going to be fine," Lavinder says again.

I stare at the monitor, like the squiggly words of the report will somehow make any more sense to me than they did a few minutes ago. The teenager, the young girl, Melanie, the one I killed — she's okay? She's *not dead*?

For the next minute, I half-expect to feel that compulsion to go after her again. Thoughts trip over themselves in my head — does this happen a lot? Have there been people I killed who didn't actually end up dead, and I just never noticed because I never stick around to make sure? Is Melanie really okay? Would she be able to see me now, like the dead woman could in her last moments of life? *Is she really still alive?*

"Still," the other officer murmurs when I begin paying attention to their conversation again. "That's a weird thing to happen when you're that young. I hope they're doing a full workup." He pauses. "Would we *want* them to find something, or nothing? It's weird with medical shit. I never know whether to say 'Congratulations, now you know' or not."

Lavinder smiles and looks up at him. "I hope you're not saying 'congratulations' whenever anyone tells you they're sick."

"Come *on*, you know what I mean. So that psychic — you're cutting her loose, right?"

"In a minute."

"No, *now*. Do I have to remind you how gullible you are?"

"I told her she isn't getting anything for this, and she's fine with that, Mike. She doesn't want to be associated with this at all. What do we lose for hearing her out?"

"*We* don't lose anything. *You*, though, lose your last six years of progress, like a goddamn alcoholic thinking one drink is okay." Mike gets up from his desk and starts heading over to the interrogation room. "You know what, I'll take care of this. You just sit tight."

Lavinder rolls his eyes. "Sir, yes, sir."

I have to go see Melanie, I decide. Right now. But the thought of the woman in the office, Andrea Relshaw, stops me — I can't just abandon her. I'm the only person — the only *thing* — in the entire world who knows anything about how she died. She may not have said as much, but I know she's counting on me to make sure Louis sees justice. Otherwise, she died for nothing, and I don't want to accept that.

So I follow in Mike's footsteps, leaving the mystery of Casey Lavinder behind at his desk.

"*Louis,*" Ara says the moment Mike unlocks and opens the door. "You're looking for a white guy called Louis, with black hair."

"Sure. Ma'am —"

"You don't have to tell me a thing, I honestly don't give a flying —"

"Ma'am —"

"— but you have a list of suspects, right? I'm telling you, you're looking for a guy called Louis. You're welcome. Now, escort me out, there's a good lad."

Mike is quiet for a few seconds, and I can't help laughing.

"Fine," he eventually says. "The only thing is, no one called *Louis* is connected to this in any way. So thank you, you know, for the waste of time, and if you think of anything else at all, please do *not* come back or call us again."

Ara sweeps out of the interrogation room and continues the conversation as Mike, gently but firmly, escorts her to the exit. "Then it's someone you haven't found yet," she says, "obviously. A coworker, maybe. A low-level filing clerk."

"Oh, great, thank you for the insight! Maybe for your next trick you can give us the murder weapon."

Ara frowns at him. "You don't have a murder weapon?"

"I didn't say that."

"Yes you did, you idiot. Are the police here all a bunch of amateurs? How do you miss a knife dripping with blood?"

Ara is naturally loud. Nearly the entire bullpen is listening to her and Mike now.

"Ma'am," says Mike, with absolutely no trace of even his fake goodwill left in his voice, "you need to leave, right now, or I'm going to have to arrest you."

Ara hesitates just before the exit, and tilts

her head toward me. "Sorry, Roy," she murmurs. "I did everything I could. I'm going home. You're welcome to join me."

She adjusts her shawl on her shoulders, pointedly, with a glare at Mike; then she walks out of the office, as graceful and dignified as she's ever been.

Mike stands motionless for a minute or two before he turns around and sees that almost half of the officers and detectives in the room are giving him weird looks. "What?" he demands.

Someone gives a low whistle. "You're *absolutely* getting cursed."

"Don't be stupid, Pence."

"I'm just saying, mate, you're getting voodooed or hexed or —"

"Yeah, okay, I'll take the risk. Show's over, everyone! Get back to work!"

There's an immediate general hubbub of people pretending to get back to work, and Mike slumps into his chair next to Lavinder's, grumbling quietly to himself.

Lavinder glances at him. "I appreciate the thought," he says.

"Shut up."

"Did she give you a name?"

"Yeah, *Louis*."

Lavinder hesitates, frowning. "We don't know any Louis."

"Yeah, no shit. Look, I'm serious about this, Casey, don't go putting any more significance on it, okay? I'm gonna have to call your sponsor if you do."

Lavinder rolls his eyes. "She still doesn't like that label."

"And I'm still gonna use it."

"What about the knife, though?"

"The what?"

"She said 'how do you miss a knife dripping with blood'. How did she know our victim was stabbed?"

Mike shrugs, unconcerned. "Lucky guess. How should I know?"

"We thought the killer took the weapon from the scene, but if she thinks it's still there, then —"

Mike gets up, puts his hands on Lavinder's knees, and swivels him around to look him dead in the eye. "Casey," he says. "Shut up."

For a second, it looks like Casey's going to argue; then he deflates and shakes his head. "You're right. Sorry."

"Don't be *sorry*. Just don't be an idiot."

"Sir, yes, sir."

Mike sits back down with a good-natured grumble, and then they start talking about a completely different crime — some robbery at a convenience store several streets away. I tune them out. I chose to stay because I was hoping they'd discuss this one, the Relshaw murder, or at the very least pull out a list of suspects so I could pinpoint more than just a single name, but that doesn't look like it's going to happen.

I stand right behind Lavinder's shoulder for a minute, just to test how far his odd near-perception of me goes. But he doesn't react at all this time, and I'm forced to leave with nothing new.

It's rare, and weird, for more than one thing to be bothering me at a time. I have no idea where to start. I need to make sure the police catch Louis, that part's obvious, and I need to try and remember what the murder weapon is. 'Knife' doesn't sound right, but all I can conjure up is a hazy memory of something glinting and sharp that Louis put down on the woman's desk right after hitting her with it. If the police didn't find it, then Louis must have taken it back, and I must have *been* there at the time, but I don't remember anything else. I probably wouldn't even remember if an earthquake had cracked a wall in two.

But that isn't the only thing bothering me. I need to go see Melanie, too, and find out if she can see me now. I have to try and work out why she didn't *die*. I have to go and make sure I didn't damage my friendship with Ara; I know how much she hates calling herself a psychic with people who aren't her clients and think she's one bun short of a baker's dozen. And I need to find out why Casey Lavinder was, however subtly, able to perceive that I was there.

If I can work out how to cover distances in the blink of an eye, that would be a great bonus.

In the end, I decide to go look at the crime scene again. It's one of only two things I can actually do right now, and the alternative — going to see Melanie — scares me too much. What if I'm compelled to finish the job? She's going to be fine; she can wait.

Justice for Andrea Relshaw can't.

CHAPTER SIX
Reality

I don't know why it didn't occur to me
that the woman's body would have been
taken away by now. Part of me expected the
office to look exactly like it had last night,
and that scene includes a dead body
slumped on the carpet by the desk.

But of course, when I get there, her body's
gone. The place where it lay slumped near
the desk is outlined in tape. Apart from a
rusty brown stain in the carpet, there's no
sign any violence occurred here at all.

Maybe I should figure out where the
coroner's office is.

… First things first.

The police don't have a murder weapon. I
know for a fact Louis used *something* to stab

her. I saw it, long and sharp, and silver. I saw him put it down on the desk, and I saw it stand up on its own. A knife wouldn't do that, so I need to focus and try to remember what it was.

Now that I'm thinking about it, how did *Ara* know Andrea was stabbed? It must be her gift, her ability to see bits and pieces of people who have passed on from when they were still alive. I've seen her do that before, once or twice, without realising until after the fact.

I'm getting distracted. I need to focus on the weapon. A statue, maybe? But there's nothing like that in the office, not even a tiny figurine on the desk.

If it can stand up on its own, it must have a base to balance on. I scan the woman's office, shelf by shelf, cube by cube. She has dozens of books, some on the stock market and other investment stuff she probably needs for her job, others on self-improvement and mindfulness meditation. No journals or diaries. The bookends are big and wooden, and definitely not what I saw last night. There are some small Buddha figurines scattered around, but they're all wooden as well, with nothing sharp on them. There's a globe on the side of her desk, next to her computer. The sleek monitor and keyboard are both black, not silver. She doesn't have anything sharp and silver that I can see, not even a small penknife or letter opener. Unless Louis put it back in a drawer, which strikes me as very unlikely, the weapon can't be in this room.

Maybe Louis *did* take it with him, like the police think, and it's gone; but I've been friends with Ara for too long to believe that. If she thinks it's still here, then it's still here, simple as that. I'm just not looking in the right places.

I hesitate, and then kneel down next to the tape on the floor, right where I was kneeling last night. Then I look up at the desk where I saw the weapon, sharp and stained with red. I must have been *here* when Louis took it away, because I never saw him among the people in the office after the murder was discovered. Why can't I remember? If I concentrate, I can conjure up a vague impression of something heavy hitting the floor, but that must have been Andrea's body, right?

My gaze falls on the globe, visible even from my vantage point on the floor.

The stand it's sitting on is long and silver.

For a moment, I forget that I'm intangible, and I reach out to try and take the globe off the stand so I can examine it better. My hands go right through, and I roll my eyes at myself with a quiet curse. But it doesn't matter; if there was any blood on it, the police wouldn't possibly have missed it.

I step outside the office, through the yellow CAUTION police tape over the doorway, past the two officers milling at the nearby water-cooler like they work for *Oath Holdings, Inc.* I walk around the perimeter of the cubicles, glancing in through the closed offices and rooms as I pass them. Two of them have globes identical to the one in the woman's office. When I check the other floors, just to be thorough, I find five more. They must be company-issue, or a really common office Secret Santa gift.

So Louis grabbed the globe stand, knocking the globe itself onto the floor, and killed Andrea with it. Then, in the aftermath, he must have swapped the stand with another one in the building, somewhere no one's expecting to look for blood. With the globe on the stand, I imagine seeing *any* blood at first glance is difficult.

Of all the bloody times to be completely intangible.

I have absolutely no idea how I can communicate any of this to the police without Ara's help, but I'm going to need to try. I *swear* Lavinder can see me, or *almost* see me, so maybe that's my best way in. Maybe if I say 'globe' in his ear enough times, he'll have the idea all on his own.

~~

I follow Lavinder home from the station that night. He gives absolutely no indication that he knows I'm there. He listens to music as he walks, and I can't hear what the music is, but I notice something interesting about Lavinder — when he's on the Tube, swaying slightly with the motion of the train, he times the swaying to the beat of the music in his ears. He's *dancing*, as subtly as he can. The side-to-side movement of his shoulders is entirely innocent unless you're watching him closely, like I am; and when you realise he's dancing, it's hypnotic. The concept of shame about dancing in public is utterly alien to me.

Lavinder lives just outside the city limits, in a tall and relatively new council estate surrounded by parks. There's a playground outside and it occurs to me: does he have kids? For some reason, that's impossible for me to imagine. Ara doesn't want kids. Maybe I picked up some of her distaste for them. The idea of going into an apartment where kids are running around is enough to give me pause and reconsider going to visit Melanie instead.

It turns out I worried for nothing, though. When Lavinder and I walk into his apartment on the twelfth floor, it's an entirely empty one-bedroom affair.

It's actually quite nice, too, I realise with a start. Far from being sparsely furnished, it looks like it could have come out of a furniture catalogue, all soft lights and warm colours. I can feel the carpet on my feet, a deeply rich brown texture. There's a silvery splashback in the kitchen and dark marble countertops that put me in mind of the starry sky outside. Lavinder flicks on the main light and I almost don't know what to examine first; he has *countless* books lining his walls, a large TV, incense burning on his coffee table. None of it is anything I would have associated with a *police officer*, let alone a single man with tired eyes and a no-

nonsense approach to conversations.

He looks even more tired as he hangs up his coat and settles in for the evening, which is odd. Home should be relaxing and rejuvenating, not exhausting, or so movies tell me. It's probably what books would also tell me, if I could read them, or what people on the street would tell me, if I could speak to them. Maybe, I reflect dryly, I don't have nearly enough experience with 'home' to be judging how anyone else treats theirs.

I sigh. "Testing," I say out loud. "Testing. One two three."

Lavinder doesn't react.

"You're not just pretending I'm not there, are you? Ara did the same thing at first."

Nothing.

I nod. "Okay, well, the murder weapon you're looking for in the Relshaw murder is a globe. A globe stand. I don't know which one, but it's definitely still there in the building somewhere. Got that? Roy to Casey Lavinder, *globe*. Globe. Globe. *Globe*. Globe. Glo —"

Lavinder makes an irritated grunt and rubs his head.

I lean in right in next to his ear. "*Globe*."

He moves away from me, but I can't tell if

that's because I'm annoying him, or if it's because he's gone into the kitchen to make himself something to eat. Maybe it's a little of both. I open my mouth to try again, and I'm cut very painfully short by the sight of a photo on one of the bookshelves.

It's Lavinder, and the woman I killed in the supermarket. The woman who first woke me up to the atrocity of what I was doing. The woman who died alone and scared before anyone found her.

It feels like I've stopped existing, like everything that makes me *me* has shifted out of touch with reality. I keep staring at the photo, because I get the idea that if I take my eyes off of it, there won't *be* any me anymore. It's a small anchor in a sea of nonexistence driving right into the core of my identity, a small safe haven to cling to while I try to remember how atoms are meant to connect. On the edges of my vision, I see Lavinder walk over to the photo, frown slightly at it, then walk away.

My identity reasserts itself. I come back down to earth with a painful start and I walk over and turn the frame face-down so I don't have to see it anymore — don't have to run the risk of *disappearing* anymore.

Lavinder turns sharply, and stares at the frame.

Neither of us move for one long, agonising minute.

"Yvonne?" he says, carefully, into the silence. If anything answers, neither of us hear it.

"I'm sorry," I say, and surprise myself with how hoarse my voice sounds. "I'm so sorry."

Lavinder doesn't hear it. He doesn't see me, either; when I step to the side, his eyes don't flicker towards me or track my movement, like Ara's sometimes do. He's just staring at the frame.

The frame I moved. With my hand.

Lavinder doesn't speak or move for a while, but it's not out of shock or fear, not as far as I can tell. He just looks like he's doing a lot of thinking. Not necessarily *quick* thinking. Just thinking. Like he's wrestling with the pros and cons of several decisions he has to make.

"Yvonne," he finally says, "if that's you, somehow, go away. You're not welcome here. But if you're — Arabetta Yeboah's... thing, I don't suppose there's any way you can let me know?"

He goes still again. I take several seconds longer to decide what to do, because the novelty of someone *talking* directly to me is so disorienting, and because I've never worked out exactly what governs the moments where I'm semi-tangible. In the end, I decide to try to be sneaky; I walk, very slowly and very quietly, over to Lavinder's side, lean in very close to his ear, and whisper: "*Globe*."

Lavinder screams and pitches sideways, knocking into his coffee table so the incense sticks go all over the carpet.

I scream and pitch backwards through the wall, so I end up in the hallway outside his apartment. One of his neighbours passes right through me, and I freeze to the spot, full of pure and unadulterated terror.

A minute later, I burst out laughing, and I could not for the *life* of me tell you why. It's probably extremely hysterical laughter. It would probably sound quite insane to anyone capable of hearing it. I seize on the insanity, and use it to propel myself back through the wall into Lavinder's living room, where he's picking up the incense sticks off the carpet with shaking hands.

When he's cleaned up, and thoroughly

rubbed his calf where his leg ran into the corner of the coffee table, he straightens up and closes his eyes. "Okay," he says. "Here's what's going to happen. I'm going to assume, for the moment, that I'm not crazy. I'm going to assume you can hear and understand me. I'm going to go see Ms Yeboah. Please... come with me."

He pauses for another few seconds, nods to himself, and retrieves his coat from the closet. I don't move, because people hearing or reacting to my presence is so very rare that it's still taking my mind several extra seconds to process what's going on. Lavinder puts his hand on the doorknob, stops, sighs in a very tired and resigned manner, and then disappears into his bedroom. He comes back carrying a Ouija Board, which he tucks under his coat as he leaves the apartment.

I follow him, and I don't manage to get my laughter under control for a very, very long time.

CHAPTER SEVEN

Recalcitrance

Ara opens the door when Lavinder knocks, and stands there looking both thoroughly unimpressed and utterly unsurprised. She doesn't say a word, not even to greet us — she just stands there with her arms folded and waits for Lavinder to explain himself.

Lavinder's shoulders are hunched and his expression sheepish. "Hi," he says, which feels like a pretty good start to *me*, at least. "I think your, uh… I think it followed me."

Ara nods. "It did."

"Oh. Good."

"It's right here, and I told you, its name is Roy."

"I don't really want to call it that."

"Why not?"

"I don't really want to talk about it, either." Lavinder shifts uncomfortably. "Can I come in?"

"You in a rush?"

"No, it's just — my parter would throw a fit if he knew I was doing this."

"What, consulting a psychic?"

"Well, he wouldn't be thrilled about that part, either, but — I guess I'm just a little paranoid."

Ara bursts out laughing. "Yeah," she agrees jovially, "I know *that* feeling. It's exhausting, you know, knowing someone else is there and not being able to see them in any way that matters. Usually it comes through my door polite as anything, but this morning it just *appeared* in my kitchen and I wasn't even *dressed* yet. It doesn't ever stop being weird. You get used to the weird, though, after a couple years."

"That's comforting."

Ara sighs and shakes her head. "Why are you here, detective? I doubt you're just dropping Roy off like it's some confused senior citizen who's had too much to drink."

"I'd like a seance."

Ara raises her eyebrows at him.

"I'll pay."

"You remember the part where I told you I don't talk to the dead, right?"

"I don't want to talk to the dead, just —" Lavinder gestures to his side, and I have to step abruptly sideways to avoid his waving hand. "And I know you can do *that*. I'll pay. Look, I even brought..." He pulled his Ouija Board out from under his coat, and Ara's face went hard. "I thought it would help," he says, unsure whether or not to be apologetic in the face of her glare. "You didn't think of using letters back at the office, so I figured you might not have one."

"Uh-huh," says Ara, in a tone I recognise as very dangerous. "And you, you just *happened* to have one lying around?"

Lavinder hesitates. "It's a long story."

"Yeah, I'll bet it is."

"Please, Ms Yeboah, I —"

"Lady Arabetta. You're askin' for a seance, you're gonna damn well use my professional title."

"— Lady Arabetta. If your friend followed me home, it stands to reason he needs to tell me something, something about the Relshaw murder, and it probably can't wait. If you won't help, will you at least teach me how to talk to him?"

"It."

"What?

"It, not he, not him."

"He's sentient, I'm not calling him *it*."

"Oh, and you're an expert on spirits now, are you? Think you know more than me? Pretty arrogant to assume it prefers 'he'. Hey, Roy, come inside if you want to be 'he'."

I stay right where I am.

"Great. Come inside if you want to be 'she'."

I don't move.

"Come inside if you want to be 'it'."

I walk inside.

Ara turns a smug expression back on Lavinder. "'It' it is."

Lavinder nods. "Fair enough. Can I come inside as well?"

"Do you want to be an 'it'?"

"If it gets me answers to this murder, sure."

Ara laughs very abruptly, and steps to the side to let him in. "Fine, we can use the bloody Ouija Board. It's not going to work, though, so prepare yourself for hours of Twenty Questions. And if *anyone* from your unit asks me about this, I'm categorically denying that this ever happened."

"Good," says Lavinder with a smile. "So am I."

~~

The instructions for the Ouija Board call for all the lights to be off, for candles to be lit, and for atmospheric music to be playing. Ara scoffs at every single one of them until Lavinder thinks to ask *me*, and I figure that we could probably use all the help we can get if we're expecting me to be able to move the pointer like I moved Lavinder's picture frame, so that's what I communicate to them. Ara grumbles ceaselessly, but at least she doesn't have any shortage of candles. Or atmospheric music.

When it's finally all set up, the only thing that ruins the esoteric scene of Ara's hand and Lavinder's hand on top of the wooden pointer in the middle of the Ouija Board, surrounded by dozens of large lit candles, is Ara's deep scowl.

"Okay," she says. "What do we do now?"

Lavinder looks at her in surprise. "I thought you were the expert."

"Not with goddamn Ouija Boards. It's yours. It's clearly been used before. *You* tell *me* what we do next."

"That was years ago. I barely remember what *happened*, let alone what the ritual is."

"Bullshit."

Lavinder shakes his head. "Can't he — it — just give it a try and see what happens?"

"I don't know, ask it, not me."

"Right. Uh… just give it a try and see what happens."

I stare at the pointer. The thought of putting my fingers so near someone else's freezes me to the spot. What if I overbalance? What if one of them moves their hand without warning? What if I actually *do* move the pointer, and Lavinder jumps like he did in his apartment and falls right into me?

Ara frowns down at the unmoving pointer, and then looks up at me, her gaze off-center and slightly unfocused like it always is when she manages to achieve something close to eye contact. "Roy?"

I take a deep breath, put my fingers on the pointer, and push. I expect my hand to go right through the table — but it *doesn't*. The pointer feels nice and solid under my fingertips.

I push again, but the pointer remains

stationary like it's nailed to the table and one paltry push from me isn't *nearly* enough to free it.

"Roy?"

I try again, and the exact same thing happens. I push with all my might, standing up slightly to put all my weight into it, but that doesn't work either. Do I even *have* weight? My instinct is no. Weight means easy exertion on the outside environment, which is not something I have ever possessed.

I leave the room briefly in order to answer Ara's question, and she sighs and sits back. "Nope," she tells Lavinder. "A dumb waste of time, and I'm magnanimous enough not to say I told you so."

"It *can*, though," Lavinder insists. "It moved a picture frame back home. It..." He frowns, and closes his eyes. "I have a picture of my ex-wife on a bookshelf. Normally I can go weeks without remembering it's there, but I noticed it today. And then when I turned around, it fell over."

"Why the hell do you have a picture of your ex-wife on display?"

"It's a reminder."

"Of *what*?"

"Of things I'd rather not talk about."

"Uh-huh. And it fell over, and you think that was Roy."

"It fell — not off the shelf, not like it tipped over. It's like when you don't want to see a picture and you turn it face-down. That's what it did."

Ara's face changes. "Oh."

"So it *can*. Maybe we need to do this in my apartment."

"Or maybe it just didn't want to see your ex-wife. You know, like a normal person, like someone who *doesn't* keep pictures of their ex around. Roy, did you want to see Lavinder's ex-wife?"

I take a deep breath, and answer: *No*.

Ara appears startled. "You've *met* his ex-wife?"

Yes.

"Roy, who the *hell* are you?"

No.

"What the hell does *no* mean?"

"It means *I don't know*," I snap, frustrated and sulky. I'd been expecting the Ouija Board not to work, I *knew* it wouldn't work, so why am I so surprised that it didn't?

"It means he doesn't know," says Lavinder, barely missing a beat, and we all stop at once, Lavinder and Ara staring at each other.

"What?" Ara finally manages. She looks, for probably the first time in the five years I've known her, like she's out of her depth. Going to the police and claiming to be a psychic is an annoying inconvenience. Meeting someone who senses more than she does, though, that's alarming and scary.

Lavinder can see that too. He takes a moment to fumble for words, during which neither Ara nor I take our eyes off of him.

"I don't know," he finally says.

"No, you said *it* doesn't know."

"I don't know where that came from."

"Out of your mouth."

"Yes, I —"

"It came from *you*, out of *your* mouth, innocent as anything, you goddamn liar."

"I just meant — realistically, that's what he probably means, that he doesn't know who he is."

"Realistically by *whose standards*, you dolt!? Who in their right, ignorant mind looks at an invisible demon spirit thing who has to *actively* answer no, and then goes 'ah, yes, of course, clearly they're expressing a lack of knowledge of what they are'? What about that has *anything* to do with logic?"

"What else would 'no' mean?"

"*Logically*, it would mean *I didn't ask a yes-or-no question.*"

Lavinder opens his mouth, then closes it again.

"Here," says Ara as she sits forward, "try this. Roy, Detective, for chrissakes neither of you *think* for this, alright? Just answer the question. Roy, what's the biggest object I have in my bedroom?"

"A crystal quartz cluster," I answer immediately.

"A crystal quartz cluster," Lavinder echoes, and the look on Ara's face actually makes him flinch away. "It's just a guess," he says desperately, "just — just a wild guess, that's all."

"*Why?*"

"Because the alternative doesn't make any sense!"

"*You're telling me!*" Ara explodes. "You spend a fucking *lifetime* practicing and honing a gift you never asked for, thousands and *thousands* of questions from malicious morons all day, every day, doin' everything you can to make sure you never have to deal with skeptics, fucking —! *Tarot* decks and

90

crystal balls and goddamn *broomsticks*, Lavinder, you think I keep any of that shit because it *works*!? I keep that shit because it's pest control spray! It deters the morons! My whole fucking *life* I've devoted to trying to understand what the hell talkin' to the dead means, and then some goddamn fucking *white guy* comes in and can *just fucking do it!?* With my *best friend!?*"

Ringing silence follows her words, heavy and oppressive. Lavinder looks utterly speechless. I, on the other hand, want to talk, a lot, about *literally anything*, just to break the stifling blanket of silence. I want to ask Ara if she really thinks of me as her best friend, because if she does, then she's been *my* best friend for years. I want to tell her she's been my *family* for years. I want to tell her that I talked to Lavinder about what I found because I thought she didn't want anything to do with the murder anymore. I want to say *so much*, too much for Twenty Questions or spelling things out with a stupid pointer that won't move, and I *can't*, and the weight of it feels like it's *crushing* me all the way into the floor. I might be crying, if I'm even capable of that. I have no way to tell.

Ara takes several long, deep breaths with her eyes closed. Lavinder doesn't move. With her eyes still closed, Ara forces a smile, and after a solid few seconds it even starts to look natural. She wipes it, takes another deep breath, and looks unblinkingly at Lavinder. "Thanks," she says, "for not saying anything. I'm cool now. I'm good. Has there been... *anything* else like this? Any time you said something and didn't know why you said it?"

"I..."

"I won't get mad again, I swear."

Lavinder pauses, looking at her with an expression I don't recognise. I can't name the feeling, but it puts me in mind of a child worried they're about to be punished. It's *wary*.

"I *swear*," Ara repeats. "It ain't fair to stick centuries of gripe all on your shoulders. Just don't start telling me how to do my job, and we're golden."

"It..." Lavinder hesitates, clears his throat. "He... no, sorry, it — uh. Let me find the words."

"Take your time."

"It said something, I think, right before it — right before *we* left. In my apartment. I think it said something."

Ara's face changes all at once, all fascinated anticipation, not a trace left of anger or sulk or grump. "What did it say?"

"I'm not sure. At the time it was... frightening." Lavinder unconsciously rubs his shin under the table. "I was paying more attention to the *sound* than to... whatever it said. I think it was *go*."

Ara looks in my direction. "Was it?"

No.

"Roy says no."

"Yeah, see? I wasn't listening properly."

Ara puts her fingers back onto the pointer in the middle of the board. "Let's keep trying," she says. "Lord knows I didn't want to be the one to suggest it, but I'm not gonna let someone who keeps a picture of their *ex* in their goddamn *living room* outdo me on this one. Floor's yours, Roy. Leave the room if you're giving up."

Lavinder hesitates, then follows suit, and I'm left sitting on the third chair Ara pulled over from the living room, wondering what on earth I'm supposed to try next.

Well, the chair's solid underneath me. I can walk *through* chairs, but I can also sit in them. The pointer's still very solid, as I discover when I tentatively touch it again. What if how solid something is comes directly from my intent? What if I can make other things in the area solid too?

I make that my first investigation, moving methodically through the kitchen and touching everything within reach — or *trying* to touch everything within reach. I quickly figure out that, outside the small circle of the table and the chairs, everything remains as intangible as it always was. I can still step right inside the fridge, although I quickly stop doing *that*, because the dark vacuum inside is disorienting and painful. But the things *on* the table, like the candles, and the board, and the pointer, stand immobile when I touch them. On a whim, I move my finger through one of the candle flames. It feels *warm*.

I can't remember the last time I felt real heat. I can remember the *feeling*, but not any of the accompanying circumstances. The scary thing about that is, when I concentrate a little more, I'm nearly convinced that spirit-me never *has* felt warm, because I usually make it a point not to step into fires or heaters. So — where does the sensory memory come from?

My attention drifts down to the pointer, where Ara's and Lavinder's fingers are still resting on its edges. If everything *else* on the table is solid...

My gut clenches, my instincts scream, but I force my hand forward to rest it carefully on top of theirs.

And I'm right. Their fingers are solid.

"Leave room for Roy," says Ara impatiently, sitting back with her eyes closed.

"What do you mean?"

"It's not gonna be able to touch the pointer if you're hogging the whole thing."

Lavinder opens his eyes and stares down at the table. "I'm not."

"You're touching me."

"No, I'm not."

Ara opens her eyes, and inhales sharply.

I try to move the pointer with a firm push, but it's as stubborn as before. What was happening when I moved the picture frame? I nearly stopped existing out of shock, I remember that, but I was firmly *there* when I turned it over. Just scared.

Maybe I need to be scared again.

Before I have the chance to think or second-guess my split decision, I put my free hand through Lavinder's shoulder. I try very hard to keep thinking through the sensation of ice water flooding every empty space inside me, and I focus all my attention on the pointer, and I *push it*.

And it moves.

Each of us pull our hands away, including me. Ara and Lavinder look at each other, and then they wordlessly put their fingers back on the pointer. I take a breath to steady myself, fancy that I can hear nonexistent blood pounding in my ears, put one hand into Lavinder's shoulder, and push the pointer with the other.

H. I.

Lavinder stands up and moves away, face pale, breathing hard.

"Detective?" Ara squints at him with concern. "You okay there?"

"Yes — just —" He focuses on his breathing, consciously and obviously, one hand on his chest. "— I just feel like I'm about to have a heart attack."

Ara stands up fast and hard enough to knock one of the bigger candles on the table over. "Roy, don't you *dare!*"

In an instant, I'm over by the wall, as far away from Lavinder as I can physically be without leaving the room, my hands behind my back. Ara tracks the movement with an unfocused but angry gaze, then nods with satisfaction and picks the candle up.

Lavinder looks at Ara with an expression of alarm on his pale face. "*Roy's* doing this?"

"I don't *know*. Probably. It did it to a customer of mine, yesterday."

"And you *trust* it?"

"Yes. With my life. Literally, with my life. C'mere, let me take your pulse."

"*Why?*"

"Lots of little reasons. First, because the last thing I need is for a police officer to drop dead in my apartment of a goddamn *heart attack*. Pretty sure that's what you call a suspicious pattern. Second, because Roy scattered when I yelled at it. I think it's as scared as you are. So come on, give me your wrist."

Lavinder offers his wrist without further argument and Ara wraps two fingers around it. I stay where I am, trying to process far too much all at once. Communicating is *possible*, except it means hurting someone. I thought I was the only one who gets hurt when I step inside other people. I didn't know other people can feel it too. I've never looked at *their* reactions.

Ara trusts me. Ara *still trusts me*. Why?

"It's a little fast," Ara murmurs, "but it's calming down. You're gonna be fine. Right — ready to try again?"

Lavinder and I both stare at her.

"What? I didn't buy into the whole spooky-music-and-candles thing this far just to give up the moment we hit an obstacle. We're gonna need to be a little more creative, that's all. Roy, did you *mean* to nearly give the good detective here a heart attack?"

I answer without the Ouija Board: *No.*

"You said you had to, with Melanie. You said something was forcing you. Did something force you to do this?"

No.

"So it was an accident. Now, the million-dollar question: do you need to do it again to use the board?"

Yes.

"Does it work like a battery?"

Yes.

"Can you use me instead?"

"What?" I say out loud, and Ara takes the lack of movement as a yes.

"Great," she says. "We're gonna do that,

then." She turns toward her fridge. "And before either of you get the wrong idea about my general baseline level of magnanimity, I'm just gonna take this opportunity to say: *I fucking told you so.* I *told* you Ouija Boards are terrible. I *told* you they're more trouble than they're worth. Why ain't I surprised to learn they need *human batteries.*"

"You're not doing it," says Lavinder.

"Got a better idea, do you?"

"Yes. We shouldn't do this at *all*. But if you're going to try again whether I join in or not, I'm going to stay and help, and I'm going to be the battery."

"You —!"

"You're older than me. You're more at risk of a heart attack to begin with. I'm physically stronger, and I'm an officer of the law — shielding citizens from danger is written in the job description. We'll stop if it gets too much for me."

Ara points a finger at him, ready to deliver a scathing rebuttal, and nothing comes. She glares harder, then throws her hands up in the air. "You know what, fine! You want to risk your own neck, I sure as hell ain't gonna stop you. Just hang on for a bit, you're shaking, and Roy probably needs a few minutes to recover too. I'm gonna make us some special tea."

"Some — what kind of tea?"

"No clue. My grandma used to make it. Spiritual strength, she said. I figure it can't hurt."

Lavinder hesitates, then sits back down at the table. "Okay."

CHAPTER EIGHT

Recharging

This time, I can feel Lavinder shuddering when I put my hand inside his shoulder. Before, there was too much pain, too much fear, too much ice water in the empty parts of my existence for me to pay attention to anything going on around me apart from the letters I needed on the Ouija Board.

It feels a little bit easier to keep my focus this time around. I don't know if that's because I'm getting practice, or if it's just my imagination.

H U R T S

Ara reads out each letter as I point to it, and her expression slowly changes into one of concern. "It hurts you, not just him?"

I point to *YES* on the board.

"Let's make this fast then. Did you know Lavinder before the three of us met in the city?"

NO.

"Did you know his ex-wife?"

YES.

"How?"

I'm losing my focus; I want to ask why Ara chose to *start* with the yes-no questions, but I don't have the energy. I push on, forging the single word on the board.

S U P E R M A R K E T

Lavinder lets out an explosive breath and stands up from the table again. He manages two steps before he collapses against the wall, breathing just as hard as before, and I can't tell how much is the physical exertion of his heart and how much is shock at my answer. I can't say I'm not grateful for the chance to recover, at least; my body feels too big for its existence again, like when I first saw the picture in Lavinder's flat. It's probably not a good idea for me to try this again. It's probably not a good idea for me to be trying this at *all*.

When I manage to pull my focus back together, Ara's kneeling beside Lavinder, that particular pinch in her face that means she's feeling more responsibility and concern than she wants to be feeling. "You gonna die on me?" she says.

Lavinder shakes his head without much confidence.

"Do you need an ambulance?"

"No."

"Good. What happened at the supermarket?"

"She — Yvonne died. They said it was a heart attack."

No one says anything as the minutes stretch further and further. Lavinder gets his breathing back under control, and healthy blood flow back into his face. Ara sits on her haunches next to him, staring blankly into the distance. She's the first one to speak, and there's more feeling behind it than her tired voice gives the impression of.

"*Shit*," she says. "And there I was, makin' fun of... I'm sorry. I was a right arsehole."

Lavinder shakes his head. "Don't be sorry." He takes a breath, and lets his head fall back against the wall. "I divorced her years before that. I wasn't sorry she died."

The silence that stretches *this* time is very, very different. If I couldn't plainly see the confusion and suspicion on Ara's face, I'd have been convinced I imagined those words.

Ara stumbles over a few different replies before she manages something coherent. "You got a therapist?"

Lavinder smiles. "Yes, I do."

"They a good therapist?"

"Yes."

"You an abusive prick?"

"I — no."

"But you're sayin' it's a *good* thing Roy murdered a woman doing her shopping?" Ara waves an airy hand at me. "Not your fault, I know, I'm sorry."

"It's —" Lavinder's voice sticks in his throat; he swallows hard. "I'm sorry. I can't talk about it."

"Mhmm, okay, sure. Sit down with me, Roy. Use me as a battery. Same question."

I leave the kitchen briefly. *No.*

"If this is about hurting me, I swear, I'm gonna knock both your damn heads together, you see if I don't —"

No.

Ara pauses, then says again, much softer: "Is it dangerous for *you*?"

Yes.

"Can we try again tomorrow?"

104

Yes. Definitely. I haven't gotten the chance to tell Lavinder about the globe stand that Louis used to kill Andrea Relshaw, and no matter what the danger is, I'll be *damned* if I let this go before I tell him everything I know.

Ara nods once, satisfied. "Good. Detective, until I get an answer to that question, you ain't welcome here, and you *definitely* ain't welcome to spend the night. Can you get home safe?"

Lavinder takes two more deep breaths, then pushes himself carefully to his feet using the wall. "Yeah," he says.

"Great. I'll come by the station tomorrow."

"No, don't — my partner's never going to let me hear the end of it."

"I'm not using that bloody Ouija Board in a public place."

"What about the London Library? Plenty of empty spaces there."

"I'm not a member."

"I am. I can bring you inside."

Ara pauses, then nods. "Why not? I'm sure contacting spirits is *exactly* what Carlyle expected it to be used for. It's gonna be the last time, though, both of you hear me? Anything doesn't get asked or answered then about that poor woman's murder, it ain't *ever* getting asked or answered. Roy, you're welcome to spend the night, if that's something you're keen on doing."

No.

"Suit yourself. Library, tomorrow, lunchtime."

It takes only a couple of minutes further to work out the details; then Lavinder packs up the Ouija Board and leaves, and I follow suit before parting ways with him at the train station. There's one last person I want to go see tonight.

~~

By the time I find the right hospital, the right ward, and the right room, it's nearly three in the morning. Not many people are up and about at 3 in the morning, not even in a hospital; but the extra time and the extra space means I feel solid and real again. I don't know if Melanie will be able to see or hear me, and I don't know how I'll be able to communicate with her if she can't do either; but part of me doesn't really care. She's one of my victims. She should be *dead*, and she isn't. Part of me can't help but feel like if I can just *see* her, I'll find some of the answers I'm looking for, as ridiculous as I

know that feeling is. For all I know,
Lavinder might have been lying, or
mistaken, and the only way I'll know for
sure is to see her for myself.

She's asleep when I step into the room.
Her hair's been brushed and braided, but
the rest of her looks exactly like how you'd
expect a heart attack victim to look — pale,
and sallow, and, even in her sleep, a little bit
tense. There's a man I don't recognise asleep
in a chair pulled right up next to her bed,
and there's a teenager on the other side of
the room near the window, wide awake,
staring blank-faced out into the night. It's
Sam, I remember, the boy who was with
Melanie when she went to visit Ara.

There's a weight around the man in the
chair. I can walk up to Melanie in the bed
easily, and I can walk over to stand beside
Sam easily, but getting close to *him* feels like
walking through cement. The air hangs
heavy, and it bars my passage. I've seen that
before, sometimes, between people walking
out on the street together; it's a sort of
tangible distance in the air that's difficult for
me to move through. I've never learned
what it means. I never really cared enough
before to try and find out. But now, with

Melanie in the mix, it's *personal*, and feeling that gravity sitting tethered between Sam's position by the window and the man in the chair makes me want to curl up in the corner hissing like a cat.

I don't, of course. I'm not a cat.

What do I do now? Two of the three people in the room are asleep, and as I recall, the one who's awake doesn't put any stock in paranormal occurrences. I doubt *he's* going to be able to tell I'm there.

"Hello?" I try softly.

Nothing in the room moves.

"Melanie?"

She stirs a little with a groan. Sam's gaze jerks towards her, but he doesn't move.

I frown, and try again. "Melanie?"

"M'awake."

"Can you hear me?"

"I said m'awake."

Sam steps over to the bed, to the opposite side of the man in the chair, moving like he, too, can feel the physical weight that hangs between them. "Mels?" he asks. "Are you okay?"

"Fine." She stirs further, and makes a small effort to hoist herself up on her pillows. "Why'd you wake me up?"

"I didn't."

"Liar."

"I *didn't*."

"'S not very funny."

Sam makes an obvious effort to keep his voice at a whisper. "Just go back to sleep, you little worm."

"Mmkay."

I step desperately forward. "Melanie, can you hear me?"

Melanie groans. "*Yes,* I'm *awake,* I can *hear you just fine.*"

Sam says something else, and I don't hear it, because for a good few seconds I feel completely and utterly weightless. She can hear me. *She can hear me.* I have a *voice.* I have *weight.* Ara acknowledges me, knows I'm there, knows what I'm forced to do, and appreciates me anyway, but *this*? I didn't realise how much it ached in my chest to be able to speak, but never to be heard, never to be *understood,* until now. I spoke, and someone understood. I'm real. *I'm real.*

"I swear, Sam," Melanie says, "it wasn't a dream, I'm not an idiot, I know what a real person sounds like —"

"Melanie," I say again, and she stops, staring straight ahead at the wall, and I *want* to give her the time to process that she's hearing a disembodied voice Sam can't hear, but all of a sudden the words pour out in a rush and I can't even begin to try and stop myself. "I'm real, I'm *real*, my name's Roy, I was there when you and Sam went to go see Ara — Lady Arabetta — she's my best friend, I'm her best friend, she was worried about you and I thought you were *dead*, but you're not, and I didn't know if you'd be able to tell I was here, and you *can*, and I —"

Sam cuts me off. "Mels, what are you doing?"

"Sam, *shut up*."

"I'm real, I promise," I go on. I must be crying, because I can hear it in my voice. "I'm real. Please, *please*, I need you to believe me. I need your help. I need your help *tomorrow*."

I stop then, because the words have exhausted themselves, and somehow they've exhausted *me* as well. I feel dizzy and light-headed and, for the first time in ten years, I feel like I could sink onto a bed and fall asleep.

I don't fall asleep, though. Every single modicum of attention in me is focused, laser-like, on Melanie's face, which has shifted between disbelief and confusion several times since she started properly listening to me. Now, it's just thoughtful.

"Mels?" asks Sam, worry clear in his voice.

"Do you have a body?" Melanie asks. "Like, can you walk around? Can you see things?"

It takes me a couple of startled seconds to answer. "Yes. Yes, that's — I mean, I can't see it, but —"

"Sam, put your hands behind your back."

Sam blinks in confusion. "What?"

"Just do it, okay? Just humour me. I had a heart attack two days ago."

"… Okay then."

"It's a game where I have to guess how many fingers you're holding up behind your back. Zero to ten."

"Seriously?"

"Serious as a heart attack," Melanie answers him sweetly.

"That is *not* funny."

"It's a little bit funny."

"You're a jerk."

"I'm a jerk who's a little bit funny."

Sam rolls his eyes and huffs out a short laugh. "Okay, fine, guess the number."

111

"So how many fingers is he holding up?"

If the situation is surreal to *Sam*, as seems to be written plainly all over his face, it's sure as *hell* surreal to me. I don't know what I expected, but usually when ghosts or spirits or demon things try to bother someone who can't see them in books or movies or on TV, the person's reaction is a lot more like Lavinder's. Screaming, bumping into furniture, that sort of thing. I'm relieved, obviously, and still exhausted, and probably still crying, but I can't help being wary as well. People who react unpredictably are dangerous.

"Five," I tell Melanie.

"Five," she repeats back to Sam.

He blinks in surprise. "How did you do that?"

"I don't know, blind luck? Do it again. A different number this time."

"Okay."

"Seven," I say. Melanie repeats it, and Sam's surprise turns into incredulity. We try again, ten different times, and by the end we're not even pausing — Sam changes the number of fingers he's holding up as quickly as Melanie guesses correctly, and Melanie and I don't miss a beat telling him the new number. After the eleventh time, Sam abruptly stops, and so do I, and so, by extension, does Melanie.

"Cool," says Melanie. "So I'm not just hearing voices. Sam, I can talk to a ghost."

Sam stares at her.

"I think I'm more of a spirit," I say. "Ara doesn't think I'm a ghost, and I don't remember dying."

"Sorry. I can talk to a spirit, Sam."

"What the *fuck*," says Sam, with a lot of very quiet feeling in his voice.

"That was the point of the guessing game. I could have been hallucinating, and even if I wasn't, there's no way in hell *you* would have ever believed me. Now we're both convinced."

"*I'm* not —!"

"For God's sake, Sam, get over yourself. Sorry, what was your name again?"

For some reason, Melanie's concern that she might have been hallucinating makes me feel better. *Now* things are a little more predictable. "Roy."

"Roy. His name is Roy, and he —"

"It."

"What?"

"I'm not a he, I'm —" I pause, and I can't

help laughing. It might be a bit hysterical.
"I'm a *spirit*. Just call me it."

"But you sound like a dude," says Melanie dubiously.

"I do?"

"Yeah."

"*Really*?"

"Yeah."

"I *sound* like something!?"

"Uh..."

"What do I sound like? Can you record me? Wait, no, that's a stupid suggestion. What's a real person I sound like? A celebrity or something, someone on TV? Hang on, do I have an *accent*? What's my accent?"

"Okay, hold your horses there, jitterbug. What do you sound like to *you*?"

"Well — nothing. I can't hear myself."

"You can't *hear* yourself?"

"I hear the words I say, but I don't hear a voice *saying* them."

"What the hell does that *mean*? Wait, no, I don't care yet. What are you even doing here? You're just as surprised about all this as I am, so if you didn't expect me to hear you, why are you here?"

"I thought you were dead. I thought —" I

pause again, because there's no way I'm telling her I'm the reason she's in the hospital. "— Ara's my best friend, and I was there when you had your heart attack, and I thought, maybe if you had a near-death experience..."

Melanie nods, like this makes all the sense in the world to her. "So what is this, then, like a Ghost Whisperer thing? You have unfinished business you want me to help with?"

"Still not a ghost."

"Right. Sorry."

"But yes, I want your help. Ara can tell I'm there, but she can't *hear* me, and I need to talk to her and the police about a woman who was killed in London yesterday."

"You want me to help solve a murder mystery?"

"No, I know who the killer is. But *they* don't, and you're my only way of telling them."

"Cool. Great. Give me, like, three hours to process that I'm suddenly in a paranormal mystery episodic adventure, and I'll get back to you."

"Okay. What's my accent? Tell me what my accent is."

"Uh, I don't know, normal?"

"Normal for what country?"

"Scandinavia. Which country do you *think*, you doofus?"

"England? You mean England? I'm English?"

"You sure sound it, yeah. Is that a surprise?"

"Yes, that's a surprise! The first place I remember is New York City!" I pace up and down beside Melanie's bed, full of nervous energy. "This is all brand-new, I've never talked to anyone before. I mean, I talk to people all the time, but they never talk *back*, which can sometimes get very depressing and take away all your motivation for ever saying anything. Sometimes I *think* I can tell, but then other times I can't, you know? It might even change depending on what country I'm in. I need to test that. I don't know *how* I'd test that unless you came with me, though. And hey, now that I'm thinking about it, there are some places where I'm a little more *solid*, like — I can flatten the grass in Ireland, you know, when you're lying down and you stand up and there's an imprint left behind in the shape of your body? In Ireland, I can do that. So I know

I'm human, or humanoid, or humanish, but I've never heard my own voice before. Could you imitate me? So I have an idea? How deep is it?"

"I'm not going to *parrot* you," Melanie says, cutting me off. "I'm *terrible* at voice acting." She takes a long breath with her eyes closed. "If you want to bring someone here, sure, I'm happy to translate, but I don't think they're going to let me leave the hospital any time soon. Heart attacks aren't supposed to happen in teenagers, can you believe that? They think I might have some kind of heart murmur. Plus, Dad's not going to let me out of his sight maybe ever again."

"Fuck what Dad wants," Sam mutters. He's still eyeing the space I'm standing in warily, having followed Melanie's gaze towards where the sound of my voice came from. "*I'm* not letting you leave the hospital, not until they say you're good and ready."

Melanie gestures at him. "So there you have it."

"I can do that," I decide. "I can bring Ara here."

"Lady Arabetta? How?"

"Creative communication, mostly."

"Oh, good. For a second there I was

scared you were going to say possession."

I laugh. "Ara wouldn't let me possess her even if that was something I could do," I assure her. "And I'm pretty sure it's not. Being inside someone hurts."

"Hurts?"

"Yes. A lot."

"You're pretty well-spoken for someone who's literally never talked to a living thing before."

"Thanks! I've had a lot of practice, I think. I talk to myself sometimes. I talk to Ara a lot. I hear other peoples' conversations all the time. It's like learning from a textbook, you know? You have all the theory and all the examples and all the discussion questions, but you don't actually get —"

"Yeah, Roy, I had a heart attack two days ago. I'm *exhausted*. Can you let me sleep?"

I cut myself off after I've tripped over a few more words. "Yeah, of course. I — sorry, I'm sorry I bothered you. I hope you have good dreams. Say hi to Sam for me."

"I think Sam probably wants to try punching you."

I glance over at Sam, and honestly, I can't disagree. He looks like exactly the sort of person who gets over uncertainty by being illogically aggressive, and the expression of startled annoyance on his face when Melanie says his name speaks volumes. "I don't like this," he says to Melanie, his entire body tense. "I don't like this at *all*."

"You're only saying that because we're talking about you behind your back in front of your face." Melanie snuggles down into her pillows, and I finally notice that her breathing sounds more strained than it did when she first woke up. That's stupid of me to ignore. She had a *heart attack*. Of course shock isn't going to help, and I don't want to be the reason she flatlines again, so I move toward the door while Sam helps Melanie get comfortable.

"Sorry," I say again over my shoulder. "Sleep well, Melanie."

"You too," she murmurs.

I have a vague memory, as I navigate the corridors of the hospital down to the ground floor, of that exact dialogue. *Sleep well. You too.* Not from watching other people, either. I'm pretty sure I remember someone saying that to *me* before.

Sleep well.

Who would have said that to me? Ara?

My entire body is vibrating with

excitement and I feel like I could leap over the moon if I had to, but I end up leaving the hospital with a lot more questions than I was hoping to have when I went in.

CHAPTER NINE

Rendevous

Nothing happens to me between leaving Melanie's hospital room and arriving at the London Library at noon the next day.

It should feel familiar. That's the story of my life — of my entire ten-year existence before this. Months of nothing happening, followed by a few days of emotional struggle as the urge to kill someone grips me, followed by more months of nothing happening. I thought I was used to that. I thought it was all I'd ever known. I told myself it was fine, it was *relaxing,* it gave me the opportunity to travel around and learn so many different things about so many different kinds of people.

Today, I find it *maddeningly boring.*

That changes when I finally decide to head over to the library to wait for Lavinder and Ara to get there. I've never been inside before, and I quickly conclude that that's a small travesty. It's a beautiful mix of magic and mundane, of old-fashioned narrow aisles twisting and turning in a maze of books and modern open-plan study spaces, of cosy reading nooks and rickety metal staircases servicing higher shelves. It's the kind of place I can almost pretend I'm real, completely alone in the stacks. The kind of place where, if I nearly bump into someone turning a corner, I say 'excuse me' without thinking. The kind of place where you could almost expect to see something truly magical if you get lost, a staircase to nowhere or a blank wall where there shouldn't be one, or a stately wardrobe with nothing in it. Inside the stacks, walking alongside books that have been bound by hand and books that were printed three hundred years ago, I can almost pretend that when I step outside, I'll be in a completely different time period.

The effect is somewhat ruined whenever you come across someone with a laptop, or a printer. But even then, I make those people into a way of passing the time. One of the people in the Writers' Room is a journalist, doing research into patterns of conflict in Syria, and she's entirely unbothered by my presence as I watch her work over her shoulder. Someone else on the opposite side of the room is a novelist, writing a story where dragons rule the sky and someone's child is recruited to prevent a war. I read as he types until he stops and stares out the window beside him, daydreaming.

All in all, while I'm still relieved when noon finally arrives, I'm certainly not bored anymore.

Once Lavinder signs Ara in as a guest at reception, he leads us both downstairs into the basement, which turns out to be a labyrinth of journals and newspapers. "The Times Room," he explains. "It's all available online, so not many people come down here. We should be fine."

"I ain't wild about the idea someone might walk in on us," Ara grumbles.

"We're not breaking any rules."

"Yeah, yeah, yeah. And try not to have a heart attack," she adds, "'cause then paramedics will need to storm the place and I don't want to answer *those* questions either."

Lavinder's mouth twitches into a smile. "Duly noted."

They don't speak again as they set up the board on the floor in a secluded corner of the stacks. Ara's mind, I know, is still on what Lavinder said last night, trying to puzzle out what on earth could make him grateful that his ex-wife died. I'm curious too, but I have far too many things to be curious about lately, and I have two very important things to communicate right here and right now, so my mind is on how to say them using as few letters as possible. I don't want Lavinder to have a heart attack any more than Ara does.

"Okay," says Ara once they're seated around the board. She glances up at the corners nearest them, which remain empty of people and noise. "Whenever you're ready, Roy. First question — "

The last time we did this, it was the first time I'd ever been able to communicate anything substantial. It had been terrifying, but also thrilling. Today, after being able to speak seamlessly to Melanie, the thrill of the Ouija board is completely gone, leaving nothing but quietly burning impatience in its wake. I take a deep breath, put my hand inside Lavinder's shoulder, and move the pointer before Ara can even form a question.

G - L - O - B - E

"Globe?" Ara frowns down at the pointer. "The hell does that mean?"

Lavinder's breathing is strained, his face drained of some colour, but I can still tell from his expression exactly when the penny drops. "Globe," he says. "There's a globe in Relshaw's office. What about that globe?"

W - E - A - P - O - N

Lavinder frowns, but doesn't ask anything else. He looks like he's mulling it over in his mind, and I figure that's the best I can do — he'll go back to the crime scene on his own and work it out for himself, now that he knows what to look for. I have to keep pressing on, so I take Lavinder's shoulder again and ignore that he stiffens with a sharp exhale.

M - E - L - A - N - I - E

"Melanie?" Ara says out loud. "She's in the hospital, ain't she? What does she have to do with the murder?"

H - E - A - R - S - M - E

Everything in Ara's posture changes. She sits straighter, stares more intensely at the board, breathes a little quicker. "She *what*?"

I don't try to communicate again.
Lavinder's leaning away from my touch,
and Ara knows *exactly* what I mean.

"That don't make any sense," Ara mutters.
"She couldn't hear you when she came to see
me. What gives?" She pauses. "Did you go to
see her at the hospital?"

YES

"How come she can hear you? 'Cause she
almost died?"

YES

Ara claps her hands together, startling
both me and Lavinder. "Great. Detective,
what's the safest way to have a near-death
experience?"

He doesn't answer her. Partly out of
surprise, I suspect, which is perfectly
understandable, because I'm *also* staring at
Ara like she's gone completely insane. But I
really don't like how pale Lavinder's face is,
either, so I'm not going to communicate
again no matter what the question is. If Ara
wants to know anything else, then she
knows to go and see Melanie. And,
hopefully, she knows not to *throw herself in
front of a bus* before she gets there, *what is she
thinking*.

"I'm serious," Ara goes on. "I can handle

126

having a heart attack. Roy, give me a heart attack."

"No!" I shout, louder than is probably appropriate in a library even if you're an intangible spirit.

"Lady —" Lavinder tries to say, but his voice is hoarse with effort and he has to stop so he can concentrate on breathing.

"Is it pills? People get their stomach pumped when they OD, don't they? What are my chances of being okay if I do that?"

"Arabetta —"

"Also, is it gonna hurt?"

"There — *isn't* a safe way to —"

"Don't give me that rubbish, people fail at committing suicide all the time. Tell me what the odds are. I'll be careful, I'll have someone with me, emergency services on standby —"

"You're insane, I won't — help you do that —"

"That's fine, I have plenty of friends I can ask."

Lavinder takes a long breath and gives Ara the sternest expression I've ever seen on his face. "I will arrest you *right* here."

Ara looks like she's going to argue, but then she deflates with an angry breath. "Just wanna be able to talk to my best friend, is all," she mutters. "Fine, fine. How are you doin'? Need a visit to the hospital?"

Lavinder pauses, assessing both his own health and how serious Ara is about relinquishing her plan; then he slowly shakes his head. "I'll be alright."

"You *sure* you don't need a visit to the hospital?"

"Yes." He rubs his hair and stares down at the board, considering. "How about this — you go see Melanie, with Roy. I'll go back to the station and see about this globe. If Roy can tell you anything else, call me. How does that sound?"

"Annoyingly reasonable."

"Actually, call me anyway, just so I know you're alive."

Ara huffs out a laugh. "You mean you won't be grateful if *I* end up dead?"

"No."

Something changes in Ara's face, and I know exactly what it is. She'd been joking — a mean joke, a prodding joke, a cruelly teasing joke, but a joke nonetheless. The kind of men who perpetuate abuse, or who wouldn't blink at a woman's death, would answer defensively. Or they'd joke back. Or they'd get angry.

Lavinder takes it completely seriously, and answers completely seriously.

I don't remember very much about the woman I killed in the supermarket. I remember how *I* felt, because it had been the first time I'd actually felt anything in response to one of my compelled murders. But I don't remember much about the woman. She'd been... tall, I think. Wearing a dress? Was it a dress, or was it yoga pants? I never thought I'd ever confuse the two, even in my memory.

What sort of woman would Lavinder not be sorry to lose?

"Alright," Ara says, slowly and thoughtfully. "I'll give you a call when I get there."

"*Thank* you. Be careful."

"You remember *Louis*, right? Found any new suspects called Louis?"

"No."

"Be on the lookout for someone called Louis."

"I will."

"And *you* be careful."

Lavinder does his half-smile again. "I will."

They exchange numbers, and I remain lost in my own thoughts as I follow Ara out of the library. I feel like I'm *missing* something, something I should know, like I have the answer to a trivia question on the tip of my tongue. But no matter how hard I strain, I can't quite grasp the shape of it, and it's bothering me *so* much more than I'd like.

~~

"Look, she'll see *me*," Ara insists, glaring at the woman behind the reception desk. "I'm a psychic, I can guarantee you she wants to see me. Tell her Lady Arabetta wants to see her and that she's got a story about Roy."

"I told you," the reception lady says, just as stubborn and far more polite, "no visitors. It doesn't matter who you are, our policy is very clear."

"It's visiting hours, though."

"The family have made it clear they don't want visitors."

"Will you just *tell* her, for god's sake? Let her make up her own mind after that?"

"I'm afraid I can't do that."

"Why the hell not?"

"Because the family have made it very clear they don't want visitors."

"It's that tit of a brother of hers, isn't it? He's told you to keep *me* out, 'cause he still thinks I poisoned her."

"Ma'am, I really can't —"

"Ask *her* what she wants, not that great big bloody —"

"Ma'am, if you don't leave, I'm going to have to call security."

Ara takes a breath, pauses, and then releases it, rolling her eyes. "Fine, fine. You don't mind if I read a magazine in your public waiting room, do you? I ain't got magazines at home and I've been dying to look at..." She leans over to see what's on the table in the corner. "... Architectural Digest."

"I certainly can't stop you, ma'am," says the reception lady with a pleasant smile. "Have a nice day."

Ara gives a sarcastic smile back and turns away. "Roy," she mutters out of the corner of her mouth, "can you do anything?"

I walk right past the reception desk and take the stairwell up to Melanie's floor.

"I'll take that as a yes!" I hear Ara call after me, her voice raised so I can hear it, and as I continue on to Melanie's room, my thoughts are preoccupied with picturing the reception lady scolding Ara down into a waiting room chair. It makes me smile and grimace at the same time.

There's a lot more activity in Melanie's room than there was overnight. The man who'd been asleep in the chair before is awake now, standing up at his full considerable height, hovering protectively over Melanie's bed. Sam is standing in the corner, once again as far away from the man as physically possible, leaving that tangible weight in the air between them. They're all paying rapt attention to a doctor who's standing at the foot of the bed, holding a clipboard, in the middle of some rambling explanation I missed the beginning of.

"… to put it simply," he says, "there *is* no cause — not one we can find. Your heart is perfectly healthy."

"You're missing a test, then," the tall man says.

"I know it seems that way, but I promise you, we have done *everything* we can. I can take you through how recovery is going to work, but after that, you shouldn't have any further problems."

"And what if she *does*?"

"It's hard to believe, but the human body

is… it's a very finely-tuned machine, and it's not unheard of for a glitch in the machinery to cause a problem like this. As long as Melanie is careful with her recovery, there is no reason for this to happen again. She'll be absolutely fine."

"Hey, Melanie," I say into the lull of the conversation.

Her head jerks towards me, her eyes wide, and then she sighs. "Really?" she murmurs quietly. "With everyone here?"

"What was that?" asks the doctor.

"Nothing. Just thinking out loud."

"Sorry," I tell her, "I'm still getting used to this. Ara's downstairs trying to get in to see you and the receptionist won't let her. She says you don't want any visitors."

"You know what?" says Melanie. "On the off-chance that someone's here to see me, can you go down and send them up?"

The doctor frowns. "What do you mean?"

"Just — you know, I want visitors. It's boring here without visitors."

"What are we, chopped liver?" says Sam.

"We don't *want* any other visitors," says the tall man, with no small measure of irritation. "Just family."

"Hey!" Melanie raises her arm. "As the

only person in this room who actually gets a say in it, I want as *many visitors as possible.* Can you just check, please? Just check the waiting room and see if anyone's here for me?"

"Melanie —"

"I am a disabled infirm, dad, and I want attention."

"I'm not convinced that *psychic* didn't try to —"

"Dad! Come *on.* Visitors are *important for my recovery.* Right?"

The doctor hesitates, looking between Melanie and the tall man next to her. "Well, I… I can certainly stop by downstairs and ask if anyone's been trying to see you, if you'd like."

"Yeah! That would be great. And if, you know, they're still *here,* just go ahead and send them up. Please?"

"Melanie," says the tall man, "I really don't think that's —"

"Luckily," Sam cuts him off, "no one gives a shit what *you* think. Just do it, she won't let us hear the end of it otherwise."

"Technically," the doctor says carefully, looking down at the clipboard, "Melanie isn't eighteen yet, so —"

"Yeah, she's been completely independent for two years," Sam interrupts him, with all the hurried irritation of someone far too accustomed to explaining that. "*I'll* go check if —"

"I," says Melanie, cutting everyone off, "am going to throw a *tantrum* if I don't get my way, and I can't imagine *that's* going to be good for my recovery, so maybe just do what I'm asking? Please?"

The doctor shakes his head with a weak smile. "Alright, alright. I'm on my way. Ring for a nurse if you need anything else, okay?"

"Yep, I know the drill."

The doctor leaves the room, and a very unpleasant silence sits around the four of us.

"Let me guess," says Sam. "That guess-how-many-fingers crap again."

Melanie gives him a brilliant smile. "Promise you're not going to get mad at her?"

"Mad at who?"

"Lady Arabetta."

Sam's face goes sour, and he opens his mouth to say something Melanie *probably* won't like, but lets it fade with an irritated grumble. "Yeah, I won't get mad at her."

"This is the psychic?" their father asks, his expression completely unreadable.

"Oh, yeah. Dad, go on a walkabout."

"What?"

"You're gonna be rude to her, and I want visitors, not drama."

"I'm not going to —!"

"Remember our deal? My terms. *My* terms. I still want to believe you, but you're *going* to make a scene, so go on a walk and come back when she leaves, okay?"

There's something about the idea of Melanie *ordering* her father to leave which chills me down to the very bones I don't have. His expression is as unreadable as ever, but I could *swear* that I'm about to see him lash out, standing right next to Melanie in her hospital bed, his fist on the same level as her face. In the corner, Sam straightens, shoulders tense, a wiry coil ready to spring.

But Melanie's father doesn't lash out. He stands very still for several seconds, and then he takes a long breath and nods. "Okay."

And he walks out, taking that heaviness in the air with him.

"*Shit*," Sam says, exhaling a sharp breath. "Do you really have to test him like that?"

136

Melanie shrugs. "You can go on a walk too, by the way, if you don't think you can be nice."

"I can be nice."

"I've never *once* seen you be nice."

"I'm nice all the *time*. You just don't see it."

"Choosing not to punch someone is not being nice."

"But punching them *is*?"

"Depends on the punch."

"I know exactly what you're trying to do, and I don't care *who* you are, I'm not punching some sick kid in the hospital."

"Coward."

"Do you want me to be nice, or what?"

They're both laughing. I'm standing awkwardly in the corner. I want to join in, in a way I've never really experienced before. I'm no stranger to feeling invisible, or dismissed, or ignored — every part of that is part and parcel of being... whatever the hell it is I am. I come across friendly banter between friends all the time. Usually I'm content just to listen and enjoy it. With Melanie and Sam, I'm not content, I'm *aching*. There's a yearn, deep inside me, for something I don't remember ever having. With them, I don't feel invisible, I feel... left

137

out.

It's weird, and I don't like it very much.

They've both trailed off by the time Ara walks into the room, and — with barely a glance around the space to take in her new surroundings — Ara lifts her eyebrows at Melanie. "You don't need to stop on *my* account."

"I'm being nice," she explains, "to prove a point." She and Sam both start laughing again. Ara looks confused, then bemused, then impatient, with her arms folded over her chest.

"So you can hear Roy," she says, which is presumably meant to cut the laughter off. Instead, it makes Melanie laugh harder.

"See!?" she says to Sam, gesturing at Ara. "Psychic! I told you!"

"That wasn't psychic, Roy told me."

"Then why do you need my help at all?"

"It's a damn sight better than watching someone get used as a battery, that's — look, would you stop laughing like a crazy loon, it is *very* unsettling."

Melanie waves a hand. "Sorry, sorry, don't mind me..."

"I *have* to mind you, you're our translator."

"Right. Yeah. Sorry. Hang on."

"Roy, what the hell did you mean when you said *globe*?"

"It's the murder weapon," I say immediately. "There's tons of them in the building, practically one per office. I think someone used the globe stand to stab her, and then swapped it out with another one on some other floor."

Melanie sobers up *very* quickly when she hears that. "Murder what?"

"The murder —" I freeze. Melanie must have been *very* tired last night. "It's a murder case, sorry. Ara and I have been trying to help the police solve a murder in London. Just tell her it's the murder weapon."

"Uh..." Melanie looks at Ara. "He says it's — no, *it* says the — can I use 'they'?"

"What?" asks Ara.

"What?" I echo.

"I don't want to call a sentient being *it*. How do you feel about 'they'?"

It takes me a moment to process what the hell Melanie's talking about. "Oh — yeah, sure. I really don't care. Tell her it's the murder weapon."

"They say it's the murder weapon."

"And —"

"And also there's a lot of them, a lot of the

139

globe things, and someone used a globe
stand to stab the person, and swapped it out
with another one on some other floor. Shit,
Roy, this is *not* what I signed up for!"

Ara doesn't answer, too busy typing
feverishly into her phone. "Got it, great.
Roy, how do you feel about Lavinder?"

"What?"

"They say what?" Melanie dutifully
translates.

Ara rolls her eyes. "Did I stutter? How do
you feel about Lavinder? Does he feel okay
to you? Do you trust him? Does he rub you
the wrong way? Lay it on me. I want your
honest opinion."

I frown at her. "Why?"

"Why?"

"Because I can't figure him out, that's
why! He's a gentleman except for how he's
glad his wife's dead, he's helpful except for
how he's a copper, he *owns a Ouija board* for
lord knows what unfathomable reason, and
he's thrown his lot in with *us*, a medium and
a vengeful spirit guide, to — what? To solve
a murder? Is he *genuine*, or is he a goddamn
prick?"

"How am *I* supposed to know that? I'm
not omnipotent."

"How are they supposed to know that, they're not omnipotent."

Ara shakes her head. "You've been following him around, haven't you? And what do you mean, you're not omnipotent? You sure as hell ain't human."

"I *am* human, really, I'm just invisible."

"They *are* human, really, they're just invisible."

Ara bursts out laughing. "Oh, so humans teleport? Humans sit on ceilings? Humans kill each other with telepathic heart attacks? Your story's ringing a bit hollow, bud."

"I —! Those were *accidents*! I can't usually just teleport around the world like distance doesn't matter, that was *weird*. It's not like I've been able to do it again."

I wait for Melanie to repeat my words, and she doesn't. When I look at her, she's staring at Ara, her face whiter than it was overnight. "Telepathic heart attacks?"

Everyone in the room is deadly quiet.

"Melanie," I finally say — at least part of my silence was because I'd completely forgotten my apologies might actually mean something here. "I'm... I've had to, for... um. Sometimes I get this feeling that I have to hurt someone, and the longer I ignore it,

141

the worse it hurts *me*. I hate doing it. I don't know *why* I have to do it. But it always — usually it *kills* people, but it didn't kill you, and I don't know why, but I was *so happy* to learn that —"

"Roy, you better be explaining," says Ara.

"They're explaining," says Melanie, "so shhh."

"— so I've been trying to stay away just in case the urge comes back, but it *hasn't* come back, and you're making me wonder if everyone I've ever done this to had a chance to survive, and —"

Melanie shakes her head. "So, what, it was an accident?"

"Well — no. No, it's deliberate. But —"

"— but you had to."

"Yes."

"Because you always have to, because you get hurt otherwise."

"Yes."

"Is it just Lady Arabetta's clients?"

"No, you're the only one who — no. Just people, random people, people I don't know, all over the world."

"Have you tried, you know, *not* killing someone?"

"Of *course* I've tried not killing someone,"

I answer, struggling between feeling offended and uncomfortably remembering how little I cared in those early years.

"What happens?"

I hesitate, trying to find the words. "It hurts. Like — like a headache, but all over. Like you're getting pushed down into a tiny bucket and there's a weight squeezing down, and it gets worse and worse and worse until I forget everything except that I *need* to do it."

Melanie digests this silently. I feel like I'm waiting on pins and needles. After a minute, she relays my side of the conversation to Sam and to Ara, with no trace of her true feelings on the subject in her face or her voice. Ara just nods, like this was all old news to her; Sam, predictably, glowers.

"I'm sorry," I repeat. "Really. It sucks. It all sucks. I'm glad you're okay. I'm *really glad* you're okay."

"Well, that makes two of us." Melanie smiles. "Warn me if you're going to do it again, okay?"

"Okay." I pause. "Just out of curiosity, what would you do about it?"

"Search me. Run, I guess? Maybe I can take a lot of fish oil all at once and give my heart a massive strength boost."

I laugh. So does Melanie. It takes her another minute to gather enough breath to be able to speak coherently again. "Okay, okay, so you said — what were we talking about before that?"

"Lavinder," Ara volunteers curtly. "We were talking about Roy's opinion about Lavinder."

"Oh, right. The copper guy."

"I think he's genuine," I decide, firmly, out loud.

"Roy says they think he's genuine."

Ara looks at the spot I'm occupying, following her strong but vague sixth sense, her gaze as off-centre as always. "Why?" she asks.

I shrug a little. "I don't know. It's not logical, I don't have any justification for you. It's just my gut. No, wait, I don't think I have a gut. Instinct? Instinct, I guess. Men like what you're thinking of don't take the existence of things like me in stride based only on the word of a woman."

Melanie translates, nearly word for word, and Ara bursts out laughing. "You've got a point there," she admits. "He's —"

"And — wait, Melanie, tell her to wait —

what you said yesterday, about how I'm your best friend? I just want to make sure you know that you're mine too. I really wanted to say that at the time. I don't know what I'd have done if I never met you. You're one of the reasons I keep *trying*, and you're the only reason Andrea Relshaw has any chance of getting justice. You're the closest thing I think I've ever had to family."

"Aw," says Melanie, "how sappy."

"You don't have to relay the sappy bits," says Ara, rolling her eyes.

"Oh, no, believe me, I *really do*."

And she does. And Ara listens, her eyes on the space I'm in instead of Melanie, which is why I can see the tears glistening before she quickly wipes them off on her sleeve and pretends like I haven't said anything meaningful to her at all.

~~

Through Melanie, I manage to tell Ara everything I know about the murder. I tell her about Louis, and the conversation I overheard right before he murdered his coworker. Ara types every single word into her phone, which I belatedly realise she's doing because she's texting Lavinder all the relevant information. Texting. *Texting*. Part

145

of me feels ashamed I forgot texting exists.

When she's done, she slips the phone back into her pocket and fixes Melanie with a piercing look.

"Young lady," she says, "I'm prepared to offer you an internship with my consultancy practice, from the moment this sterile prison lets you go until such a time as I work out how to develop your unique set of skills."

Melanie laughs. "You'll *what*?"

"I'm offerin' you a job."

"What, really? A paid job?"

"That's what 'job' means."

Melanie laughs more, and stops when she realises Ara isn't laughing at all. "I'll — I'll think about it? Sure sounds like more fun than catching up on schoolwork."

Sam scoffs. "Blow off the rest of the year."

"*Sam.*"

"I'm serious. Tell them you had a heart attack. Drop out, get better, do your A-levels next year."

"What a *fantastic* brother you are."

"People would kill to have their brothers tell them that, you ungrateful little snipe."

"People killing other people is why some people would need brothers like you at all, you giant-eared cretin. I'm *not* dropping out,

146

but I will *consider* asking for a couple of weeks off."

Sam grumbles, but he's clearly learned better than to argue. "Fine."

Melanie brightens. "Hey, do you think I can get extra credit for the police acknowledging I helped crack their case wide open?"

"The police ain't gonna admit any such thing," says Ara. "Lavinder's keeping this quiet. You can probably guess why."

"But what about my five minutes of fame?"

"Tell a TV station you had a heart attack at seventeen."

"I want five minutes of *fame*, not five years of infamy."

"And you think you'll get that if the headline's 'Local Girl Translates For A Ghost'? Grow up." Ara gathers herself up. "Now *you* are gonna recover, and *then* you're gonna give me a call just in case we need your help again, sound good?"

"I could die first and *then* give you a call."

"No, you can't. What the hell kind of logic is that?"

"Fiiine. Then it's a deal."

Sam is uncharacteristically difficult to

read as Ara and I leave the room. I can tell
he's upset, but I can't tell what he's upset *by*,
because for once, it doesn't seem to be Ara.
Maybe he's just generally pessimistic and
doesn't know how to deal with good news.
Their father turns the corner into the hall
just as Ara disappears down the stairwell,
and I take a brief pause to study him. He
looks like Sam. Sam probably hates that. I
take a tentative step towards him, and that
same heaviness in the air blocks me from
getting too close.

What *is* that heaviness? Who is he? Why
had I been so convinced he'd hurt Melanie?

Sam thought he was going to hurt
Melanie, that was obvious. Maybe I just
picked up on that. Maybe everything about
the man is so unnerving to me that I
immediately imagined the worst-case
scenario. Either way, I don't really feel like
giving him the benefit of the doubt. Frankly,
I'm amazed *Melanie's* willing to do that.

Thinking about it, I actually feel a little bit
scared. I don't know what's scaring me, but
I recognise the signs. When I thought he
was going to hurt Melanie, it wasn't Melanie
I saw in the bed. The trouble is, I'm not sure
who I *did* see, and I don't know if what I

saw was a memory, my imagination, or
some other quirk of being whatever the hell
it is I am.

And I don't even know where to *begin*
looking for answers.

CHAPTER TEN

Rescue

Lavinder comes over to Ara's flat again that evening, once he's off-duty. Ara begins interrogating him the moment he steps inside, even as she puts together some tea and brandy for them both.

"So how did it go?" she demands. "You find anything?"

"There's no one called Louis who works in the building," Lavinder answers, taking the interrogation completely in stride. "Not so much as a janitor. Is Roy sure that he was a coworker?"

I answer *yes*, in Ara's leave-the-room style of communication. Once Ara nods toward me in confirmation, though, I immediately begin second-guessing my certainty. Andrea

150

specifically talked about *firing* him, I
remember, and I told Ara as much earlier in
the day through Melanie. *Start looking for
other jobs*, she'd said. What else could that
possibly mean?

But the more I think about it, the less sure
I am. She talked about an excuse to turn him
down, and an excuse to start an
investigation. Maybe I'm missing some
important context. Maybe Louis is *related* to
Oath Holdings, Inc., but not an employee.
Maybe he's friends with someone who
works there. Maybe he's a business partner.
Maybe someone erased all evidence of his
relationship with the company.

Maybe this is all giving me a headache.

"Could be a nickname," Ara suggests.

"That's what I think," Lavinder agrees,
nodding. "You said *scamming* in your text.
Whoever the guy is, Louis might not be the
name he's going by now. The only other
lead is that they were looking for an excuse
to fire him, and, surprise surprise, no one on
the board wants to talk to us about who
they're planning to fire. I can't get much
further without someone else at the precinct
to help who believes that my 'hunches' are
solid fact."

Ara laughs. "Don't suppose anyone else there would believe a *psychic*, hm?"

"Not enough to investigate what a psychic tells them to investigate, no."

"Why the hell not? What do they have to lose?"

"Reputation. Time. The luxury of not having to deal with frauds who all think they can do the same thing and earn a reward for it. Dignity. Pride."

"They're all stupid. So this is all we have to show for our hard work? A bunch of stubborn morons and dead ends?"

"Not quite. We found the murder weapon."

Ara stares at him. "Then why didn't you lead with *that*!?"

Lavinder smiles a little. "You sound like my captain."

"*You take that back.*"

"Okay. You don't sound like my captain. We found the murder weapon, that globe stand. It got swapped with the one in the CEO's office, believe it or not. There's a partial print, but no match in the database, so it's not quite as helpful as you might think."

"So get the fingerprints of all the

employees and compare them."

"Mike's working on a warrant for that, but it's going to take a couple of days."

Ara blows out a frustrated breath and slams the teapot down a little too harshly. "Your job is terrible."

"You don't have to tell *me* that."

They both fall silent for a moment, and I'm gripped by an urge to talk just to fill that silence. Hardly any point in it if no one can hear me, though. I'm starting to think Melanie might already be spoiling me.

It's several minutes before anyone says anything, and it turns out to be Lavinder, breaking the silence by uncomfortably clearing his throat. "So," he says, "you told me yesterday that you can see pieces of people from when they were alive."

"Yep," Ara answers. "Sure can. The blood, or the guts, or the kidneys, or the brain. You name it, I can see it."

Lavinder gives her an odd look.

"I'm joking. Christ Almighty, Lavinder, grow a sense of humour. I can see parts of their existence from while they were alive, yeah. Why?"

"How much does a session cost?"

Ara takes a long gulping slurp of her tea

before she answers. "Why?"

"Because I'd like to pay you for a session."

"Why?"

"Well, because it's not fair if I don't."

"Cut the crap, you know what I mean. It's your ex-wife, right?"

"No," Lavinder says immediately. "No, I — no. There's nothing about her I want to understand anymore. No, it's someone else. From a long time ago."

"Colour me intrigued. I ain't gonna charge you for that, you moron. It's outside work hours, and you can't afford my overtime rates."

"Lady —"

"Call it the friends and family discount. Also, we're sittin' in my living room drinking tea my grandmother used to make. You don't have to use my full title anymore."

"… Ara?"

"Yep."

"I'm not going to take advantage of your services. Let me pay you *something*."

"Give me a backrub, we'll call it even."

"Really?"

"Lavinder, this is *not* an argument you're gonna win. Accept your defeat with dignity. It's obvious it's the real reason you came over."

"I —"

"So *cut the crap* and let's get started, sound good?"

Lavinder is quiet for a minute, that particular look on his face a lot of people get when they talk to Ara — a confused pinch in the brow, bemused and uncertain, like they've just been left behind in their own plans. "Yeah," he finally answers. "Sounds good. What do I need to do?"

"Nothing. Just sit there and look pretty. Who am I looking for?"

"I — hm. Do you need a name?"

"Nah, just their relationship to you."

"My brother."

Ara gives Lavinder a single confused look, and then lightly shrugs, settles back in her chair, and closes her eyes. The room is silent once again.

I prepare to wait for the several minutes it usually takes Ara to find anything. To my surprise, she opens her eyes less than thirty seconds later, breathing sharply, blinking up at the ceiling with an expression of utter shock on her face.

"Ara?" Lavinder asks.

"I'm fine. I'm good. I'm fine. Hang on a

155

minute."

She does not look fine. She looks like I just tried to kill her, slick with sweat, her gaze darting fearfully all over the ceiling — but since she's at least coherent, neither Lavinder nor I make a move.

"So," she says, and then stops. Lavinder waits patiently for her to continue. "So. So... uh, fear. Heaps of it. Might even go so far as to call it terror. I... honestly, I don't even know how to begin to describe this, Lavinder. It's like I'm seein' the moment he died, but that's not what I *do*. I don't see *death*. I see life. This, right here, is exactly why I'm *glad* about that."

"Are you okay?"

"Don't know. Ask me again in a few minutes." Ara closes her eyes and takes a deep breath. "He died in a lot of pain, and a lot of fright. What *happened*?"

"A lot of pain and a lot of fright," Lavinder answers softly. "You didn't — there's nothing else?"

"It's right *there*, I don't have to reach for it, it's... it's so easy for me to see, like some kind of stalkery ex waitin' outside your favourite coffee shop, but I... I *can't* see it. Tryin' to see more hurts. Making heads or

tails of it is like pulling a hen's teeth. Real
strange."

"Does that... happen often?"

"*No.* Even people who die violently, I
reach for 'em, and I have to *reach*, and any
fear I feel is background noise. Like — like
muted static on a TV. Life's always bigger
than death. Life has gravity, life has... noise.
Death doesn't. Someone passes on, and the
passin' on bit really doesn't matter to them
anymore. *Life* matters. Family matters. Love
matters. Accomplishments matter. Not
death. With this, it's more like... I dunno,
like the death got stuck so bad that *life*
doesn't matter." Ara opens her eyes and
wraps her arms around herself. "I don't like
it."

I can't take my eyes off of Lavinder's face.
He's usually difficult to read — barely even
smiles, and I've certainly never seen him
laugh. Now, though, the emotions on his
face are like reading words on a page. Fear.
Shame. Guilt. His face looks as pale as it did
when I needed to use him to move the
pointer on the Ouija board.

"Like — like a ghost?" he asks.

"Nah. No such thing. Not like you mean,
anyway." Ara sniffs and then looks hard at

him. "You *do* know how genuinely scared I am right now, yeah? You're glad your ex-wife is dead —"

"I never said I was *glad* —"

"— and then when you ask me about your dead brother, the connection I get to you is *terror*, and meanwhile you look guiltier 'n a cat with a feather on its face. Anyone with a lick of common sense would think you're *exactly* as guilty as a cat with a feather on its face."

Lavinder blinks, confused, and then grows a look of dawning horror. "You think *I* killed him?"

"I think that's possible, yeah."

Lavinder opens his mouth, closes it again, and exhales slowly. "I can leave, if I'm scaring you."

Ara bursts out laughing. "You are the weirdest cop I've ever met!"

"Sorry?"

"You don't *deny* anything, even when it's blindingly obvious you're innocent."

"You just said —"

"Guilty people don't ask psychics to contact the spirits of their dead victims! Unless, you know, they're stupid. You're a lot of things, but you ain't stupid."

"I —"

Someone rings the doorbell.

"Who the fuck is that?" Ara demands, pushing herself up off the sofa. "It's after eight, you goddamn hooligans, go home, don't *make* me call your parents."

"I'll get it," Lavinder says, jumping to his feet and beating her over to the bead curtain. "You just take it easy."

"I ain't *infirm*," Ara objects, but she sinks back down into the sofa anyway. Her grumbles trail off into something barely audible. She's had this sort of thing happen fairly often — she doesn't advertise, but neighbourhood kids know what she does anyway. I've tried to tell her to stop answering the door, but obviously, that hasn't worked. One day I came to visit, only to find her door plastered in toilet paper, and Ara *still* goes and answers the door whenever they play Ding Dong Ditch *anyway*, just to yell after them down the hall that they've been cursed and they're going to turn into great big ugly werewolves.

"Hello," I hear from the hall, "I'm looking for —"

I recognise the voice *instantly*. I blink, and I'm on the ceiling again, shock and fear freezing my thoughts into little icicles trying desperately to weigh me back down to the floor. Time moves slowly. A ra's gaze slides by agonising inches up to where I've attached myself to the ceiling, and past Lavinder, in the doorway, I see Louis.

I don't think I'd have recognised him on appearance alone. In the aftermath of the murder, all I cared about was the woman he murdered, and trying so very hard to make sure she knew that she wasn't dying alone. But I know his voice. *I know his voice.* I know that note of panic right on the very edge of his words. I know how dangerous that note of panic is. I know he's capable of murder when he's panicked, and he's standing there, in the doorway, mere *metres* away from *my best friend,* staring at Lavinder with an expression of mixed shock and panic.

For a moment — a lifetime — no one moves. A ra's looking at the space I'm occupying with both suspicion and concern. I'm trying to move, trying to launch myself at Louis, trying to lodge right into his heart and stay there until he's convulsing on the floor, but the ceiling might as well be a magnet.

Lavinder says something, but time goes by so slowly that I can't make out a single word. Ara cuts in angrily, rising to her feet. Then Louis has a gun in his hand and everyone's shouting at once and Lavinder moves *towards* him —

I tense up and lunge.

I'm inside Louis now, and I hear him drop the gun, and the distant *bang* of a gunshot. I hear Ara shouting, something I understand this time, because it's just one word — "*Roy!*" — interspersed with the deafeningly loud beats of Louis's heart. I don't know if I can kill without first getting the compulsion to kill, because my targets die with a single brush against their shoulders, and Lavinder stayed alive with my entire hand inside his shoulder — but I am damn well going to *try*. I brace hard against the wracking pain, and keep myself wrapped tightly around his heart. The beats slow down, and I don't move. Louis falls to the ground, and I don't loosen my grip. I can feel *myself* beginning to splinter, and I still don't stop. I think I'm screaming.

Then, abruptly, like a TV screen losing power, everything stops.

~~

I don't know where I am.

It's a gorgeous summer day, fading into my awareness by degrees. I'm lying on my back looking up at the undersides of swaying tree branches. The sun is just beginning its lazy descent somewhere off to my right, tinging the entire world with golden light.

It feels familiar, and yet completely alien. The world around me is enjoying a slow, lazy peace, but all I can feel is my heart hammering against my ribs and my hands clenched into fists. I'm scared, and I'm angry.

Well, of course I am, I think to myself. Someone just tried to kill my friend.

Which friend?

I can't remember. I squint up into the deep blue sky, thinking hard.

"Mum's going to kill you."

"I don't care," I hear myself saying.

A boy steps into my line of sight, his head blocking out the light above him. "Come on," he says, pleading. "You can't just stay out here forever."

"Watch me."

"If you just say you're sorry —"

"I'm *not*. I didn't do anything wrong!"

162

I can hear myself saying the words, and even think the thoughts that are leading me to say the words in the first place, but I have no idea what's going on. I try to voice that, and nothing happens. My lips don't even move.

"Please," the boy says.

"No."

"I don't want her to tell Dad."

I wince. I don't know why. "Then stay out here with me."

"I can't. I'm scared."

"Nothing out here's gonna hurt us worse than they do."

"But there are snakes. And spiders."

"You ignore them, they ignore you. Come on, *please*." I sit up in the grass, growing suddenly excited. "We can make a camp! We can be like Lewis and Clark, or that guy who went round the world in a hot-air balloon. We can be *explorers*. We can pretend we've never been here before, but we know the people in that house are bad, so we're making camp in the woods instead."

The other boy sits down cross-legged next to me. I can tell my excitement is infecting him, even though he still looks frightened. "But then in the morning we have to go back, and it's just gonna be *worse*."

"Who says we have to go back?"

He stares at me. "We're kids! We can't just *leave*."

I wasn't being serious — at least, not at first. But the look in the other boy's eye galvanises me, as if the more he resists and reminds me about the consequences, the more I'm convinced we can make it so there *aren't* any consequences. "We could go to New York!" I insist. "We could see the Empire building, 'cause Billy says it's the tallest in the whole *world* — and we could see all the shows on Boardway too, like that movie from last week, and —"

"Stop! We can't do any of that!"

I grip him by the shoulders and look him straight in the eye. "Yeah," I tell him, "we *can*. We can do *whatever we want*."

"What about — what about if it rains and one of us gets sick? What if we get lost? What if someone says 'where are your parents'?"

"We'll find out when we get there!"

"Do you even know how to make a camp?"

"I —"

"Or how to get to New York?"

"It's across the ocean," I answer proudly.
"You gotta take a boat. We can take a boat!
We've taken boats *loads* of times."

"But we never —"

I shake him slightly, growing more and
more agitated that he can't see the
possibilities like I can. "It doesn't *matter*!
We'll learn! We can *do* it, I promise we can. I
don't want to go anywhere if you're not
coming with me."

He looks at me, wide-eyed, and opens his
mouth to answer, but the scene dissolves
slowly in front of me and all I hear is low,
grating static.

CHAPTER ELEVEN

Rude

I've never slept before. I've never *lost time* before. It's always boggled me how people can fall asleep, and then wake up without any memory of when they lost consciousness. I suppose if it's normal, you don't give it a second thought, but if *I* think about it too hard, I make myself really paranoid. What if Ara never wakes up? What if she drifts off, her memory shut down, and then just... never gets her consciousness back?

As far as my muddled thoughts are concerned, I shouldn't be conscious right now. I shouldn't *exist* right now. I was inside Louis squeezing his heart into pulp — then I was dreaming, I think, something

166

about being explorers and making camp to sleep outside — and now I'm here, in Ara's living room, lying next to her doorway, staring up at her ceiling with utter silence all around me. As far as my memory is concerned, not a single second has passed between any of those three moments, and that's *not normal*.

Which makes it all the more unnerving when I sit up and there's no one around.

It's not evening anymore, either. The curtains over the window have been pulled back, and there's bright sunshine filtering in through the glass.

I get up and quickly search the apartment, but neither Ara nor Lavinder are anywhere to be found. There's the remains of a very simple breakfast on the kitchen table, not cleared up, which is very unlike Ara and more than enough to worry me. I search a little more, and I find the spot where the bullet Louis fired lodged itself into the wall, just near the ceiling. The bullet itself is probably long gone, but I can still see the hole in the wallpaper. Touching it makes me shiver.

My first thought is to go and find Melanie, because she's the person best equipped to help me make any sense of where the missing time went. And because no better thoughts present themselves, I go and do that first, making my slow and painstaking way over to the hospital where she's staying. It takes two trains and a short walk along cobblestone paths, dodging people in my way with a lot less caution than I normally have.

Turns out, it's a wasted trip. When I finally make it up to her room, it's empty, and the bed is freshly made, ready for a new patient. No sign of Sam or their dad, either, or any of their belongings. She must have been discharged. I don't know her address.

The precinct is the next place I think to try, right in the city, tucked away down one of the busier side streets. Lavinder isn't there, though, and I'm getting desperate enough by this point to search *thoroughly*. Not in evidence lockup, not in any of the interrogation rooms, not near the holding cells. Plenty of other officers are there, at their desks working or milling around discussing cases with each other, but I can't ask any of them where Lavinder is, and no one's casual conversation happens to clue me in on that information. A dead end.

The crime scene, maybe?

No. When I get there, the police tape has been removed, the office has been cleaned, and there's no longer any sign a murder happened here at all. Case closed, I hope. Louis should either be dead or in custody, and the fact he had a gun *at all* should be evidence enough that he's the one who killed Andrea Relshaw. Innocent people don't have guns.

A gentle tugging sensation begins in my gut, as familiar as it is sickening, and for a moment I seriously consider the prospect of trying to recreate what just happened in Ara's apartment — trying to kill myself wrapping around some random person's heart. Even if I only lose a little bit of time again, that would still be better than doing nothing, right? I don't know how much time has passed, I don't know where Ara is, I don't know where Lavinder or Melanie are, and the compulsion tugging me gently out of the building is like that phone call from your boss right after a vacation has just reminded you of what life could be like, *should* be like. *Back to work*, the call says. *Back to killing strangers you don't know. Come on, up and at them.*

I can't stand the idea that everyone's moved on without me and all I have left, all I will *ever* have left, is this constant, cyclical, murderous *drudgery* that will *never ever stop*.

But I can't try to kill myself. I don't have any guarantee it would even work, and besides — I don't have enough information yet. Ara might have just been running some errands. After all, what's she meant to do, if I disappeared on the spot? Come into the void of nonexistence after me? What a ridiculous idea.

Cautiously, I make my way back to Ara's building, testing where the compulsion is dragging me and how far out of its way it'll let me go before my head starts to ache. To my surprise, it's pulling me in the exact same direction. That's convenient.

That's really disturbingly convenient.

I get all the way to Ara's apartment, and the compulsion doesn't pull me away. But there are voices, coming from inside, and one of them is *definitely* Ara's, and my heart can't figure out if it wants to leap with joy or sink with growing suspicion. It's making me feel sick, so I bite the bullet and step through the door, just like I've done hundreds of times before.

The conversation inside stops dead, and Ara's on her feet in seconds. "*Roy?*"

My suspicion is right. It's Ara. The compulsion is dragging me towards Ara.

"Roy! Holy *shit*, Roy, you had me so — so *angry*, I was *furious* at you, what the hell were you thinking diving into him like that!? What the hell *happened* to you? You had me worried *sick*, you bloody big ingrate!"

I stay right next to the door, as far away from her as I can get without leaving the room entirely. "Yes-or-no questions," I mutter, like she could possibly hear me, feeling numb with fear. "I can't do anything with questions that aren't yes-or-no questions."

"Uh, hi," says Melanie, sitting on the sofa. "Yeah, you can."

The numb breaks all at once, like ice splitting on the surface of a lake. *Melanie.* I hadn't even *seen* her, I'd been so focused on Ara. I'd just assumed whoever was with her was a client, but — of course, Ara doesn't do her seances out in the living room. Either I'm just that scared, or stepping out of existence for several days left a lot of my common sense behind. Melanie. *Melanie.* I can warn Ara I'm dangerous, a live wire, and… maybe together we can figure out some way to make that stop. Like that whole two-heads-are-better-than-one thing. I have to believe that's true, because I truly and sincerely do not know what I'll do if there's no alternative to killing my best friend.

"Don't come near me," I say, the words all spilling out of me at once. "You're the next target. Tell Ara she's the next target. If I touch her, she's going to die."

"Oh," says Melanie. "I guess — time for the fish oil, then?"

"*Tell her.*"

She does, haltingly. Ara's expression does not change one bit.

"Great," she says, like I've just told her a piece of moderately good news she's been waiting on for a while. "Are you killing yourself trying to resist?"

"Not — not right now." I take quick stock of how I'm feeling, and although the compulsion is still *there* and impossible to ignore, my intention to stay as far away from Ara as possible for as *long* as possible isn't hurting me. "I'm okay right now. But I don't know how long that's going to last."

"Uh-huh," says Ara, after Melanie translates. "Okay. Is this why you disappeared for the last week?"

"No."

"Then why the fuck did you do that?"

"I don't *know*. It hurts, doing that kind of thing, and I've never done it before meeting you and Lavinder, and I think it... killed me, somehow, only I can't die, so I just came back once I was fixed. It's been a whole *week*?"

"It's been a *long-ass* week is what it's been, Roy. You'll probably be happy to know Louis isn't dead, though. Just comatose."

"Oh," I say sourly. "Yeah. That's great."

"That was sarcastic," Melanie clarifies for Ara. "Like, that *dripped* sarcasm."

"A being after my own heart. Lavinder thinks you saved our lives, Roy. *I* think you were a stupid goddamn *idiot*, and Lavinder is *trained* to take down *gun-toting madmen*, and next time, *leave it to the goddamn professionals*."

"I wasn't thinking," I say desperately.

"Yeah, no kidding!"

"No, I mean I literally wasn't thinking! I *couldn't*. There wasn't any *room* for it. I just saw him, and you, and then the gun, and I did not have room inside me for thoughts, Ara, I couldn't hear anything, I couldn't feel anything, I don't know how I could possibly have made a different decision. There was just... I was just scared. Just *so* scared."

"You're mighty talkative when you have a way to talk," Ara mutters. But she doesn't say anything else, not for a long and very tense minute, and I've known her long enough to recognise reluctant affection when I see it. She understands I didn't have a choice — not that other choices were worse, but that I literally *did not have one* — and it's fighting with her own fear that I was never coming back. Neither Melanie nor I say anything at all until Ara takes a deep, decisive breath.

"So what's the plan?" she says. "You just gonna keep resisting killing me until it kills you instead?"

"I don't know," I answer. "I really don't know."

"Well, I do. Go ahead and kill me."

"What?"

"What?" Melanie says at the exact same time.

Ara pulls out her phone. "We'll call 999 first, get 'em on their way. I'm gonna fight tooth and nail to stay alive. They're gonna resuscitate me. I'm gonna live. Roy won't have to kill me anymore."

"Ara, are you *insane*!?"

"And I'm *seconding* that," Melanie adds to her translation. "I'm not going to be party to this! Nowhere in your job description did it say 'stop your boss from dying after she commits suicide'!"

Ara puts her phone, displaying the digits '999', face-up on the table. "Look," she says, her tone suspiciously reasonable. "I didn't wake up this morning planning to have a heart attack, but here we fucking are. I'm not losin' Roy again. We have proof it doesn't always *kill* someone, if help comes fast enough, so I'm making sure help comes fast enough."

"Melanie is young and healthy," I argue, "and you're *not*."

"Excuse me?" Ara demands once Melanie furiously translates.

"You can't deny the facts, Ara, you're in the *exact* age range where a heart attack is a major risk, you don't exercise — and what if you're right, but you go comatose, like Louis?"

"Then I'll wake up and kick your ass. Look, Roy, do you still feel compelled to kill Melanie?"

"No."

"Exactly. You tried, and you failed. You don't have to *succeed*, you just have to *try*, and I've got a stubborn streak a mile wide."

"You're not even looking at other options! You — for god's *sake*, Ara, you just want to be able to hear me!"

"I ain't denying that's a factor contributing to my decision, but I *also* don't want you *permanently* dead, and if you're gonna be forced to do it sooner or later *anyway*, then we may as well make it on our own terms, yeah?"

Melanie stands up. "Wait," she says, "*wait. This is me talking, not Roy. If we're going to make sure help comes fast enough, why don't we just *drive to the hospital* and do it right in their emergency room?"

Ara and I both stare at her.

"What? Tell me it doesn't make sense. Ask literally any heart attack victim in the history of the world if they would have gone right to a hospital if they had advance warning. Show me *one person* who would say no."

"Not everyone has access to a hospital," I point out.

"For the love of god, semantic much? You

know what I mean. Let's go get the help before we actually *need* the help. Just go to the emergency room and say you're having trouble breathing, and then Roy can do their thing right while they're taking your blood pressure."

Ara bursts out laughing. "I knew I hired you for a reason," she says, taking her phone back. "What do you say, Roy? Think you can manage that?"

I'm beginning to feel the ache in my head, the warning pulse not to do exactly what we're planning. That probably means it's going to work.

"Yeah," I say. "But — you go on ahead. I'll catch up."

"What do you mean? What are you doing?"

"Staying as far away from you as I can."

Ara pauses. "Tell me honestly, Roy. Are you going to be okay?"

"*No.* But neither are you, and that doesn't seem to matter, so just *go.*"

She hesitates on her way to her bag, phone in her pocket, gaze on the space I'm occupying right next to the door. There are a lot of emotions that cross her face, and probably a lot of things that she wants to say, but she ends up saying none of them and just gives me a nod, her lips a tight line.

~~

Waiting in the apartment is agony, both physically and mentally.

It's also something of an interesting experiment.

I recognise the pain, now, because I felt it on fast-forward when I dive-bombed Louis's heart. And I *stayed* in Louis's heart, even through all that pain, which is all the evidence I need to know that it's completely possible for me to resist long enough that I stop existing. So right here, right now, I test the boundaries a little.

One step away from the door makes the pain worse. One step towards it makes the pain better.

Planning to stay in the apartment for the rest of the day makes the pain worse. Idly considering the door and how to step through it makes the pain better.

I wonder if I can take advantage of that, if I can be next to a target I'm compelled to kill and manage to resist purely based on strategic thinking. If I promise myself I'll brush up against them in two hours, will that reset my resistance level, even if I don't end up doing so? If I make enough plans that I don't follow through on, will making plans eventually stop working as a strategic thinking tactic?

I have absolutely no idea, and intellectually speaking, it's interesting.

Practically speaking, I'm not going to perform dangerous experiments on living people. I'm not some corporate pseudo-scientist.

I wait long enough for Ara and Melanie to be halfway to the hospital, like we agreed on before they left. Then I head out, and down the stairs, and out onto the street, following my compulsion as easily as if I had a GPS installed in my head. The pain vanishes completely, so I slow down my pace, and it presses in on my head again urging me to go *quickly*. I slow down more.

It's the longest, most agonising trip I've ever made in my life.

By the time I reach the hospital, my vision is cloudy. All I can see, all I can manage to think about, is the laser-clear route I need to take through the emergency doors inside. I've sped up without noticing, and even the *thought* that I should slow down a little dies in its inception, leaving just a little cut of pain where it occurred. I practically run, dodging around EMTs bringing someone in on a stretcher from the ambulance bay, and then there's a room with a nurse and Melanie and Ara and I brush up against Ara's shoulder before I can notice or process anything else about the room.

Immediately, like Ara's shoulder was some sort of switch, my mind clears up. There's no more pain, no more one-mindedness, no more laser vision. I can hear what the nurse is saying with crystal clarity.

"— Your vitals all look good, ma'am. Are you still having that difficulty with your breathing?"

Ara spares me a sideways glance. "Nope," she says. "Nope, that's cleared up."

"When did that stop?"

"Oh, I don't know, five minutes ago? But you should probably know, I'm about to have a heart attack."

"You're — I'm sorry?"

"About to have a heart attack."

"Do you have pain in your chest?"

Ara nods slowly. "Chest hurts, arms hurt, I'm feeling sick, I'm — feeling dizzy —"

She's white as a sheet, and *now* it's pretty clear she's having trouble breathing. The nurse is immediately on her feet calling for help and Ara bends over double, shaking hard, one hand grasping Melanie's with what even *I* can tell is an extremely weak grip.

"Ara?" I say, kneeling down right next to her, my face right by hers, as close as I can be without touching her. "Ara, can you hear me? Can you hear this? Ara?"

She forces her eyes open and, for the very first time, her gaze locks perfectly on to mine. She tries to say something, but she doesn't have enough breath left for me to hear it, and then her eyes roll up in her head and she slumps, unconscious.

I back away immediately to give the medical personnel room to save her life. Melanie is asked to leave the room, and she doesn't object or put up a fuss, and I follow Ara through every single step of the process, from stretcher to resuscitation to emergency surgery, even though all I can do is pace anxiously in the corner and wait to hear if I've killed her.

CHAPTER TWELVE

Revelation

They manage to save her life.

I don't leave Ara's side until I'm completely convinced she's going to be okay. It's touch-and-go more than once — I don't understand many of the details, but I understand urgency when I see and hear it. I also understand what flat-lining means. I'm dancing from one foot to the other each time I hear the steady beep of a flat-line, and I don't stop speaking the entire time, just in case Ara can hear me now and some part of her will understand the words I'm saying.

I don't remember *what* I said. Probably nonsense, just strings of nonsense phrases and sentences, interspersed with some variation of 'don't you dare die on me', over and over again, like a morose life coach.

But it works.

And it probably wouldn't have, if Ara hadn't been *right here* in the hospital when it happened.

"Cool," Melanie says when I tell her that. "I can add 'saved someone's life' to the karma bucket list. You think this would count?"

"Absolutely," I answer. I'm shaking, I realise. I didn't even know I could do that. I clench my hands together to try and calm them down.

"You still feel that compulsion?" Melanie asks. She can't see me, so she doesn't know I'm sitting right next to her, and she addresses her question at the blank wall opposite. She has her phone out and by her ear, so the one-sided conversation doesn't arouse any suspicion or concern.

"No."

"Maybe we can use that. The next time you have it, I mean. Maybe Ara and I can tell whoever it is what's up, and we can make sure they're in the hospital when you do it."

I laugh, shaking my head. "That would be wonderful, but I don't think whatever

makes me do this would be okay with that. I
don't know how many more times I can
resist like I did today. Besides, the
compulsions lead me all over the world, and
I don't think it's fair on you or Ara to expect
you to hop on a plane whenever it happens.
I know for a fact Ara couldn't afford it."

Melanie's quiet for a bit. Then: "Why us?"

"What?"

"Why me, and why Ara? What's the
pattern? It can't just be random, because it's
a whole lot more efficient for you to kill
whoever you happen to be next to. Which —
don't do that, by the way."

"I'll do my best."

"So what's the pattern? Were we going to
die *anyway*, and you just helped it along, or
is it like punishment for something? Are you
an angel of mercy, or vengeance? Or is
someone *making* you do this?"

"I'm not an angel. What do you mean,
punishment?" I stare at her. "Punishment for
what?"

"I don't know, dude, you tell me. What
kinds of people do you kill?"

I start to answer, and then stop, because
— I don't know. Most of the time, I try *not*
to learn anything about my victims. But the

few times I have, they've generally been bad people. Like that CEO from before all of this started, with his dangerous lack of empathy, ruining so many lives he'd never otherwise have touched.

"Roy? You still there?"

"I don't know," I finally answer. "I don't know what kinds of people I kill. I usually don't want to learn more about them. I think — you might have a point, because sometimes I've noticed the people are... bad. But that *can't* be it, because that doesn't explain you, or Ara. You're easily the youngest I've ever... and Ara wouldn't hurt a fly."

"I'm the youngest? Really?"

"Yeah."

"Well, *would* Ara hurt a fly? They're really annoying. Most of us wouldn't think twice about swatting them. Would Ara swat them?"

"What does that have to do with *anything*?"

"I dunno, dude, maybe God's a fly."

We both burst out laughing. Some of the other people in the waiting room give Melanie odd looks. At least one of those looks is outright hostile, so she quickly tries to stifle her laughter in her sleeve.

"Are you seriously trying to say that *you've* ever done anything worth punishing?" I ask, once we both have ourselves back under control.

Melanie gives a little shrug. "Maybe that's why I survived, though, because I haven't. Maybe that's why Ara survived. Maybe some wires got crossed somewhere with us."

"But it doesn't explain Lavinder's ex-wife, either." I pause, remembering Lavinder's reaction to finding out I'm the reason she's dead. "Then again," I add uncomfortably, "I don't really know anything about her. How *is* Lavinder, by the way? Is he okay?"

"Probably."

"What do you mean, probably? You've met him, right?"

"First of all, no, I've never met him. Second of all, he hasn't really talked to Ara since that whole thing with the murderer. From what I heard, his partner got wind of him being friends with a psychic, and he's just trying to lay low for a while."

"What does his partner have against psychics?" I wonder aloud.

"What does *anyone* have against psychics? People don't like feeling duped."

"No, it's more than that. He didn't even want to let Lavinder *see* Ara. He said something like 'don't make me call your sponsor'."

Melanie raises her brow. "What, like he's addicted to psychics?"

"I guess so."

"That's dumb."

"Maybe his ex-wife was a psychic."

Melanie laughs. "Sure, and his partner's trying to stop him from replacing her. *That* makes total sense. Case solved."

We talk each other around some more circles, trying to make sense of why I'm compelled to kill and *who* I'm compelled to kill, and what Lavinder's deal is. But there's nothing either of us can answer just by talking, so eventually we lapse into silence, and we spend the rest of the night in that waiting room.

Melanie's brother calls her a few times. He doesn't sound happy, and although I've never *heard* him sound happy, I also understand it in this case — he's probably wondering why Melanie's attracting heart attacks all of a sudden. She doesn't tell him I'm there with her, I notice, and I don't ask her why. Twice, Melanie's dad calls, and

both times Melanie ignores the call. I don't
ask her about that, either.

~~

The moment a nurse comes out to let
Melanie know Ara's awake, I take off. I
know the way, because I followed her all the
way into recovery, and Melanie doesn't
need two people telling her where to go.
She'll understand.

And then I pause just outside Ara's
doorway, terrified.

What if she can see me now? The very
first words out of her mouth are going to be
some kind of disparaging insult about it,
because I know Ara well enough to expect
that before I get anything sincere or
heartfelt. I don't want to find out what I
look like through one of Ara's disparaging
insults. I don't want her to treat me any
differently, either. Maybe I'm overreacting,
because Melanie went through the exact
same thing and all she gained was the ability
to hear my rambling, but Ara's... Ara's *Ara*.
She can talk to the dead, however
roundabout her methodology. Right before
she lost consciousness, she *saw* me. She
locked eyes with me.

So did Andrea when she was murdered in

188

her office.

Would it be different, for different people? If Lavinder had a near-death experience, would he be able to feel me as a solid object?

I'm just stalling now.

I take a deep breath and walk inside. Ara's sitting up in bed, fluffed up against about four pillows, her hair pulled back and looking oddly thin without her usual headscarf. But her eyes are as bright as they always are, and the moment I step into view, she looks directly at me.

I freeze. The words I *had*, all prepared in my mind to fend off that disparaging insult, evaporate. But Ara looks just as scared and uncertain as I do, and it's so out-of-character on her face that for a moment I wonder if I even have the right room.

"Roy?" she says, and her voice is the first thing about her to give away that she had a brush with death. It's weak, and hoarse. Just as uncharacteristic as the uncertainty on her face.

"Ara?"

She inhales sharply, and then her face splits into a grin. "'Bout time, you piss-poor excuse for a ghost. I was expectin' to wake up to you right *here*. I think I might be offended."

I take it all back. Disparaging insults are absolutely fine. Relief floods through me and puts a smile on my face. "Are you okay? How do you feel?"

"Like I just had a heart attack, what kind of question is that?"

"It's payback for all the questions *you* asked that I couldn't answer."

"You know what, that's completely fair. Let me fix that right now. Why *weren't* you right here when I woke up?"

"I wasn't going to just leave Melanie on her own, was I?"

"Melanie's headstrong and resilient! She'll get over it."

I grin. "In that case, so will you."

"I acknowledge your compliment, but I'm also disownin' you as my best friend."

"Tough! After everything we went through just to get to this point? You're never getting *rid* of me."

"You better start paying rent."

"Do you take invisible currency?"

Ara laughed, and quickly stopped, and then gestured at me. "Get the hell over here, then, so I can see you properly. Eyesight ain't what it used to be."

"Ara, you have perfect vision."

"*Get over here.*"

I laugh, and I can't stop laughing, even as I step over to her bedside. It's funny — for all that I'll ramble endlessly at someone who can't hear me, I don't think I've laughed all that much. It's like there wasn't any point to laughing before someone could hear it. More than that, I know for a fact I've definitely never made *someone else* laugh, and hearing Ara laughing at my stupid joke makes delight balloon in my chest.

But then Ara reaches out to touch me, and I shy away, the laughter dying in my throat. "*Ara.*"

"What?"

"You just had a *heart attack.*"

"Yeah, I know, I was there. Come here so I can feel your hand."

"You're crazy if you think I'm going to let you risk *another* one."

"I can *see* you, you great big paloonka. How do you know I won't be able to touch you properly?"

"Really?" I ask skeptically. "You can *really* see me now? Are you sure?"

"Lookin' right at you, ain't I?"

I hold up a fist. "How many fingers?"

"What?"

"How many fingers am I holding up?"

Ara hesitates. "Four?"

"I'd say that's close, but you're only one away from being as wrong as it's possible to be. Good job."

She rolls her eyes with an exasperated groan. "Okay, fine, I can't see you *clearly*, but I can see you. Gimme your hand."

"No."

"Just for a second."

"No."

"If I go through you, we'll stop. There's no danger."

"Were we at the same Ouija Board night where Lavinder nearly killed himself trying to talk to me?"

"Obviously, we weren't, because he didn't."

"You were about to call an ambulance."

"Lies and slander."

"We are not experimenting with putting even *more* strain on your heart, and that's final."

"Come *on*, Roy, it's like putting your finger through a candle flame. Sure, fire's dangerous, but a candle flame is safe enough you can put your finger quickly through it and feel nothing."

"You bring up a very good point," I tell her, nodding. "Let's try that."

"Great!"

"*After* you recover, after you're discharged, and after you're safe at home with Melanie there to keep you steady."

Ara slumps back in her bed with a short exhale of a laugh. "You're no fun," she mutters. "I thought you'd be more fun than this."

"And I thought you'd be *smarter* than this, so I guess we're both disappointed today."

She laughs again, harder this time, and I can't help it — I laugh too. A part of me had been worried that once Ara was able to hear me, everything about our friendship would change. I wasn't exactly *wrong*, but I hadn't taken into account that things could change for the better, too. Talking with Ara like this, I'm starting to wonder how on earth I stayed sane for a whole five years of one-sided conversation.

I think I left a lot. Back then, Ara was more of a refuge than a *friend*. She'd been a home base, a comfort zone. It wasn't until more recently I started craving more, and it wasn't until Ara pointed it out that I realised it was because I felt crushingly lonely.

I wouldn't trade this moment here with Ara in the hospital for *anything*.

"So what *do* I look like?" I ask, immediately intensely curious.

Ara sobers very quickly, and she watches me thoughtfully. "You don't know?"

"No. Why would I?"

"Never seen your own reflection?"

"No."

"If you look down at yourself, what do you see?"

"Nothing."

"When you reach out to touch something, and you look down at your hand, what do you see?"

"*Nothing*. I know it's *there*, I can feel it, but I don't *see* anything there."

"Do you feel human?"

I pause, considering. "Sometimes. I walk the way people do, I run, I take the stairs, I lie down. Except —"

"— except when you're suddenly on my ceiling?"

"Yeah."

"Or walking through my closed door?"

"Oh, I forgot about that, yeah."

"You *forgot* about that?"

194

I shrug. "It's a normal thing for me. I do it all the time."

"I bet." Ara takes a deep breath. She's worried about something, I can tell. "So if I asked you to *guess* what you look like, what would you say?"

I've had ten years to think about this, and my answer is much the same as it was when I first woke up in the streets of New York City. "Like a human. Like a person. Tall, short hair. I — I don't know if you can *feel* like a particular race, but I think I'm probably white, because I don't think about it all that much." I hesitate. "Am I wrong? Do I — do I look human?"

The fact that Ara has to consider her answer carefully makes my heart sink all the way into my feet.

"Yes," she says finally, "and no. You ever see those old cartoons where something's moving very fast and it's just a black streak? That's what you looked like when you went into Louis, both Lavinder and I saw that. Terrifying, I don't mind telling you. Like something right out of a horror movie. Right now, that's what you look like, like — some sort of vague black blackness hanging in the air, right there —" She frames me with her hands. "— lookin' *vaguely* human, with two legs and two arms, but all rough and blurry around the edges. I can tell where your eyes and mouth are, but I don't *see* them, it's more... sort of obvious they're not there. Make sense?"

"Uh, no."

"You look like a human, but you don't look *human*."

"So I'm either a black streak or a shadow?"

"A shadow! That's it. Yeah, you look like a shadow."

I don't give myself any time to process that. "What about —? You said 'right *now*, that's what you look like'. Did I look different before? When you saw me during your heart attack, did I look different then?"

Ara whistles. "You're sharp."

"Thanks, I've had a lot of time to learn."

"As a matter of fact, you did."

I wait, but Ara doesn't elaborate. "So what did I look like *then*?"

"You seen my phone anywhere?"

"Your — what?"

"My phone. I know I had it on me when I came in, but it ain't here now, so the nurses probably took it. Can't say I blame them, but I want it back now. I have to make a

call. Go tell them to give me my phone
back."

"You... Ara, I can't ask the nurses to give
you your phone back."

"Why not?"

Silence hangs uncomfortably on top of us.

"Oh," Ara says. "Right. Damn, this is
gonna be weird to get used to. Where's
Melanie?"

"Probably getting told a lot more about
how you —"

Right on cue, there's a knock behind me,
and I turn around to see a nurse and
Melanie coming hesitantly into the room.
"Are you happy to have visitors, ma'am?"
the nurse asks with a bright smile.

"Happy? I'm *demanding* visitors. Get in
here, Melanie."

Melanie grins. "Yes, ma'am."

"Can I get my phone back, too?"

"Of course you can," the nurse says, "all
your possessions should be in the cupboard
over there. Are you settled? Feeling any
pain?"

"All settled," Ara replies as Melanie goes
to the cupboard in question, "no pain."

"That's great to hear! If you need any
help, just —"

"— press the button right here, I know,
I've been told that five times now. Thanks
very much for saving my life, I really do
appreciate it, now skedaddle and look after
the patients who ain't a young spring
chicken like I am."

The nurse laughs. "You have a good visit,
ma'am," she says, and then leaves the three
of us to it.

"So you were clinically dead," Melanie
says immediately as she dumps all Ara's
clothes on the foot of the bed. "Like, three
times. Roy and the nurse both said if you
weren't *right here*, you'd be dead. I'll take my
Nobel Peace Prize now, thanks."

"That doesn't sound like the sort of thing
you're supposed to tell me," Ara says
skeptically.

"Oh, it's not. The whole conversation was
very conspiratorial. They think I'm your
granddaughter, by the way."

"Of course."

"And they only told *me* because I'm gonna
be your caretaker for the next month,
apparently, so I'm supposed to make
absolutely sure you experience no stress or
elevated anxiety levels for the next week,
and then take it easy until your check-up."

"My what-up?"

"You know, so the doctors can make sure you're properly on the mend."

"No one told me about a check-up."

"I just did."

"Screw a check-up. Gimme my phone."

"Say please."

"Gimme my phone."

There's something in Ara's tone that makes Melanie realise this part *isn't* playful banter, and she doesn't say anything else before finding the phone in one of Ara's pockets and handing it over. Similarly, Ara doesn't say anything while she navigates to the contact she's looking for, puts the phone on speaker, and places it face-up in her lap for both me and Melanie to hear.

The call's picked up almost immediately, and it's Lavinder's voice on the other end. "Hello?"

"Hey, it's me. You're on speaker. Thought I should let you know — I just had a heart attack."

There's silence for several seconds, filled with static that sounds a bit like wind on the other end. Then: "Ara?"

"Yep. Sorry, yeah, it's Ara. Thought you'd know the lilting sound of my voice by now."

199

"You just — you just had a heart attack?"

"Yep."

"Are you in the hospital?"

"Yep."

"Are you going to be okay?"

"So everyone tells me."

"Is this Roy-related?"

"In *exactly* the way you're thinking. It's right here, by the way, say hi."

"Hi." Lavinder pauses. "So it's back, then?"

"As of this morning, yes. Scared the hell out of me. Apparently, it stopped existing for the week, and then came back once it was fixed. Don't ask, I have no idea, and I don't think Roy does either."

"Is this —? Did you... was it deliberate?"

"How the hell do you think it could have been an accident?"

"I mean — did you *ask* it to?"

Ara pauses, and then comprehension dawns on her face. "*Oh*, you think I —! No. No, I swear to you, Roy came back and I, completely coincidentally, became its next target. Melanie and I figured my best shot at surviving was to be in the hospital when it happened. You have her to thank for the fact I'm still kicking, by the way."

"You're welcome," says Melanie.

"And Roy's right there? You're not still the target?"

Ara looks at me. "Am I still the target?"

"Nope."

"It says no."

"Right," says Lavinder, after several more seconds of silence. "Well… thank you for letting me know."

"Come visit me."

"Now? I'm on duty."

"Whenever you're off-duty, then, none of us are going anywhere. If you can't visit a friend when they've just been clinically dead three times, when *can* you visit them?"

"I — Ara, it's… it's really not a good idea."

"That you talking, or is it the asshole Mike?"

Silence.

"You gonna let other people dictate what you can and can't do for the rest of your life? Besides, you still owe me that story."

"No, I don't."

"We made a bet, and you lost it."

"We — when? I don't remember —"

"God's sake, Lavinder, just come visit when you're off-duty. It ain't hard, and I'll never forgive you if you don't. Wait, hang on, no — that's a joke, Lavinder, of course I'll bloody forgive you, the choice is up to you, but I'd *really like it* if you chose to come and visit me."

"I'm — I'm sorry, Ara, but it really isn't a good idea."

Ara nods, her lips pursed. "Would you answer a question for me, then?"

"Yes."

"Do you happen to know why Roy looks *exactly* like you?"

There's silence again, utterly and completely, on both sides of the phone.

"I'm off-duty in two hours," Lavinder says. "I'll come over then."

The call disconnects, and Ara looks at me, and I stare back, lost for words.

CHAPTER THIRTEEN

Recurring

You would *think* the next logical thing to discuss among the three of us would be *why do I look exactly like Lavinder,* but Ara doesn't let us. She refuses to answer any questions Melanie or I have, and cuts us off whenever we try to talk about it without her. "Just wait 'till Lavinder's here," she keeps telling us. "I ain't explaining everything twice."

"You say that like you have *any* idea what's going on," I tell her impatiently.

"You say that like you have *any* idea what's going on," Melanie repeats. Ara gives her a look, and she frowns. "Sorry. Force of habit."

"*What* force of habit? You've done this for exactly *two days*."

"I don't know! I guess habits ingrain faster when they're *supernatural*. Plus, if you count the week in between, it's actually nine days."

"I always know exactly what's going on," Ara retorts to me, ignoring Melanie's argument. "Sometimes I like letting other people explain it, is all."

"Ara, I've known you for *five years*," I tell her. "I know when you're full of it."

"Christ, it's really been that long?"

"It's been five years, two months, and thirteen days. Why do I look exactly like Lavinder?"

"Just wait 'till Lavinder's here, I ain't explaining everything twice."

There's a small mirror above the sink in the corner of the room. Since Ara is being the opposite of helpful, I move over to that mirror, like anything will have changed in the last twenty-four hours and I'll be able to see my reflection. The mirror remains as empty as it always does — no Lavinder, no face, no streak of black shadow. Just the wall and medical machinery behind me.

I try to imagine what it would be like, to see Lavinder's face staring back out at me, but it's *impossible* to imagine. He's not me. I'm not Lavinder.

Am I?

Lavinder was the first person to be able to hear me, before Ara, before even Melanie. Being in his apartment was the first time I was able to move a solid object. He *knew* I was there, even before he knew I existed, looking at his computer screen over his shoulder. Is there something he's not telling us? Why did he change his mind so suddenly after he heard I look exactly like him?

"Do I *sound* like Lavinder?" I ask suddenly as I turn around.

"Just wait 'till Lavinder's here, I —"

"No," Melanie says firmly. "Nuh-huh. Not even slightly."

"You said you've never met him."

"I haven't, but he's old, right? You don't sound old. You sound really young. Like, fourteen or fifteen. Younger than me."

I stare at her.

Melanie can't see me, but she can hear the silence, and she can infer that I'm surprised. "Dude, why do you think I was so weirded out by you talking about murder? You talk like a cop, but you *sound* like a kid."

"Now that you mention it," says Ara, frowning, "you're right. It's like an adult and a child both trying to talk at once."

I'm mildly offended, but I'm not sure which direction I'm offended in. Technically, I've only been self-aware for the past ten years, so it *should* make sense, but something about me is offended anyway. I don't feel ten. I feel ageless. I feel older than everyone in the room, Ara included.

"Oh," says Melanie, "and speaking of murder, which is not a sentence I ever thought I would seriously say, guess what we figured out while you were gone? The woman who died, Andrea Relshaw, is my aunt."

I turn and stare at her. "*What*?"

"We weren't close," Melanie says quickly. "I haven't seen her in — god, over five years. I didn't know her well at all. She was my mum's sister, and she didn't even come to Mum's funeral, so... you know. Still, that's a hell of a coincidence, right?"

"It sure is," I agree absently. My thoughts *want* to race off to some conclusion I can't see the shape of, but because I can't see the shape of it, there's no direction for my thoughts to follow. Louis kills a woman, hours after I try unsuccessfully to kill that woman's niece — is that really just a

coincidence? Is *Ara* just a coincidence?
Trying to untangle three separate
connections in my head is a lot more work
than I thought it would be. "Do you know if
you're related to Lavinder?" I ask Melanie.

"God, no. Definitely not."

"Wait 'till Lavinder's here," says Ara, "I
ain't explaining everything twice."

I grumble a little and sink into the chair
over by the window.

~~

We don't end up waiting the full two
hours for Lavinder to go off-duty. Either he
cut his shift short, or my sense of time
passing has gone uniquely haywire, because
it feels like barely an hour later when he
appears, very hesitantly, in the doorway of
Ara's room. For all that he looks like he
wants to enter without fanfare, the moment
Ara spots him, her smile and energy fill the
entire room.

"Lavinder!" she says cheerfully, and
gestures him inside. "Get in here, we're
having an argument."

"*You're* having an argument," Melanie
says, her voice a little muffled because her
chin is resting in the palm of one hand. "Roy
and I are trying to pursue the noble art of

scientific inquiry, and you're stifling us."

"I'm not the government, Melanie, stop bein' so dramatic."

"*I'm* dramatic? I'm not the one who goes around wearing a giant beaded sign that says 'I practice voodoo'."

"You're a teenager. You're dramatic by nature."

"You also have crystal balls and broomsticks in your —"

"Alright, alright, we're both dramatic arseholes. Lavinder, get in here, *now* we're having an argument."

"Please," I say, "*please* tell me you can hear me now, Lavinder?"

"Roy's askin' if you can hear it now," Ara translates.

For a moment, it looks like Lavinder doesn't understand the question; then he shakes his head. "No."

Ara groans. "*Fuck*, this is going to be annoying. Alrighty then. Get in here, sit down, and tell us the entire story."

Lavinder has always looked smaller than he actually is. He isn't shy, but it's like he never grew properly into his own person. His confidence is quiet, and eager not to draw any attention to itself, but it's still *there*.

You can't be a police officer without knowing for a fact you can rely on yourself. It's just that right now, in the wake of Ara's demand, Lavinder looks like he's never had any of that quiet confidence in his life. He looks lost.

Something about it sticks uncomfortably in the back of my mind.

"I'll start for you, shall I?" says Ara. She's gentler, now, like she noticed the same thing I did and she's decided to take pity on him. "I can tell Roy the bits I already know."

Surprise settles on Lavinder's face. "You haven't told it yet?"

"I don't go around blabbin' other peoples' secrets, and I'm offended by the notion you think I would. You okay with Melanie being here?"

Lavinder glances in Melanie's direction. "Your... apprentice?"

Melanie grins. "Or, you know, her assistant, when we're at home and not being stuffy ponces. If this has to do with Roy, I want to stick around. I'm kind of involved now. You could argue I was kind of the first one to *get* involved."

"Now hang on, how do you figure *that*?" Ara snaps. "Roy couldn't talk to *anyone* before it met me."

"But Melanie's the first time I was able to tell you what that meant to me," I point out, and Melanie and I both laugh when Ara glowers.

"Traitor," she mutters under her breath. "How 'bout it, Lavinder? It'll give you some time to remember you're a proud cop and not some schoolboy gettin' called into the principal's office."

Lavinder starts, and finally steps properly into the room, closing the door behind him. "Is it necessary?"

"Roy killed her, so yeah, I'd say it's pretty damn necessary for it to know how it did a public service."

"I did a what?"

"They did a what?" Melanie echoes.

Lavinder takes a long breath and slumps against the wall. "Fine. Go ahead."

Ara takes a deep breath, and then proceeds to mince absolutely none of her words. "Yvonne was an abusive prick and an unrepentant murderer. The divorce was *messy*, she stalked Lavinder for months afterwards, vandalised his door, shit like that. If the choice was between her and someone else in that grocery store, then it's no wonder you chose her."

"A —" I stare at Lavinder, who stares down at the floor like it's the most interesting thing in the world. It isn't; I've checked. It's off-white tile. "A *murderer*?"

"Hit and run," Ara clarifies. "Lavinder found out, turned her in, she threw a hissy fit, they got divorced. Sounds like she was a nightmare even before that, though. She pretended to be a psychic, can you believe that? Preyed on folks' needs for closure, then married the first gullible idiot who kept goin' back. No offence, Lavinder. So! You can rest easy, Roy, our friend here isn't corrupt or abusive or an arsehole. I'm reservin' judgement on him being a prick, though."

Melanie gasps and waves one hand excitedly in the air. "Oh! Oh! Roy and I were talking about this!"

"About Lavinder being a prick?"

"*No*, about why Roy has to kill people. We thought maybe there's a pattern to the people they kill, like they're all guilty of something, you know? Like Roy's a spirit of vengeance."

Ara puffs up. "*I* ain't guilty of *anything*, thank you *very much*."

"Well, neither am I!" Melanie retorts. "But you could be punishment for *Roy*, 'cause, you know, Roy probably isn't supposed to go erasing itself from existence for a week at a time, and maybe killing you was meant to be a lesson for *Roy*. And I — I could just be a fluke."

"I dunno if I believe in gods, but I ain't a fan of the idea they're that malicious," says Ara. "Or that careless."

"It would make sense, though, right?"

"That doesn't make it the only possible explanation. What are you thinking, Roy?"

Personally, I'm still very much stuck on the fact that the woman who made me rethink everything about my poisonous existence was a *murderer*. "But," I say, and have no words to add for several seconds, until I breathe and try again: "But, she's the reason I started feeling *anything*, at *all*. Before her I wasn't… thinking, I wasn't *me*, I was just doing whatever I felt like. And then I killed her, and there wasn't anyone else around, so she died completely alone. That changed things. I started making sure no one else ever dies alone, ever. I started caring, I started *feeling*."

Ara nods slowly. "And her bein' an

abusive arsehole takes some of that away, is that what you're saying?"

"Well — yes."

"So really you should just go back to being an unfeeling force of nature, then."

"No! Maybe. I — I don't know. I'm not suddenly feeling less, but... but I don't know if it would have happened if I knew she wasn't a good person."

"Probably a good thing you didn't know that, then."

"Is that why Mike hates you so much?" I ask as the thought suddenly strikes me. "Because you're a psychic? Is it because he thinks you're going to do that to Lavinder again?"

Ara smiles at me. "That's exactly it! He thinks I'm tryin' to sink my hooks into a gullible idiot and milk them for all they're worth. Moron thinks he's protecting Lavinder by telling him what to do. I don't think he realises that makes him just as much of an abusive prick."

"He's not," Lavinder cuts in. He looks a little more in control, with some colour back in his face, but he's still using the wall for support. "Mike's not like that."

"Not on *purpose*, and I'm not having this

stupid argument with you again. Anyway, just thought you'd want to know that, Roy. You did a good thing back then."

Did I? From where I'm standing, it looks like all I did was set Lavinder adrift, clinging to whatever reassurance he could get from anyone willing to give it, or to *reminders* of Yvonne, never changing, never growing. I swallow hard and ask: "Why does he have a picture of her in his living room?"

"Oh, that's actually a good question. Lavinder, why do you have a picture of her in your living room?"

Lavinder smiles a little. It's such a startling change in his expression that I'm momentarily taken aback. "It's a reminder," he answers.

"Of *what*?"

"That from the outside, things can look happy, and you can think you've achieved everything you wanted to achieve. And that doesn't say anything at all about what's really going on under the surface."

We're all quiet for a minute.

"Who's his sponsor?" I ask abruptly.

"Who's your — what, *sponsor*?" Ara repeats, giving me a puzzled look.

"My what?" Lavinder blinks at Ara, and then his eyes widen in recognition. "*Oh. That's* — it's one of Mike's jokes. I see a psychologist. He calls her my sponsor. Like a — like it's an addiction thing."

"Oh."

I don't know what else to say. *Was* killing Yvonne a good thing? I can't tell anymore, except that it would be wonderfully easy to believe that of *course* everyone I try to kill deserves it. Of course I'm doing the right thing.

It doesn't explain Melanie, and it doesn't explain Ara. And it doesn't explain why it feels so terrible, each and every time, even when I've seen direct evidence that my victim hurts all the people around them.

"Okay," Ara says, once it's obvious no one's about to break the silence. "So that's all *I* know. Time for you to talk, officer. Why does Roy look exactly like you?"

I tense as I remember the *real* reason we called Lavinder here, and for a moment I'm dumbfounded that I was able to forget it at all. Lavinder tenses as well, imperceptibly, except when you know what you're looking for. It's all in his shoulders and neck, not in his hands. His hands stay loose and ready.

"I don't know," Lavinder admits softly.
"But... he — it — it looks like the way I
do... right now?"

"As opposed to what?" says Ara.

"As opposed to — a child."

Melanie raises a hand again, like we're
sitting in an English class. "They do sound
really young, if that's what you mean."

"But it *looks*," Ara adds, "*exactly* like you,
right here and right now. So stop stalling
and *talk*."

"It's — I'm sorry. This is hard."

"We can be patient. Look at us all, sittin'
here, being patient. Well, you'll have to take
my word for it Roy's being patient."

"Roy doesn't know?"

"Know *what*?" I demand. "Can we assume
until further notice that I don't know
anything?"

"No," Ara translates. "Extremely firmly. I
think I may have been mistaken about Roy
being patient."

Lavinder nods once, opens his mouth, and
there comes a knock at the door to cut him
off. Ara releases a low stream of expletives
and yells out: "You have the worst timing in
the history of the Isles, go the hell away and
come back later! I ain't in any danger of

dying!"

The door opens a crack and a nurse pokes her head in. "Sorry, Arabetta, you have another visitor."

"I do?" Ara blinks at her with confusion. "Who?"

The nurse opens the door a little wider, and a man steps in behind her. He's old, with deep lines on his face and streaks of grey in his hair, but he doesn't act that way; he stands perfectly straight wearing a crisp, tailored suit with a smile on his face.

He looks oddly familiar, and I don't like that smile. It's not warm like Ara's, or fond like Lavinder's, or full of delight like Melanie's. It's more like a mask of a smile, with sharp corners and something dark lurking behind it.

"Lady Yeboah?" he says.

"Technically, but only on official papers. Who the hell are you?"

"My apologies," he says with a curt nod. "My name is Spencer Dowlen. I believe you knew my brother. I just wanted to come and pay my respects in person."

"Is everything alright, Arabetta?" the nurse asks. She hasn't left yet — maybe she sees the same things I do, and it's causing the same unease to sit in the back of her mind.

"No," Lavinder answers before Ara even opens her mouth. He straightens too, suddenly every inch the guardian and protector of the community, with no further trace of the uncertainty or the fear. "You're not welcome here. Please leave."

There's a short, startled pause.

"Detective," Dowlen says, surprised. "I almost didn't recognise you. I promise, I'm not here to cause any trouble."

"In that case, you'll have no issue with leaving."

"Lady Yeboah, I assure you, I'm only here to visit —"

"His brother is a coma patient who suffered a heart attack," Lavinder tells the nurse. "Arabetta and I were both there when he suffered his heart attack. Mr Dowlen has made it clear he blames Ara for what happened. If he doesn't leave right now, please call security to escort him out."

The silence this time is far less startled and far more emotionally charged.

"I'm here to visit my brother," Dowlen says, and to his credit, his tone and general demeanour hasn't changed one bit. "I thought I might drop in on Lady Yeboah while I'm here, to try and get a clearer sense of what happened. Honestly, Detective, what is it you think I might do?"

"Sir," says the nurse. "I'm afraid I *will* need to call security if you don't leave."

Something flickers through Dowlen's expression, but then the smile settles right back in place. "Of course. Forgive me. I hope everyone has a pleasant day."

He turns and steps politely past the nurse back out into the hallway.

"Holy *shit*," Melanie says under her breath. "Was anyone else getting vibes of a Bond villain?"

Ara bursts out laughing. "Thanks heaps for that, Melanie."

"No problem."

"If you see him again, let us know," says the nurse. "I'll make sure everyone knows he's not on the visitor list."

Ara nods at her. "Thank you."

The moment the nurse has left and gently closed the door behind her, Lavinder says: "I need to go."

"You need to fucking *what*?" Ara jumps from subdued and a little afraid to furious in less than one second flat. "Listen here, you overgrown —"

"I'm sorry, Ara, I really am, and I would explain more if you hadn't just had a heart attack. There's something I need to take care of."

"I don't care if there's been a *mass murder*, Lavinder, you ain't just leaving us here hanging like this! You owe it to Roy, it saved our lives!"

"Roy," says Lavinder, "will you come with me?"

"That depends," I answer. "Can you hear me now?"

He doesn't reply.

"I can come with," Melanie offers. "Play translator."

"No," says Lavinder, "you can't. It's police work. There is no story I could give them that would make it okay for a teenager to be coming along with me."

"Well, Roy says they aren't coming if you can't hear them, so that means you've gotta leave Roy behind too. Take it or leave it."

"Okay, that's fine. Thanks anyway, Roy. I'll come back after dinner."

"*Casey Lavinder,*" Ara snaps, pushing herself up to be as threatening as she can possibly be, "*you come right back here this* —!"

He leaves the room before she can finish, without another word or a backwards glance. Ara deflates all at once, and stares sullenly down at her bedcovers. "Damn it, damn it, damn it, damn it... You sure you don't want to go after him, Roy? You can find out what he's up to and report back to us."

I shake my head vehemently. "No. If it's all the same to you, I just tried to kill my best friend, right after a week of not existing, right after killing myself *saving* my best friend, so I don't really want to go running around following people who can't tell I'm there. I want to stay here. With you. He said he's coming back."

Ara nods contemplatively. "Fair enough. Thanks, Roy."

"Man," says Melanie, "when you lay it all out like that, I feel like I've stepped into a sci-fi show. And not a *good* sci-fi show. You know those shows that take really interesting supernatural concepts and turn them into the most boring mundane shit and then keep churning on that for like ten seasons? *That* kind of show."

I laugh. "Sorry I'm not more entertaining."

"*You're* plenty entertaining. Could have done without the Bond villain guy, but you take what you can get, I guess. What's for dinner?"

"Nuh-uh," says Ara. "You aren't having a single *bite* of any of the food *I* get."

Melanie pushes herself to her feet. "Was someone going to remind me that I'm spending dinnertime with a thing that doesn't eat and a patient getting waited on, or was I just supposed to remember that myself? God dammit. I'm gonna go get something from the vending machine, back in a few."

"I like her," Ara tells me.

I sink into the chair by the window, watching her leave. "So do I."

CHAPTER FOURTEEN
Rush

The fading light outside the window casts ugly shadows across the parking lot. As I watch, those shadows lengthen into proper dusk, and then I can hear the sound of crickets in the bushes lining the edge of the scraggly lawn.

"Kitchen," says Mum. "Now."

I'm grateful she doesn't see me flinch. The only thing that makes her angrier than disobedience is the idea that she might be a monster. I turn away from the window too quickly and knock my elbow against the windowsill, and I have to squeeze my eyes shut against fresh tears of pain.

Mum's cooked dinner tonight, and the food smells as delicious as it always does. I

223

sit carefully at the table, trying to be on my best behaviour, trying not to touch anything with the arm that hurts. It feels stiff and numb where I rest it gently in my lap. Doctor tomorrow, Mum promised. But the novelty of having a cast, of being able to ask classmates to sign it, wore off a while ago.

There's four places at the table, even though Mum and I are the only ones here. Dad isn't home yet, and neither is my brother. There's a sick dread paralysing me, because Mum hasn't said a word about where either of them are, and it's a silence I recognise as too dangerous to break.

I don't want to go anywhere if you're not coming with me.

We made a promise that day. The two of us against the world. I *promised* I was never going to leave him on his own. But we're both powerless when Mum or Dad orders us to do something, and I didn't put up a fight when they left because they always come back. They're *always* back in time for dinner. We have to be; someone's always punished if we're not.

Mum curses, suddenly and loudly, making me jump in my chair. She gets up, scraping her own chair violently back over the tile, and goes over to the phone. I stay quiet, and I avoid her gaze.

"What the fuck is *taking* so long!?" are the very first words out of her mouth when the dial tone ends.

I can hear Dad's voice on the other end, but I can't make out what he's saying. All I know is it makes Mum go quiet, and give me a steady look I pretend very hard I don't see.

"Have you been talking to your teacher?" she asks.

I don't reply.

"You *have*, haven't you? What did you tell her, you little brat?"

I don't reply again. *Nothing*, I might have answered, once upon a time. I don't anymore. Mum hates that word. She hates it especially when I use it.

"You come on home," Mum tells Dad, but she doesn't take her eyes off me. "Just leave it, for now. We can get a lawyer."

A lawyer. I remember those, from the books I read. They only ever get involved when something bad happens.

Mum hangs up, and every instinct in me is *screaming* to go up to my room and lock the door and wait for the storm to blow over, but I have one last bit of bravery left, and I know exactly how to use it.

"Where is he?" I ask Mum.

Her gaze snaps to me. "What?"

"Where is he?"

"That's not any of your *goddamn* business."

"Please —"

"Did you *hear* me!?"

She takes a step forward, and I retreat immediately, running for the stairs. My arm jostles with every step and I can't help hissing with the pain, but I don't let myself cry. I learned a long time ago never to let myself cry. The steps in the ancient staircase creak right in the middle, but I don't want to risk jumping over them, so I just *run*, eyes shut as though that will somehow block out the noises giving away exactly where I'm going.

"Hey!" I hear Mum's footsteps and her voice at the bottom of the staircase. "*Hey! What the fuck do you think you're —!?*"

~~

" — doing? Roy? *Roy!?*"

I sit bolt upright, breathing hard, my head and vision swimming.

"Roy! What the hell was *that*?"

"I just — I'm sorry, I just wanted to know

—"

I cut myself off when I remember where I am and what I'm doing. I'm in Ara's hospital room, I'm sitting in the chair by the window, and we're waiting for Lavinder to come back or to contact us to explain what's going on. Ara's left a few messages for him in the last couple of hours. None of them have worked so far.

But I'm breathing hard — I'm *breathing*. And the truly weird part is that remembering I don't need to breathe doesn't fix the problem. I'm still sucking in air like there's no tomorrow, like there's something I need to run from and oxygen I need in order to do it.

There's a meal tray over Ara's bed. I don't remember that happening. She's almost finished dinner, but I don't remember seeing her dinner come in in the first place. Melanie's on the other side of the bed, her phone in one hand and an energy bar partly unwrapped in the other, both completely forgotten as she stares intently through me at the chair I'm sitting in. When did she come back with that energy bar?

"Roy?" Ara's looking at me, her gaze dead-straight on mine, looking scared and worried. "You okay?"

"No," I answer honestly. Am I feeling light-headed? Is *this* what being light-headed feels like? "What happened? Where did your food come from?"

"It came while you were sleeping."

"While I was — *what*?"

Ara hesitates, squinting contemplatively at me. "It came while you were sleeping."

"But — but when — *how* —?"

"I'm guessing that means you don't normally sleep," Ara says, her phrasing and tone very much a non-question.

"No, I don't *sleep*!"

"You sure looked like you were, all slumped in that chair. Didn't seem like you were havin' a good dream, either."

Dream. Dreaming. I put my face in my hands and try to think. "I was really *sleeping*?"

"Do you remember what you were dreaming about?"

"I think — I think I had one after I tried to kill Louis. I don't remember it. I don't think I was alone, and... I remember talking about New York, but that's it."

"What about this one?" Ara asks. "Do you remember this one?"

I nod slowly, hugging myself. "Yeah."

"Want to talk about —?"

"No."

"Fair enough. Listen, Lavinder said he was coming back around dinnertime. It's getting late and I can't get a hold of him. D'you think you'd be able to —?"

"Yes." I stand up. "I'll go find him."

"You sure?"

"Yes." Anything not to sleep, or to *dream,* again. Anything to keep moving.

"Okay then. Take Melanie with you. She might be helpful."

Melanie crosses her arms. "*Hey.*"

"Not you, you dolt, obviously *you're* going to be helpful. I mean it might be helpful to have someone along most people can see and talk to."

"Lavinder's not going to like that," I say.

"Lavinder can kiss my bedridden ass. Got my phone with me, let me know if I can help from here."

CHAPTER FIFTEEN

Regression

"Are you still there?" Melanie asks for what's got to be at least the eleventh time since we left the hospital.

"Yes," I answer flatly. I've progressed from amusement through to exasperation and finally to indifference. "I would *tell* you if I was suddenly not going to be there."

"I know, I know. This is just *really weird*. You've had like a decade to get used to it, I've only had a few days. Besides, you might not *know* you're suddenly not going to be there. You vanished for like a week on us and Ara didn't get any warning."

"Mhm."

"What do you think's up with Lavinder? Do you think he knows why you look exactly like him?"

"I don't know."

"Do you think he *actually* had an important case come up, or was he just stalling?"

"I don't know."

She pauses. "Can you touch my shoulder, or something?"

"No."

"For the love of — okay, you know what, we're talking about it."

I look at her, surprised. "Talking about what?"

"The dream thing you had. Do you have any idea how *different* you sound right now? You were light and upbeat and cheerful before, you wouldn't *stop* talking, and now you're all brooding monosyllabic Batman. Which is fine, you know, normally that would be fine, people process shit differently and it's none of my business, but I think you've made it pretty clear that when your mental health goes *phwoom*, you also go *phwoom*. Or, you know, someone *else* does. So in the interest of public safety, spill it, Casper. Tell me about the dream. I don't want to go *phwoom*. I've already gone *phwoom* once."

I burst out laughing.

"Yeah! See? Exactly like that!" Melanie looks inordinately pleased with herself. "*That's* how you should sound! It's working already! So *spill*. Get me more of that musical laughter."

"It's not — talking about the dream isn't going to make me laugh, though."

"*Duh*. But it'll make it more likely. You need a therapist, and since the closest thing you've ever had to one is Ara, which — don't get me wrong, she's great, but she's very *blunt*, you know? — I'm offering to take on the role. Temporarily. Hit me."

We're on a train into the city, and for the moment the train car is nearly empty, so I've been pacing up and down the corridor while Melanie has cheerfully talked at no one without getting any funny looks for it. Now, even just *thinking* about having to describe what happened in the dream makes the swaying of the train that much more unsettling, and I lose my balance twice on my way to go sit down next to Melanie.

"I don't know where to start," I admit. "It wasn't the kind of dream where *things* happened."

"Do you have dreams where *things*

happen?"

"No."

"Then why did you put it like that? Like you know how dreams normally go."

I hesitate. "I... don't know."

"It's interesting, right? Anyway, sorry, I interrupted you, carry on."

"It was more just... feelings. There's a... there was me, I think, only it was some little kid, not a spirit or a ghost. And they're sitting at a dinner table with their mum, and usually their dad and brother are there too, only not this time, and that's... scary. It felt scary. It felt like it was the end of the world. Then mum gets a call and it makes her angry at them — at *me* — and there's... something about hiring a lawyer, I think, I don't know, I just remember being so scared that I felt sick. And I go up to my room, and — wait, my arm's broken, I remember that. It hurts. It keeps jarring. And mum's chasing me upstairs, and..." I spread my hands. "That's it. That's the whole thing. Psychoanalyse away."

Melanie doesn't say anything for a minute. We sit in silence, listening to the rhythmic noise of the moving train.

"Okay," she says slowly. "So, first of all,

are we assuming that's a memory?
Something that actually happened to you?"

I shrug uncomfortably. "That's what it felt
like, but I don't see how it can —"

"If that's what it felt like, that's what we're
going to assume. Do you know how old the
kid is? Or — was?"

I shake my head, take two seconds to
realise Melanie can't perceive that, and
amend: "No."

"How young? Like, toddler, or primary,
or...?"

"No, not a toddler, I wasn't that young. I
— the *kid* understood what was going on. I
don't know, maybe eight? Ten?"

"You said the mum got a call, too, so it
can't be that far back in the past. I don't
know, when were telephones invented?
Whatever, doesn't matter. Here's the real
point. What you're describing sounds an
awful lot like how my brother and I grew
up."

"What do you mean?"

"You met our dad, right? He was in the
room when you first talked to me. He left us
before I was born, then came back like 5
years later. He's always been into some
shady shit. I have this one really clear

234

memory of Sam with a broken arm, and I
have a lot of vague memories of bruises. A
lot of bruises. And… I remember Sam left
once when I was in primary school and I
was fucking *terrified* that he'd just left me on
my own, or that something happened to
him. But he came back. And then I went to
go live with him, and we cut off all contact
with Dad. Then I had this stupid heart
attack, and Dad came to visit me in the
hospital, and he was just… *bawling*, like, in
floods of tears, he kept saying he was sorry
and he wanted a second chance, so I told
him he could have one as long as he
promised it was on my terms. Also that he
can't go anywhere near Sam. It's… this
wasn't the point, this is a super long tangent,
sorry about that. Back to the real point. The
real point is that your dream sounds pretty
much exactly like a day in the life of little
me. Being so scared you feel sick. Parents
yelling at you for things you don't even
understand, let alone things that aren't your
fault. Parents not letting you have your
space, not respecting your boundaries or
your privacy. A brother going missing.
Parents blaming *you* for their own shitty
stuff. Getting hurt. Getting hurt a *lot*."

Melanie falls silent for a minute, staring out the window opposite. I don't say a word. Melanie's phone buzzes; she stares blankly down at it, then sighs and turns it off.

"Sam and I had years of therapy to get over all of that," she says quietly. "And I didn't even get the worst of it. By the time I was old enough to yell right back, Sam was old enough to *punch* right back. And — I'm pretty sure Sam's still in therapy, actually. He doesn't tell me much. He's functional, just — he has so many triggers, you know? And with you — at least Sam knows what his triggers *are*. You don't. It… it *sucks*, that you can't do that. I'm sorry."

"Down," I say suddenly.

Melanie looks up. "What?"

"Sorry, I — all of that is terrible, but thinking about it in relation to me is terrifying, so I'm trying to think about something else, and I just realised: what Ara said, the first time you met her, the word she got from your mum. Down."

"What about it?" Melanie asks, frowning.

"What if it was meant to be Dowlen?"

"The Bond villain?"

"Yeah. If Andrea Relshaw is your aunt —

236

she definitely knew her killer. And she definitely said something about her killer's brother, too, which we know now is Spencer Dowlen, right? So if your aunt knew Dowlen, maybe your mum did too. Maybe your mum was trying to warn you about Dowlen."

Melanie digests that slowly, twisting her phone in her hands. "But — where would Mum have met someone like that before? Dad's into that kind of shady shit, not her..."

She lapses into silence again, and a large group of people board the train, robbing us of the privacy Melanie probably needs to say any more. The sick feeling of fear in my gut doesn't go away, which makes me very grateful when we finally reach our stop and we can start moving again.

~~

I make a very quick tour of the precinct bullpen when Melanie and I arrive, but I can't find any sign of Lavinder — or of his partner Mike, for that matter. I tell Melanie exactly that when I make it back to the waiting area at the front.

"It's a good thing you've got me, then," she says, rubbing her hands together. "High school drama class, don't fail me now."

237

The officer behind the desk doesn't look up until Melanie taps on the glass. She looks busy, and tired, with long black hair pulled back in the sort of bun that was probably perfectly straight originally and then only got more crooked and messy with stress and time. "Can I help you?" she asks.

"Yes, please." Melanie pitches her voice a little higher than usual, so she sounds afraid and desperate. "Please, I'm looking for... oh no, I forgot his name. I'm looking for the detective who's helping me with my case."

"What case is that, ma'am?"

"Someone broke into my flat last week. It's been... so *scary* ever since then, you know? I'm not sleeping, like, at all, and I have a baseball bat right next to my bed all the time now. I don't even play baseball, I had to borrow it from my brother."

Sympathy flickers briefly across the tired officer's face. "Can you describe the officer who helped you?"

"Sure, I can try." Melanie pauses, visibly steeling herself. "I'm sorry, I was just — so upset, at the time. I think he had brown hair? He was really gentle."

"Did he wear glasses?"

"No, I don't think so."

"DC Wright?"

"No, that doesn't sound right."

"DC Lavinder?"

"Yes!" Melanie lights up so quickly that for a moment even *I* forget she knew the name from the beginning. "That was it! I remember thinking it sounded exactly like a plant. Please, I need to talk to him. He said to let him know if I found out anything else was stolen, and now that I'm not so upset anymore, I realised a ton of other things are missing. Can I talk to him?"

"Give me a minute, I'll find out where he is." The officer gives Melanie an affirming smile and starts tapping on her keyboard. I step through the desk so I can look at the computer screen and see what she's doing.

Reading is as hard as it ever is, but when I focus, I can make out an address. It helps that it's a familiar suburb — one less thing to memorise — and when I'm sure I have it I step back over to Melanie again. "I got it!" I tell her excitedly. "It's Spencer Dowlen's address, I'm about 98% sure, and I got it!"

"He's out, I'm afraid," says the officer. "Maybe you could tell me what was stolen, and I can put it in the report."

Melanie's eyes go wide with fright and

she shakes her head violently. "No. I'm sorry. It's... really embarrassing. I *really* don't want to tell anyone else. Please."

"Did he give you his number?"

"He did, but he's not answering." Melanie wrings her hands in the air — actually *wrings her hands* — and fixes the officer with the most desperate look she can manage. "*Please.* If you could just tell me where he is, I'm *happy* to go and find him there, especially if it's on my way to work."

"Melanie," I say, confused, "I *have* the address."

By her side, out of eyesight of the officer, Melanie shoots me a quick thumbs-up.

"I can't do that, miss," the officer replies, completely oblivious to my presence. "I can pass on a message, or you can wait here for him to come back —"

"How long will he be?"

"Honestly, I don't know. But if you leave me your number, I can have him call you back."

"I'm happy to wait, if it won't take too long. 30 minutes?"

"Oh, definitely not, he's —" The officer stops herself, but Melanie presses on.

"45 minutes?"

"No —"

"Will it be more like a few hours?"

"Traffic coming back from Forest Hill can be —" The officer stops herself again, and sighs. "I'm sorry, ma'am, but I think the best I can do is pass on a message for you."

Melanie pretends to think about this, taking several calming breaths, and then gives the officer a watery smile. "No, it's alright. I'll just come back tomorrow."

"Are you sure?"

"Definitely. Thank you!"

Less than a minute later, before we're even properly out of the station, Melanie drops character completely and exhales sharply with a soft cheer.

"I *had the address*," I remind her, but I'm amused in spite of myself. "You didn't have to go and do that."

"I know! Damn, that was an *adrenaline rush*." Melanie, grinning from ear to ear, hoists her bag onto her shoulder as she walks out of the station. "Did you see that? I was *awesome*. Shit, maybe I shouldn't have given up drama. I could be a star by now. I could be living in Hollywood. You're still there, right? Roy? Roy, you haven't left yet?"

"I'm still here," I assure her.

"You saw all that, right?"

"Absolutely, and you're right, it was awesome, and maybe you shouldn't be bragging about it before we're out of earshot of the officers?"

"Oh, right. Sorry. No, I'm not sorry, I haven't been arrested yet, so in your *face*, you — ghost-spirit thing. I just wanted to see if *I* could do it. You know, in case I decide I want to solve mysteries when I grow up and you won't always be around. I got the suburb, did you hear? Forest Hill!"

"Yes, I did hear, and I think I need to repeat, I have the *exact* address."

Melanie finally deflates a little, taking a steadying breath. "Okay, *fine*, you have the *exact address*. So, onto the villain's lair, right?"

"Call Ara, let her know."

"Why? All she'll do is tell me not to go."

"And, you know, maybe she'll have a point."

"Oh, come on! It's not like he's going to *kill* me, not with police officers right there."

I stare at her as we walk. "Melanie, the fact that you jumped *right to the possibility of him murdering you* is *exactly* why you shouldn't go! Better safe than sorry, right?"

"What if he kills you?"

I let some silence hang in the air between us.

"I'm fucking serious! What if he does the same thing Louis did to you?"

"Louis didn't do *anything* to me. *I* tried to kill *him*."

"Okay, but what if this guy forces you to do the same thing? What if he pulls a gun on Lavinder?"

"Lavinder is trained to take down people with guns — I shouldn't even have touched Louis the first time. Believe it or not, I've learned from that! I won't touch this guy, I promise. Besides, even if I did, how would you being there help?"

Melanie makes a very loud, angry noise. "This isn't *fair*!"

"You're like twelve years old, Melanie, you've got a whole life to try and make things fair —"

"I'm not *twelve* —"

"Thirteen, whatever, I don't understand anything about time, will you just call Ara and tell her where I'm going?"

Melanie doesn't answer immediately, too busy shifting angrily from one foot to the other and taking long, deep, rhythmic

243

breaths. Then she sighs and slumps all at once. "Okay, fine, whatever. Tell Lavinder if he doesn't call her *right away*, though, he and you are *both* on notice."

I smile. "Duly noted. Thank you."

"Yeah."

"Besides, you're still recovering from a heart attack. Shouldn't you be avoiding dangerous situations for the next several years?"

Melanie scowls. "Go before I change my mind, you pansy-assed translucent moron."

I laugh, and I leave her with that sound, since she'd said on the train she loved the sound of my laughter so much. I feel a lot less like laughing once I'm properly on my way, but I refuse to let myself think about what *else* Melanie said on that train. It can wait. The mystery of who I am, and of what Lavinder isn't *telling* me about who I am, can wait until I'm sure that Lavinder's safe.

CHAPTER SIXTEEN

Retaliation

It occurs to me, as I walk towards the train station, that I keep acting like I'm a flesh-and-blood human being. The 'human being' part is debatable, but the 'flesh-and blood' part isn't. A flesh-and-blood person would need to get on the train, spend a little money, and wait for the full hour or so it takes to get to Forest Hill, by which point Lavinder and his partner might not even still be there.

When I needed to get to Ara and tell her I'd just witnessed a cold-blooded murder, I'd stepped right over to her apartment in the blink of an eye.

Maybe, if I practice, I can do something like that again. Deliberately.

I've never been to Spencer Dowlen's house before, so I have no image of it in my mind, no idea what the outside of the building looks like or what the inside of it smells like. But I have a very clear image of Spencer Dowlen, all sharp smiles and sharp suits. And I have a very clear image of his brother, Louis, who might live with him. Maybe that'll be enough. I walk along the pavement, dodging people walking in the opposite direction, and I try to imagine that I'm standing right next to Dowlen.

Nothing.

Well, obviously it wasn't going to be easy. I try again. When it still doesn't work, I try a third time. Still nothing.

Melanie's words on the train drift through my mind. *"Which is fine, you know, normally that would be fine, people process shit differently and it's none of my business, but I think you've made it pretty clear that when your mental health goes phwoom, you also go phwoom, or someone else does."*

Everything I've achieved in the last few weeks, I achieved because I *felt* something. Fear, or anger. Thinking calmly about things has never brought me anything but frustration. Why would my imagination be any different?

I try to imagine Spencer Dowlen killing Ara in her hospital room, but that doesn't work — he didn't. But he *might*, I try to remind myself, at *any* point in the future, especially now that she's alone back there. Unfortunately, that's still a remote enough possibility that I don't really feel anything.

Maybe that's because I *also* tried to kill Ara.

That, I tell myself sternly, is *singularly* unhelpful.

What if Spencer Dowlen tries to kill Lavinder? His brother had a gun. Spencer Dowlen might well also have a gun, and he *really* doesn't like Lavinder. That was a feeling I got from him plain as day back in the hospital room, for all that he tried to hide it behind a placid expression. What if he and Lavinder are talking right now? What if Dowlen's reaching for that gun, *right now*? What if Lavinder is distracted and doesn't see it? What if Dowlen is, right now, *pulling the trigger* —

Space distorts, the buildings around me vanish, and the next thing I know I'm on the ceiling of a ground-floor living room clear on the other side of London, Lavinder and

Mike standing at one end, and Spencer Dowlen standing at the other. The moment my awareness of things snaps back together I *launch* myself from the ceiling down at Dowlen and I crash hard against some invisible force surrounding his chest.

"— any evidence," Spencer Dowlen is saying, completely oblivious to me and my bumbling presence as I fall over backwards. "If you did, I believe you'd be arresting me. Am I under arrest, Detective Constable?"

"No, sir," Mike says shortly. "But as you and your brother are both suspects, I'm obligated to tell you that if you try to leave London, we can and *will* arrest you. We still haven't gotten an alibi for your brother, either."

"How convenient he's a suspect, when he's utterly unable to defend himself."

"Mr Dowlen —"

"Doctor."

"Dr Dowlen, as I told you before, if you're accusing my partner of attacking your brother, you're welcome to come down to the station and fill out a report. Anything short of that is, if you'll pardon my French, bullshit."

"And the report would go somewhere, of

course? Someone would take it seriously?
There would be an inquiry?"

"We take accusations against our
detectives *very* seriously, Dr Dowlen."

"Yes, I'm sure you do."

Lavinder takes one very small, very quiet
step forward. He isn't quite smiling, but he
looks calm, utterly and completely sure of
himself. "Dr Dowlen," he says, "I *know* the
evidence to convict you exists."

Dowlen starts to look irritated. "And how,
pray tell, do you know that?"

"You're crowing."

"I'm what?"

"Crowing. Bragging. You don't *honestly*
believe I or Ara did anything to your
brother, because if you did, you would have
filed that report immediately, and you
wouldn't be entertaining *any* conversations
with me, let alone this one. But you can't
resist the opportunity to brag, can you? You
can't resist the chance to lord over us how
immune you are. This is a game to you, and
it wouldn't be a game to you if there wasn't
a chance of you losing. Therefore, there
must be a chance of you losing. Therefore,
evidence to convict you exists, and every
moment my partner and I don't find it, you

grow more and more confident. That's impressive, but ultimately, it's going to be your downfall. Good people don't take the time to crow."

A short silence fills the room, with both Dowlen *and* Mike looking at Lavinder, and when Dowlen's face begins to twist, I steel myself and try to plunge my hand into his shoulder. Whatever invisible force is protecting his heart, it doesn't extend any further than, specifically, his heart, so my hand sinks into his shoulder quite easily and I can feel my existence begin to scatter as Dowlen begins to grow pale.

"I trust," Dowlen says, his voice hard and his breathing erratic, "that you gentlemen can see yourselves out?"

"No," says Lavinder. "I think you'll need to help us. I have a terrible sense of direction."

"Let me — rephrase that question, then. *Will* you —" Dowlen stops, grunts in pain, and points at the window. "*Out.*"

Mike and Lavinder look at each other. "Sir?" says Mike, stepping forward. "What's the matter?"

"*Nothing's* the —!" Dowlen hunches, falls against the wall, and I move with him, keeping my fist firmly inside his shoulder, keeping my focus entirely on one of the creases in his shirtsleeve, determined to *stay* there until he was *dead*.

I hear Mike cursing from somewhere behind me, and hurried footsteps. Seconds stretch out into forever, and then I hear Lavinder's voice right next to my ear.

"Roy, *stop*."

"He told Louis to kill Andrea!"

"You're going to kill yourself, Roy, *stop*."

"Rich arseholes like him don't get convicted!"

"Mike and I are going to make sure he *does*, Roy, please, *stop*!"

I don't stop. A few seconds more, that's all I need, Dowlen's almost on the ground with his face completely drained of colour —

Lavinder steps right into the space I'm occupying. I let go and reel away from them both, and against the wall Dowlen gasps and sinks all the way onto the floor. Lavinder's gaze follows me, full of both fear and conviction, and the only sign he felt anything at all from stepping right into me is how his next few breaths sound like he needs to drag them up his throat.

"I don't care about him," he says. His

251

voice is hoarse and cracked. "I care about *you*."

"Casey?" says Mike from the other end of the room. "Buddy? What are you doing?"

Lavinder's gaze falls away from mine. "We talked about this, Mike," he says. "You're not my therapist."

"That's a therapeutic technique, is it? 'Cause it looks an awful lot to me like you're talking to someone who isn't there."

"I am. It's a projection technique. Good for anxiety."

"'Roy', huh?"

"Do *not* start."

The fierceness of Lavinder's reply surprises me, and it clearly also surprises Mike. "Okay," Mike says, hands up. "Okay. Ambulance is en route. He still conscious?"

Lavinder looks down at Dowlen, slumped against the wall on the floor, deathly pale and breathing hard. "Yeah," he says. "Still conscious."

"How," Dowlen manages slowly, and if *Lavinder*'s voice had sounded hoarse and cracked, Dowlen's sounds positively broken, "the *hell* did you —?"

"For your own safety," Mike cuts him off as he walks over, "I'm gonna have to ask you not to say another word. *Especially* if your next words are going to accuse my partner of attacking *you*."

Dowlen falls silent, but the look he gives Lavinder brings chills to the spine I don't have. It's not hatred — hatred, I would understand. It's something with more levels than that. Something with a very clear purpose behind it, like the physical manifestation of the feeling I get when I know I need to kill someone.

He knows, I realise with a slowly creeping dread. He can't see me, can't sense me, but he knows I'm there. He knows the attack was mine. He has some kind of safeguard around his heart, and — that question he was about to ask. Not *what* the hell, but *how* the hell. As if, unlike Mike, he knew *exactly* who Lavinder was talking to, and *exactly* how Lavinder was able to attack him.

I don't take my eyes off Lavinder in the entire five minutes it takes for the ambulance to arrive, like I'm expecting him to drop dead the second I look away. This time, Lavinder never spares me a glance.

~~

"Lavinder?" I ask. "Can you hear me?"
He stands silently in Spencer Dowlen's

entranceway and doesn't answer. All around us, the bustle of the EMTs carrying Dowlen outside continues, flashing lights of the ambulance reflecting off the brick walls of the townhouses along the street.

"Why," I continue, "do you only *ever* hear me when something dangerous is going on?"

Lavinder still doesn't answer.

Mike steps up next to him and puts a hand on his shoulder. "Casey," he says, "I want to warn you, there are going to be questions."

"About which part?" asks Lavinder. "The interview turning into an interrogation, my sanity, or how two different suspects have had heart attacks while I was with them?"

"The last bit." Mike hesitates. "All the bits, but the last bit especially. No one's going to be able to prove anything, and obviously I'm going to tell them nothing *happened*, but there's going to be questions. You'll want to prepare yourself for that."

"I'm not worried about the questions," Lavinder says. "I'm worried about Dowlen recovering enough to tell everyone I attacked him."

"That's baseless, and he knows it."

254

Lavinder shakes his head. "Doesn't matter. You know it doesn't matter. He's rich. He has connections. He could easily get me fired."

Mike doesn't reply, probably because there's no counterargument to make.

"You should have let me kill him," I grumble, watching the EMTs load the stretcher into the ambulance. "It would have done the world a favour."

"That's not how we —"

Lavinder stops, and Mike looks at him. "What?" he asks with a frown.

"Nothing," Lavinder murmurs. "Look, you go on ahead. I need some fresh air — I'll take transit."

"You sure? That's still like a five mile walk."

"I know. You want some coffee? I'll grab some on the way."

"You're a weird, weird guy, Casey. Sure, I'll have some coffee."

"You got it."

Lavinder stays quiet while Mike gets into the squad car and drives away. He talks to the EMT, not to me, as they exchange information, and then the EMT jumps into the ambulance and they drive off. It's not until we're definitely alone on the street that he glances sideways in my direction. "Roy?"

"Yeah," I say. "I'm here."

"I can't —" He blows out a breath and runs one hand through his hair. "I can't *hear* you, but... it's like I know you're there. Like I know what you just said."

"Really?" I look at him. "So what am I saying now, then? Beans."

"See, that's the problem — I don't know for *sure*. I don't hear it, so it's... hm, how do I say this. I can't tell if it's something you actually said, or if it's something I'm just *imagining* you said. I don't even know for sure I'm talking to you right now. You might have left after what happened, and I only think you're standing right next to me."

I lean in close to his ear. "*Beans*. Beans beans beans."

He huffs out a laugh. "Yes, alright, I got that. Beans."

"Man, that's *weird*."

"You're telling me. I can't think of *anything* more surreal than this. It's like arguing with an imaginary friend."

"Speaking from experience there?"

"A little, yeah."

"Did sort-of hearing me only just start

happening?"

Lavinder thinks about it. "No, I don't think so. I think — well, ever since I met Ara down at the station, I've been feeling it. Like sometimes I'm not alone, even when I'm sure I am. But it's easy to dismiss. And if I think too hard about it, then I stop being sure you said anything at all. If I didn't know for sure you exist, I'd probably still be dismissing it."

"Huh." I stare down at the pavement we're walking on. "I wonder why that is?"

"Well, most people don't deal with ghosts, so most people would be dismissive, I think."

"No, not that — *obviously* you'd still be dismissing me. I mean, I wonder why you can tell I'm here at all? Melanie could only hear me after I almost killed her. Same with Ara. But I've never met *you* before any of this."

Lavinder's expression grows oddly fixed. I study him very carefully, but there's not a hint of *any* emotion in the lines around his eyes. "Have I?"

"No. I — see, I can't tell if you just asked a question or not, but if you did, no." Lavinder pauses. "You're not saying 'beans' again, are you?"

"No."

"See? This is useless. Hang on a minute."

Lavinder pulls out his phone, dials Ara, and puts it on speaker. It rings out as we walk down the street together, drawing at least one irritated look from a passerby, but Lavinder doesn't try to put it away or find us a little more privacy. Part of me is oddly proud of him for that.

"*Lavinder,*" Ara explodes the moment she answers. "Being all enigmatic and mysterious is *my* thing. You owe me *copyright.*"

I lean in. "Ara, can you hear me?"

"Yes! Yes I can. Clear as a bell. You have Roy there with you, Lavinder."

"Yes," says Lavinder, "I know."

There's a brief pause on the other end of the line. "Oh," says Ara, sounding almost jealous, if I didn't know any better. "You can hear it now?"

"No. No, it's more like… have you ever practiced a conversation with someone in your head so often than you can almost hear what they're saying?"

"No." A beat. "Do you practice conversations with people in your head a lot?"

"Yes, I do. It's like that."

"So you can hear it, but you can't *hear* it."

"I understand it, but my ears don't. It's giving me a bit of a headache, actually."

"Yes, we know, it's all very weird," I cut in before Ara has a chance to reply. "Before we talk about anything *else*, though, Spencer Dowlen had a thing around his heart that —"

"Do you still need me to translate?" Ara interrupts me.

Lavinder laughs a little. "God, yes. That'll help me practice."

"We got any idea *why* you can sort of hear it?"

"No."

I stare at the phone, nonplussed. I'm using to being talked over and ignored, but I'm not used to being systematically and deliberately *interrupted*. "Ara!"

"Yes, I know, I'm sorry, I just wanted to make sure we're all on the same page. Go ahead."

"Can I claim discrimination? Or... species-ism?"

"What species are you?"

"Uh..."

"Then no. Go on, don't keep us in suspense. Spencer Dowlen has a thingy around his heart. Didn't seem like he had a heart to me, so this story is already full of holes."

I take a deep breath. "Spencer Dowlen had some kind of force field around his heart that wouldn't let me touch it like I did with Louis. And before you get mad at me, he was threatening Lavinder, so I had *every right* —"

"He wasn't doing anything of the sort," Lavinder interrupts. "He was... being a little annoying. Those are two different things."

"*Roy* —" Ara begins in a very dangerous tone of voice.

"It *didn't work*, so let's skip the lecture, okay? I tried giving him a heart attack, and that *would* have worked, except Lavinder stepped in to save him, and now Lavinder might get fired because —"

"I stepped in to save him because you were about to kill him," Lavinder objects.

"Yeah! He deserved to die!"

"*No one* deserves to die without warning like that, *ever*."

"I — I know that!" I falter a little, suddenly unsure of my own point. "But —

but he knows. He *knows*. He knows I exist. He knows I tried to kill his brother."

There's a ringing silence in the air for several seconds.

"Back up a minute," says Ara, her voice crackling with some minor static. "How in the *hell* do you know what he knows?"

"He had some kind of safeguard around his heart, Ara. Ten years, and I have *never* felt anything like that before. It's like diving into a swimming pool, only the pool's empty."

"Great, thanks for *that* mental image. So he's got something that makes him special, so what? I could tell you were there long before any of this chaos began, and I had no idea what the fuck you were, so why would he?"

"He knew Lavinder was talking to me," I insist, feeling oddly desperate. "He didn't say *what* the hell, he said *how* the hell. He *knew*. And he keeps accusing Lavinder of attacking his brother — what if that's because he knows something *did*?"

"I dunno, Roy, that all seems like a bit of a stretch."

"No," says Lavinder quietly. "It doesn't."

Gratitude temporarily envelops me.

"*Exactly*. Thank you. He's weird, right?"

"Weird, definitely. But Roy — why does that mean he deserved to die?"

I open my mouth, and close it again. "Roy?"

"It's not saying anything," Ara tells him.

"It wouldn't happen to be singing Bohemian Rhapsody, would it?"

I give Lavinder an invisible look of befuddlement. "What? No."

Lavinder sighs. "Thought I got it out of my head yesterday. Roy — it just seems odd, to me, that... You're trying so hard to stop killing *anyone*, even people you feel might deserve it. Louis Dowlen you only attacked to save our lives. Then a stranger comes along, you meet him all of twice, and you're confident he deserves to die. Why? Have you met him before?"

"I — no. I don't — *think* so. I don't recognise him."

Lavinder nods, like that's exactly the answer he expected. "Do we believe that you only started existing ten years ago, or that you only *remember* the last ten years?"

"*Well*," Ara cuts in firmly, "we *might* be able to *work that out* if you would just *tell us why it looks so much like you.*"

Lavinder hesitates. "Oh. Right."

"Yeah," Ara snaps. "*Right*. Roy, where's Melanie?"

"On her way back to you," I answer.

"Great. You both come back as well. Group pow-wow."

"I'm still on duty," Lavinder points out.

"What duty? Your two main suspects are in the hospital. Volunteer to guard 'em, or something. I am *not* letting you off the hook this time, not if we can't trust Roy not to kill anyone."

"Yeah," says Lavinder, "that's fair. I'll see what I can do, and I'll meet you over there."

They talk a little bit more, but I don't hear it. I seem to move almost on autopilot, drifting next to Lavinder, my heart and mind stunned.

Not if we can't trust Roy not to kill anyone.

CHAPTER SEVENTEEN

Revenge

The next couple of hours pass in a blurry haze. I'm still present, I think, still drifting along in Lavinder's wake, but it's bloody difficult to hear anything — or, for that matter, to *see* anything. I feel almost like I'm just a dream, like I'm an imagined conversation inside Lavinder's mind, making no mark on the world around him. I'm vaguely aware of when we've reached the police station, and then of Mike's voice, and then of a heated argument, and then of the sound of rain falling straight through me, but I have no real sense of time passing in between any of those events.

Trying to listen hurts. Trying to *focus* hurts.

I can't tell if something specific happens to pull me back into solid reality, or if it's simply that enough time has passed for me to be able to reconstitute myself. Whatever the reason, it's a very abrupt and very painful transition — one moment I'm so much vapour in the atmosphere, and the next I'm sitting solidly in the back of a speeding car. I have to take several deep breaths before I'm level again, which is *weird*, because I don't even have to breathe. I've tested it. Whatever part of me is human panics if I hold my breath for too long, but I don't black out or die, which probably means the human part of me doesn't know what the hell it's talking about.

Mike's driving the car, and Lavinder's sitting in the passenger seat. Rain falls in sheets down the windows. Neither of them say a word.

"Are we on our way to Ara?" I ask.

Lavinder's head tilts back in surprise. He hesitates, then hums an affirmation.

Well, at least that's something. I sit back and experimentally put my hand through the upholstery I'm sitting on. It moves through just as easily as it does *anything* I try to touch. So why, I wonder idly, am I able to sit in the car at all? Is it just a matter of expectation? Intent? I really need to experiment with that further.

My head's still aching from the brief sojourn into the edge of nonexistence, but I think that might be because I'm trying very hard not to think about the thing that put me there in the first place. That's what causes headaches, isn't it? When you want to have a thought very badly, but it's all plugged up in your head and you can't think it?

Like Melanie said. When my mental health goes *phoom*, I go *phoom*. I need to be a lot more careful.

Lavinder sits right in front of me, broad shoulder visible around the edge of the seat, and as I stare idly at it I realise there might be another reason why my head aches. Maybe there's someone who needs to die. That could also be why my hand is drawn to Lavinder's shoulder, actually, trying to fulfil that inexplicable compulsion I haven't noticed until right just now.

I pause for a moment — comprehension hits me like a lightning bolt — I swear wildly and throw myself out the side of the car. Vehicles and heavy rain pass through me, then the guardrail, then trees, then asphalt, and I land heavily and somehow *painfully* into a pile of prickly thorn bushes edging the road. For a while it's difficult to think *any* thought, let alone the two thoughts I very desperately am trying not to have, but then I hear Lavinder's voice far too nearby for me to ignore it.

"*Roy!*"

"N —no —" I feebly try to wave him off. "Go away — go *away* —"

"Roy, what's wrong?"

"Need to kill you, don't want to kill you, *go away!*"

I can feel Lavinder stopping in his tracks, staring at the bush I've landed in. Weakly I think he must have gotten Mike to stop the car. That's a lot of explaining he'll have to do. Maybe I should have said something before I hurled myself into the street. I pick myself off of the thorns, wince, shake out my limbs, wonder if I could somehow be bleeding. I back away from where Lavinder still hasn't moved.

"Wait," Lavinder says. "Please."

The pressure in my head increases with every step backwards I take, and *that's* why I stop, not because of Lavinder's plea. Or at least, that's what I tell myself. "*Go away.*"

"That's not going to work, Roy, we both know it —"

"I can stay here, I can stay in one place, you can *go*, you can get as far away from me as you possibly —"

"— and you would get to me eventually no matter what, so it *won't work*. Listen to me. We're on our way to the hospital already. Follow us, outside the car, and when you get there, give me the heart attack. I'm going to be fine."

"You're going to die."

"If Ara can survive it, so can I."

"What if you don't?"

"I will."

"*But what if you don't?*"

"Then you won't spend the rest of whatever existence you have driving yourself mad with pain. You have a second chance, and *I'm* not going to be the reason you ruin it."

What the hell are you talking about? is what I mean to say. Somehow, the words get tangled, and what actually comes out is: "I'm not going to be the reason you ruin *yours!*"

"I've had 24 years of a second chance, and

you've had *ten*."

"No, *you* just don't care if you live or die,
and that's *stupid*, 'cause —"

"Nothing out here's going to hurt me
worse than they did, not even you."

I'm stunned into silence. Neither of us say
anything for several seconds, and for a short
moment, I don't even feel the painful
pressure in my head.

"Casey," says Mike from beside the car.
He looks completely different in the rain,
with his hair flattened against his head.
"Dude. Buddy. What's going on."

"You're the boy from the dream," I say
slowly. My voice sounds very faraway. I
can't even be sure I said it out loud, and all
at once I understand what Lavinder means
about only sort-of hearing me, and being
unsure I even said anything at all.

"Sorry, Mike," says Lavinder, turning
away from me like I've already agreed to his
plan. "Thanks for stopping. We're good to
go."

"Uh," Mike says, "no we're *not*. You're
having a full on nervous *breakdown*, do you
realise that? A full on Hollywood-style
PTSD break from reality. We're not going
anywhere until you slow down and *talk to*

me."

Someone stuck behind the parked car honks angrily, but all three of us ignore it.

Lavinder nods. "Okay. I'll make you a deal. If I correctly predict what's going to happen to me in the next hour, will you do me the courtesy of hearing me out?"

"What the *hell* are you *talking* about?"

"We're going to the hospital, to find out how Dowlen's doing. While I'm there, I'm going to have a heart attack."

"You *what*?"

"I'm going to have a heart attack. It's a prediction, for the future. If I do, then I'll tell you everything, and you won't have any choice but to believe me. If I don't, then you're right, I'm having a psychotic break, and I'll go get all the help I need. Does that sound fair?"

"Does that sound —! Casey, are you fucking *nuts!*?"

"If you stall us, I'm going to have the heart attack right here, and I'll probably die from it."

"Damn it, Casey, you're not making any sense! Make *sense*, and then we'll go!"

"I really don't know how I can be any clearer than this. Hospital first, then heart attack, *then* I'll tell you everything."

Mike flounders for words. Lavinder nods, once, and holds out his hand. "Alright then. Give me the keys, I'll drive."

"You are *not* fucking driving!"

"Then I'll walk. You might as well come with me, because at least that way, you can make sure I stay safe. And I swear to you, I *will* tell you everything, one way or the other. It's up to you what we do after that."

Mike flounders for words a little longer, then makes his decision with an aggressively aggravated noise. "OK! *Fine*! Get in the goddamn car, and we'll go to the goddamn hospital!"

"Thank you."

"*No*. You don't get to thank me until we end the day with you outside of handcuffs and a straitjacket, alright?" Mike jingles the keys as he walks over to the car. "And I am *not* stopping in the middle of traffic again, either."

Lavinder follows him over. They both get in, and drive away, and I stay rooted to the spot, staring after the car, trying in vain to process everything that's just happened.

~~

Lavinder is the boy from the dream.

271

For a while, that's the only thought I can have, over and over and over again, until I can practically see the words hanging in the air around me. *Lavinder is the boy from the dream.*

They don't fit anywhere. They don't connect anywhere. They're just *there*. Rain that won't fall, clouds that won't part, a conclusion that won't come. I almost feel like I'm drowning in the thought, until I finally manage to pull myself together and let the words fall to the ground around my feet, so my thoughts can finally move forward.

I don't know what *I* am, but clearly, Lavinder does. The more I replay our conversation in my head, the more I'm certain of that. Lavinder knows *exactly* what I am. Maybe he's known from the beginning — or maybe he didn't at first, but that's changed now, and he never bothered to tell any of the rest of us.

I guess, to be completely fair, he *couldn't* really tell me. He didn't even know I was there until today.

So what *am* I?

The questions hangs nearly solid in the air, until I consciously move my thoughts forward again.

The way Lavinder and I argued, the way *I* argued, so desperate and scared, is oddly familiar. I've seen that kind of argument before. So many times. Family. Family who all care so much about each other that it hurts. *Family* argues like that, where they care so much it makes them angry, where they care so much that they want to *drag* each other to good health. It's how Melanie and Sam argue. It's how Ara and I have *started* arguing. It's how I always felt about Ara, from even before we *could* argue.

What am I?

Casey Lavinder must be the boy from the dream. In the first dream, I argued with him. In the second dream, it was *his* safety I was worried about. We had the same parents. We had the same *awful* parents. We had the same mother I was terrified of. The same bedroom.

But —

— but it *can't* be true. It's *not true*. I'm *ancient*. I'm *formless*. I don't *have* family. I've *never* had family. No one has ever hurt me the way Casey was hurt. *I* hurt people. I kill people. I exact vengeance. I am *ancient* and *formless* and *vengeance incarnate*. I don't have

273

a name, I am barely even *comprehensible*. I
can trace my beginnings to the very first
sentient thoughts of the very first sentient
being.
I *don't have a name*
except my name is Roy.
I *don't have family*
except I argue with Ara like she is.
I *don't have friends*
except Melanie cares about me.
I *don't care* about *anything*
except I cared about Andrea Relshaw.

I am **ancient** and **formless** and **vengeance
incarnate.**

I'm a child sitting against the door digging
small heels into rough carpet so the door
will stay closed.

I kill people.

I *was* killed —

**Nothing has *ever* touched me and
nothing *ever will*.**

But Casey —

I feel nothing, I want nothing, I AM nothing.

Casey is the boy from the dream —

I REMEMBER NOTHING.

~~

I'm in the hospital. Bright buzzing lights line the ceiling. There's a steady beeping coming from several rooms at once, unhurried, unassuming, unalarming. Sterile is everywhere, in the air, in the walls, in the masks on some faces, in the sinks in some rooms, but sterile doesn't touch *me*. I'm wherever I need to be. First, over by the desk; then, in a room. Nothing unmakes me, not the sterile atmosphere, not the buzzing bright lights, not the steady beeping. Not the thing that pokes awareness at the sight of the consciousness in the bed.

Two people speak quietly together over by the glass. I appear next to them, and I move through the target to break it.

The target... doesn't break.

I move through it again. There's a catch in the air, a sizzle, a spark. The target still does not break.

I stand within it. The sizzle grows. It grows and grows until there is no space for both it and for me, and I, an unmovable uncaring *force*, give no ground, even though it shaves at awareness, even though it sizzles within *me*.

The target starts to break. Light begins to fade. A little more time, that's all I need. Just a little more time.

The sizzle grows until it consumes my awareness, and then I lose all track of vengeance.

CHAPTER EIGHTEEN
Reprieve

Something glitters in the great expanse of nothing, which is really the only warning I get before a voice cuts into me like an icy wind.

"Wow," it says. "Ara wasn't exaggerating. You really *do* look like me."

I don't know what my thoughts, my feelings, my body, *or* my consciousness is doing. For an eternity, I just drift.

"Roy?"

Roy. Memories cascade. "... Lavinder?"

"Yes. I mean — if you like. But I think I'd prefer Casey, if that's alright with you. It seems... a little more appropriate, like this."

Awareness comes back in by degrees, like when sunlight's streaming through your window and someone's pounding angrily at your door, but the very *last* thing you want to do is wake up and face a world that doesn't want you in it.

"Like what?" I ask. There's nothing around us — all I see is Casey Lavinder, a few metres away from me, looking exactly like he did when we argued outside his car. Everything else around us is just... blue. Endless sky. Endless colour.

Casey shrugs, looking up at nothing. "Like... well, whatever this is. You wouldn't happen to know where we are, would you? I think I'm unconscious. Or possibly dead."

"*Dead*?"

"No, not dead," Casey says quickly.

"I *told* you it wasn't going to work —!"

"I can hear Mike. I wouldn't be able to hear him if I was dead, right?"

"How the *hell* do you know that?"

Casey shrugs uneasily.

"Where are we?"

He shrugs again, this time with a gentle smile. "I was hoping you would know. If I had to guess — inside my head, or my soul? Or maybe on *your* plane of existence? Somewhere that isn't real."

I look at Casey. It's not often I feel like the

only one who *doesn't* know what's going on, and it doesn't take long for me to decide I don't like that feeling. At *all*. "Am I a ghost?"

"No," Casey says immediately. Then, softer: "I don't think so, no. If you're a ghost, you can't possibly be the *only* ghost, and if all ghosts can kill like you can — I looked up the statistics for people who have heart attacks younger than 35. Different people say different things, but overall, the rate is *decreasing*. It's not nearly a big enough number. Whatever you are, I think you're unique."

"What *am* I, then?"

"I don't know."

I narrow my eyes. "Yeah, you do. You know me. You *know* we've met before."

Casey smiles abruptly, startling me. It's not a happy smile. It's more like the mask of one, the mask people learn to wear when they need something to cover up their grief. "That's true," he says. "I still don't know *how*, but I know that's true."

"Am I *you*?"

"No."

"Then *tell me*. Please."

Casey nods, swallows. Looks up at the complete lack of a sky once more. "When I

279

was growing up," he says, his voice hoarse, but firm, "I had a twin. An identical twin. Our parents..." Here, he falters. "... weren't great. Grown-ups at school started to notice. We were absent a lot. You — my twin, he was — *they* were — injured a lot. One day, our father took me to school, and everyone at school wanted to know why my twin wasn't there. One thing led to another, they called the police, and... I wasn't allowed to go back home. By the time anyone went to go find you, they were too late. Our mother..."

Casey's words tumble over themselves in the rush out of his mouth, right up until his momentum fails him and his voice chokes off.

"... killed me," I finish for him.

Casey puts a hand over his face and doesn't answer.

My words had the confident ring of memory behind them when I spoke, but I still don't *remember*. All I remember is the dream. Casey's mother chasing me furiously up the stairs, the door slamming, the painful jerk of my broken arm. I try, but I don't reach any memory of what happened afterwards. My head still isn't convinced that the dream *is* a memory. I don't feel any attachment to anything Casey just described.

No, I remind myself silently. I *do*. Why else would the dreams affect me as badly as they did? Why else did I throw myself out of the car the moment I realised Casey was in danger? Why else did Melanie's descriptions of how *she* grew up resonate so strongly at my core?

"So," Casey says, startling me — I didn't expect him to be *able* to speak again. "I don't know what you are. I don't know if you *are* my twin, or... just something wearing their face, but — I thought you deserve to know that much."

I think about this. I think very quickly, and I come to about twenty different possible conclusions. "Casey?"

"Hm?"

"Are you sure you or your twin never met Spencer Dowlen before?"

"I can't be completely sure. We were eight, when... I might have met a lot of people I don't remember. But I don't think so."

"Then why do I want him dead so badly?"

Casey shrugs again, but this one is less dismissive and more thoughtful. "You still do?"

"Yes. Definitely. *More* so now."

"Did something cause that?"

"You."

"What do you mean?"

"He — he tried to kill you. He tried to use *me* to kill you."

Neither of us speak for a bit.

"Okay," I say conclusively, "you know what? I'm just never going to think about my answers ever again. I'm just going to answer every question anyone asks me immediately, without thinking, because that's gotten me a *lot* further than *thinking* about anything."

Casey chuckles, and abruptly I never want him to stop laughing ever again. I *love* the way it changes his whole face, makes him look younger and joyful. He looks like a completely different person, for just those few seconds, laughing at my half-serious joke.

"But really," I say, once he looks serious again and the moment has passed. "You almost died. We're still not sure you *didn't* die. This could be purgatory. Dowlen has to *pay*."

"I don't understand," says Casey. "What

does Dowlen have to do with any of this?
He can't have ordered you to do anything —
he's in the hospital with heart disease."

"I don't *know*. I'm just telling you what I
feel."

"Hm."

We lapse into silence again, and I stare at
the blank space all around us. No, not even
space; space implies something could, one
day, occupy it. Around us, there's just
nothing. Empty vacuum. A dreamscape, if
dreams had never touched it. It should be
unnerving, I think, or at least a little bit
discomforting, but to me, it feels normal.
Familiar. Like I could disappear into it for a
millennium and leave all of these mysteries
for someone *else* to solve.

An idea occurs to me. "Casey, what did
that house look like?"

"What house?"

"Where your twin died. What did it look
like?"

I almost regret asking, because Casey's
face goes worryingly blank. "Why?"

"I want to test something. Humour me?"

It takes a moment, but then Casey sighs.
"It was a townhouse," he says. "Two-level,
red brick, on a wide street. Or, well — wide

for an eight-year-old, I suppose. It had a tiny garden, low fence. Our mother grew hydrangeas along the wall. They blocked a lot of the view out the window." Casey closes his eyes. "Brown front door, but it wasn't made out of wood. The back yard was big enough to have a lawn to mow, but nothing else. There was a hole in the back corner fence that took you straight back into the woods — that's where we spent most of our time."

In the empty vacuum around us, a red brick townhouse flickers into misty view. Neither Casey nor I move, but as he speaks, we seem to shift through from the front to the back of the house anyway. It's like a child's drawing, half-filled in, half-remembered. I can see the lawn and the hole in the fence and the back door, but the rest of the house is blank, lost to time.

"What about the woods?" I ask.

Casey smiles slowly. "There was a creek, narrow and deep right by the house, but wide and shallow further out. If it hadn't rained for a while, half of the creek was just pebbles. *So many* pebbles. You taught me how to skip them. And — there was a place where the bank curved sharply, above the water, and there was a rabbits' warren right above it. We saw them once, in the hole, two baby ones. On the other side of the creek there were fields of wildflowers and if you caught the wind right on a blustery day, running across them felt like *flying*. We made our own kite once. It got stuck in a tree. For all I know, it might even still be there."

We shift from the townhouse's back yard to the woods, crafted in near-perfect detail around us, like a camera focused only on the important bits and blurring the rest out.

"I don't know what's beyond that," says Casey. "We always talked about trying to find out, but — neither of us were brave enough."

"We *are* in your head," I murmur. "Look."

Casey opens his eyes, and stumbles a step in surprise. "What the —?"

"I know that field," I say, pointing. "That's where one of my dreams happened. You and — and your twin, lying in the grass there, talking about taking a boat to New York City."

Casey stares with wide eyes. "I *remember* that. We talked about running away."

I take a step towards the field, crisp

autumn leaves crunching under my feet. "I was so sure that would *work*," I say, watching the wildflowers dance in the breeze. "I was so sure that New York would solve every single one of our problems."

"You said you woke up in New York," says Casey.

"Ten years ago." I swallow hard, past a thick knot in my throat. "I — I know this is terrible, but I almost wish — I 'mean, look, let's be honest with ourselves here, I *can't* be your twin, because they didn't die only ten years ago, because you're not *eighteen*. So I have to be something else. Wearing their face, like you said. But — I almost wish I was. Even though it means having *them* as parents, and having a crappy life, and being *murdered*, and just, in general, forever being eight years old, I still wish —"

"I know," Casey says softly. "Me too."

For several minutes, we stand in companionable silence, watching the woods and the fields around us. It could almost be a real day, with the way the wind blows at grass blades and branches, and the way the sun shines down through deep green leaves to dapple the ground. Blurriness shifts with Casey's focus, first the wildflowers in sharp

Responsible Revenge | Amari Amson

relief with the trees blurred, and then the trees clear in the late afternoon sun while the flowers are barely visible through blurred fog. It's fascinating to watch.

"Can you still hear Mike?" I ask, when I stop feeling like the silence is helping.

Casey shakes his head. "I don't hear anything now."

"What do you feel?"

"Peaceful, mostly." Casey rocks his head from side to side. "A little uncomfortable. I'm pretty sure I'm in a bed."

"Are you okay?"

Casey thinks about it for a little bit, and then nods. "Yes."

"Great. I'm glad *one* of us is."

He chuckles again. "I don't think you have to be here."

"What?"

"It's my head, not yours. You should be able to leave whenever you want."

"How?"

"Haven't the foggiest. How do you usually get around?"

"Walking."

"Well, maybe try that."

I stare at him for a moment, and then we both smile at the same time, and it feels *weird*, like static electricity sparking between two people.

"But," Casey says, "just in case I *am* dead and this is the last time I ever get to see you — or hear you, or feel you, or… anything. I just — well, first of all, don't blame yourself, because I *asked* you to do this. It's my fault, not yours. Second of all, thank you."

"For what?" I ask, startled and afraid.

"For caring. For… appearing, and caring, and answering questions, and making the last week a week worth living."

Fear continues to cloud my thoughts, but I force my awareness through it. "You're welcome. And thank *you*, for… being the closest thing I'll ever have to an answer."

"You're welcome."

"You're *not* dead, though."

"How do you know?"

"I can't talk to the dead. I'm not Ara." I smile, imagining Ara interjecting to remind us that she *can't* talk to the dead, that's not how it works, and shame on me for simplifying an immensely complicated and personal matter of psychic connection. "You're going to be fine, and then we can *keep* pursuing answers together, you and me. Okay?"

Casey blinks, then gives me a long and considered look, then nods. "Okay."

And I walk, out over the fields past the tree line Casey said we never got past when I was alive, walking until the entire scene fades to nothing and my consciousness is caught and buoyed upwards.

~~

Casey was right. When awareness comes back to me, I see him lying in a hospital bed, next to one of those machines that make the steady 'nothing is wrong here' beeping noise. Mike's there too, leaning against the wall by the sink and cabinet, looking both terrified and distant, a million miles away.

A branch taps against the window, and Mike jerks like the sound was a gunshot. I can't help laughing a little. Casey told him that he would have a heart attack at the hospital, and lo and behold, Casey had a heart attack at the hospital. Mike probably has no idea what to make of it. The poor guy is probably having an existential crisis, rethinking every single opinion he's ever had about the supernatural. I leave him to it, with one last look back at Casey breathing steadily under the hospital sheets, and I head off to find Ara.

When I walk into the room, Melanie —
thank *god* — is there with her.

"— isn't something I'll ever touch with a
ten-foot pole," Ara says, tapping her phone
against her blanket with each syllable for
emphasis. "Too many complications. My
sister swore by it, right up 'till it killed her.
Always more looks than sense, that one.
That's my first and only *valid* piece of advice
you're ever gonna get from me, Melanie —
do not ever reach for more than you're
comfortable with. *Ever.* Some discipline may
seem like — hi, Roy, one minute, gotta finish
this thought — some discipline may seem
like it's total hogwash, and most *are* total
hogwash, but that ain't no reason to go
around messing with stuff you don't
understand. Look at Ouija boards. Total
hogwash. They're mass-produced by *toy*
companies, for Chrissakes. But Lavinder
and I used one to talk with Roy, and it
would have killed Lavinder if we didn't
know *exactly* what we were doin', so don't
take chances even with the hogwash stuff. It
ain't worth it. *Ever.*" Ara stretches her arms
up and lays back, grinning at me. "So, what
happened?"

"Casey had a heart attack."

"Casey — *what*!?"

"Wait, wait, wait, wait, wait." Melanie gets immediately to her feet, waving her arms. "*Hold* on one bloody minute, here, *both* of you. How's a girl supposed to process half of this stuff?" She takes a long breath. "A, is voodoo *actually real*, that seems like an important thing I should know if I'm gonna be doing any of this? And B, who's Casey."

"Lavinder," I clarify.

"Shit, *what*?"

"Lavinder had a heart attack. I caused it. He's okay, he's sleeping now. I'm... *pretty* sure it's not a coma. Ara, did you know he had a twin brother?"

Ara and Melanie both struggle to speak, but Ara recovers first. "Did you cause it by *accident*, or is it one of your jobs?" she demands.

"Jobs. I don't think I *can* do it by accident. If it's not a job, it takes a lot of effort. Ara, did you know he had a twin brother?"

"I don't give a flying fuck right now Roy, ex*cuse* me for making sure all of my *friends are okay*. Did you *tell* him?"

"About what?"

"About him being one of your jobs, you absolute *moron*."

"Yeah, and he insisted I do the same thing we did for you. So blame him if something goes wrong. Ara, *did you know* —"

"So he had the heart attack here in the hospital?"

I groan with impatience. "*Yes.*"

"And he's safe."

"Yes."

"And he's okay."

"Yes."

"Are *you* okay?"

"I am *now*, yeah."

"What in the everlasting name of the holy fuck does that *mean*, Roy?"

"Which part?"

Ara hesitates. "Well, *all* the parts, but specifically — you *do not* get to answer 'are you okay' with 'I am *now*' and then *not explain yourself.*"

"Well," I say, growing snappish, "*you* said over the phone we couldn't trust me not to kill anyone, so I wasn't okay. But then I stopped thinking about it, and I was okay. Then I got the urge to kill Casey, so I wasn't okay. Then I threw myself out of the car to get away from him, and then he confronted me *anyway*, so I wasn't okay, but then he told me he'd be fine if I did it while he was

in the hospital, and then I argued with —
something, myself, I think? — and I
completely forgot who I am, so then I *wasn't*
okay, *again.* Then I tried to kill him and
something blocked me so it wouldn't work,
and then I was inside Casey's head, and
then we talked and he explained what I am,
so I'm *okay* now, and then I left his head and
came up here to see you both, so I'm *extra*
okay. Ara, *did you know he had a twin
brother?"*

Melanie throws her hands up and sits
back down. "I'm in a fucking TV show," she
mutters to herself, folding her arms and
looking uncharacteristically sullen.

"Roy," Ara says slowly, "are you *trying* to
give me another heart attack?"

"No."

She takes a long, deep breath, clearly
struggling for patience. "No," she says
evenly. "I had no idea Lavinder had a twin
brother. Now, if you're happy, please take
me and Melanie through it all again, step by
step, with about an ocean's worth more
detail."

So I do. I explain, for Melanie's benefit,
what happened with Dowlen. I explain how
I felt only half-real after Casey's

293

conversation with Ara. I explain throwing myself into the street, Casey coming after me, my existential crisis, and how I lost myself right up until Casey managed to drag me into his head.

"Stop," says Ara. "Go back. *What* were you arguing with?"

I shrug uncomfortably. "I don't know. Something... big?"

"Vengeance incarnate, eh?"

"Yeah." I pause, thinking about those few moments where I stopped being real and started being not-Roy, where my feet left the pavement and the pavement left the atmosphere. "It was me, but it wasn't. It was like..." I snap my fingers. "It was like arguing with a child! You know that age where they start to realise they *can* talk back, but they don't have logic or common sense or even really a strong memory yet, so they argue just because they can, and they think getting louder and louder means they win? It was like that. It was like a child with no logic or sense *really wanted* Casey dead, and when I wouldn't do it, it threw a tantrum."

"Its mental health went *poof*," Melanie mutters. "So *you* went *poof*."

"Yes. *Exactly*."

Ara looks at us both. "What?"

"Roy's mental health is what screws things up for it," Melanie answers. "Didn't you notice? Every time it needs to confront something scary, something goes wrong, or it scatters."

"Oh. Sure." Ara looks at me thoughtfully. "You know, that almost sounds familiar. Vengeance incarnate. Vengeance incarnate..." She looks annoyed for a moment, then flaps her hand. "Eh, it'll come to me later. Probably in the shower, that's the way shit seems to happen to me. Keep going, Roy."

I keep going. I explain being in Casey's head, and our conversation. I explain how I left, and how I saw Mike keeping watch over him, probably *bursting* with questions. Then I finish, and neither Melanie nor Ara say anything for a while.

"I suddenly feel really lucky," Melanie says, unconsciously hugging herself. "How messed up is that?"

"It's not messed up at all," I assure her instantly.

"It feels... inconsiderate, though. Offensive?"

"I don't remember enough to *be* offended."

"And even if it did," Ara cuts in, "it is *never* inconsiderate to feel lucky. All that means is you understand how bad someone else had it. Seems pretty damn considerate to me."

Melanie nods absently. "I kind of want to find Sam and hug him forever."

"Nothing's stopping you."

"He's mad at me. You have to let him cool off before you engage, when he's mad. He never learned how not to be mad."

"Fair enough. Roy — let me go through this from the beginning. First, you know I didn't mean we can't trust *you*, right? You know I didn't mean it that way."

"Yeah." I hesitate. "Well — I didn't *then*, but I didn't really have time to think then. I do now."

"Good. Second — and this is just me spitballing, so don't tell me it's a stupid idea, because I *will* find a way to whap you upside the head — what if Dowlen has you on some kind of leash?"

I stare at her. "*What?*"

"No vanishing or scattering on me, now."

I raise my hands. "Scout's honour, I'm still here and I feel fine, just *really confused*. What are you talking about?"

"I'm talking about how you wanted to kill Dowlen, and *only* Dowlen, with no obvious reason why. I'm talking about how Lavinder and I were there when his brother went down, Dowlen blamed *me*, and when you came back, you had the order to kill me. I'm talking about how *you* said Dowlen knew you were what Lavinder was talking to. I'm talking about how, after Dowlen's threats didn't work on Lavinder, you suddenly had the order to kill *him*."

"But — I'm not denying all of that makes sense, but he couldn't *see* me."

"So? I couldn't see you either, and I knew you were there. People discover supernatural things all the time and think that makes them goddamn experts. Give someone a genuine voodoo doll and they think they're fucking Marie Laveau."

Melanie points at her. "So voodoo *is* real!"

"Don't go messin' with shit you don't understand, Melanie, we've been over this."

"Yeah! That would be a lot easier if I knew what to *avoid*, don't you think?"

"You think Dowlen has his hands on some kind of voodoo magic?" I ask, confused.

"Oh shit, no. Voodoo's real specific. You don't just point at some random folks and go 'give them heart attacks'. No, whatever he has, I don't recognise it, except that the patterns make sense. Someone pisses him off, he decides he wants 'em dead, and he doesn't much care *how* they get dead. Probably wouldn't even bother gettin' his hands dirty if he didn't have himself a mighty fine and easy way to do it."

"A leash," I say. "On me."

"As an example, yeah. I don't know where Lavinder's brother fits into this — maybe he's right and you're just wearing his face. Gotta do some research. Dowlen probably doesn't even realise what he's using is sentient. What do you think, Roy? Does it match up?"

I sit down heavily in the chair. "*Shit.*"

"Yep."

"I always assumed — I don't know, it sounds ridiculous now, but I always thought it was… something divine? Justice or something. I always thought there had to *be* a reason, that I just couldn't see the shape of it."

"I know," Ara says, a little softer this time. "That would have been simpler."

"What? No, no, *this* is simpler. Now we can kill just one person and I'm *free*."

"No, Roy. No. *No, Roy.* No. *No.*"

"Why not?"

"For one thing, we don't know for sure you *would* be free — you might cease to exist, or get bound to someone else, and all of this is even assuming we're right in the first place. For another thing, if I'm right about the leash, that's usually a *thing*. An object. Something we can take away from the fucker before Lavinder arrests him and puts him behind bars for the rest of his life."

"Arrest him for what?" says Melanie. "For existing while random people all around the world have heart attacks?"

Ara thinks for a minute, then shrugs. "Tax evasion."

Melanie bursts out laughing, almost drowning out the sound of Ara's phone ringing on the bed by her knee. Ara raises her brow at Melanie until Melanie manages to stop laughing, and only then does she answer the phone. "So," she says cheerfully, thumbing the speaker so Melanie and I can hear as well. "You're awake, then."

"Hi, Ara." Casey sounds a little rough around the edges, but otherwise just like his old self. "Is Roy up there with you?"

"Yep."

"Would it come down and help me talk with Mike?"

"Yes," I say immediately. "*Yes*. Melanie, come with me."

Melanie starts. "What?"

"Come over to see Casey and Mike with me."

"Um, why?"

I shrug. "Fun?"

Melanie thinks about that, and then shrugs. "Works for me."

CHAPTER NINETEEN

Removal

For the tenth time, there's silence in Casey's hospital room, broken only by equipment and low conversations in the hallway outside.

"Again," says Mike. He both looks and sounds extremely determined and very focused.

"Again, Mike?" Casey very nearly sounds exasperated. "How many more times do you —"

"*Again.*" Mike shifts into the very corner of the room, where no one could possibly see behind his back, and the number of fingers he's holding up can't possibly be reflected onto a surface anywhere. "Go."

"Five," I say. I've been standing in that

301

corner the whole time.

"Five," Casey and Melanie both say at the same time.

Mike shifts his fingers again.

"Eight," I say.

"Eight," Casey and Melanie echo simultaneously.

We keep going like this, keeping up a steady rhythm — four, two, zero, nine, four, nine, six — until finally Mike lets his hands drop and stares at the wall above Casey's bed, looking completely lost.

"Yeah," Melanie says sympathetically. "I know the feeling."

"Shit," says Mike.

"Yeah, I'm pretty sure I said the exact same thing."

"Can you tell him to move?" I ask. "He's squishing me in here, and I don't want to accidentally stand inside him."

Casey relays my request. Mike stares at him for several seconds, like he can't even begin to process it, and then he *jumps* out of the way towards the window, staring at the space I'm occupying with terror in his eyes.

"Come on, Mike," says Casey. "I keep telling you, it's safe."

"It *put you in that bed,*" Mike says, very

loudly, with a punctuated gesture.

"I asked it to."

"*Why*?"

"Because it was going to resist doing anything to me otherwise, and that hurts it, and it's my friend."

For the eleventh time, there's silence in Casey's hospital room, broken only by equipment and low conversations in the hallway outside.

"Shit," Mike murmurs. "Shit, shit, shit, shit, *shit*. What does this mean? Does this mean — is that woman's whole shtick real? Does she actually talk to the dead?"

"Yeah," I say. "She does."

"No," Melanie says, rolling her eyes, "she doesn't. She *feels* the dead. Believe me, she is *extremely* clear on that point. Not talking. *Feeling*. She gets snapshots of the lives of dead people, and their feelings and things, and she spins a tale out of that."

"But she talks to —" Mike points at the corner I'm in. "— *that*."

"Yeah, Roy's not dead."

"Roy's Casey's dead fucking brother, how in the hell is it *not* a fucking ghost?"

"We're still a little unclear about that," Casey says softly. "I don't think... if it's a

ghost, then why didn't it appear back then?
It doesn't look like a child, either, it looks
like me."

"You can *see* it!?"

"No. That's just Ara."

Mike drops his face into his hands again.
"Shit, shit, shit, shit, shit... shit, do you think
there's, like — an X-files department? Is
there a Mulder and Scully to handle shit like
this? Should we be reporting this to MI-6?
Do I need to buy salt? Do I need to get
religious? What the hell am I supposed to *do*
with this?"

"Nod, and accept it, and pretend your
life's turned into a TV show," Melanie
informs him. "It helps."

"Fucking off into la-la land *helps*?"

"Well, it helps *me*."

"You know what would help me?" Mike's
helplessness hardens into sharp-edged
anger. "It would help, a *lot*, to have a list of
every single person this *ghost* has ever killed,
so I can look into their lives and figure out
why the fuck each of them *deserved to die*."

"Oh," says Melanie, raising her hand and
bouncing excitedly on her toes, "about that,
Ara has a theory. She thinks Dowlen got his
hands on some kind of supernatural object

Roy's bound to, and that *Dowlen's* been the one killing all those people, not Roy. Kind of like Roy's a hitman, you know? You arrest the person who ordered the hit, 'cause *they're* the killer."

"We don't just *let the hitman go*," Mike snaps.

"No," Casey agrees, "but you could make a case in court that if the person had been brainwashed, or blackmailed, then they're not at fault."

For the twelfth time, there's silence in Casey's hospital room.

"Okay," says Mike. "Okay. Fine. Whatever. This is fine. Finding out ghosts exist is fine. Finding out your partner is haunted by the ghost of his goddamn twin brother, that's fine. You know what isn't fine? Spencer fucking Dowlen. Where's Dowlen."

"He should be here too," I point out. "In the hospital, I mean. On account of… how I almost killed him."

Melanie relays that, Mike's lips press so tightly together that they vanish into pale white skin, and he disappears out the door.

"Well," I say brightly, "that went well."

Casey chuckles once, and then his face

goes blank again. "He'll be okay. He comes on strong, but he's a good man. He'll think things through and work it out on his own time."

"I'm just glad I got to watch someone else freak about all this," says Melanie, grinning. "*That* helped. You're only insane if no one else is insane."

"Who else knows, now?" asks Casey. "Me, you, Ara, Mike...?"

"That's pretty much it." Melanie frowns, and then brightens. "Oh! And Sam. Shit, I can't believe I nearly forgot about Sam. Sam knows. Or — well, he *halfway* knows. He knows enough that he knows he doesn't want to know anything else, you know?"

"Yeah," says Casey. "I do."

We lapse into silence again.

"Do you remember I was in your head?" I ask Casey abruptly. "A couple of hours ago?"

"Sort of," says Casey, completely unsurprised. "Like it was a dream."

"What was your twin's name?"

He doesn't answer, for long enough that I don't think I'm going to *get* an answer, but then he smiles sadly at my corner. "Troy."

I stare at him. He doesn't do me the

courtesy of noticing.

"Shit," says Melanie. She paces up and down the room, waving her hands wildly in the air. "Shit. Shit. *Shit.* Then that's *exactly* who you are. You *are* the twin. You *have to be the twin, Roy.*"

Casey stares at her, looking mildly alarmed by her jerky movements. "What?"

"Because — because Ara named you! You know that thing she does where she gets bits and pieces of people from when they were alive? She doesn't always know she's doing it! A lot of the time, she *doesn't* know she's doing it! And she can *only* do that if there's something there to *find,* if there's a connection to the person somewhere in the room with her. I mean, what if she just got a piece of 'Troy' and didn't notice it was someone who used to be alive? What if she just thought she made it up?"

Neither Casey nor I answer her.

"Roy?" she asks. "You're still there, right? You didn't go *phoom?*"

"Yeah," I say. "I'm still here."

No one says anything else until Mike comes back, looking sullen and angry and ready to arrest the first person who asks him what's wrong.

"What's wrong?" Casey asks. I wince.

Mike's gaze snaps to Casey, and it softens a barely perceptible amount under the anger. "The bastard's in a coma," he says angrily.

"Who? Dowlen?"

"*Yes*, Dowlen, who else would I be talking about?" Mike runs one hand through his hair and sighs. "A woman gets killed, then the person who probably killed her gets stuck in a coma, and then his *brother* gets stuck in a coma. If that isn't some Egyptian curse bullshit, I don't know what is."

"I'm not Egyptian," I murmur without thinking. Melanie laughs; Mike shoots her a dirty look.

Casey shifts suddenly and pushes himself up. "Mike, can you —"

"Stay in that *fucking* bed, you idiot. Can I what?"

"Can you go through Dowlen's possessions? See if there's anything he had that his brother might have handled as well?"

"Why?"

"Ara thinks there's an object Roy's bound to. Dowlen would have it somewhere in his house, wouldn't he?"

308

"Why do you think the brother might have handled it?"

"You said it yourself," Casey answers with a light shrug. "Some Egyptian curse bullshit."

"No," I say slowly. "No, I don't think Louis ever had it. I don't think Louis even knew what it was. If he did, he wouldn't have killed Andrea himself, or gone after you and Ara with a gun. And besides — I could get into Louis's heart. I couldn't get into Dowlen's."

Casey nods. "That's true. But we need *some* way of narrowing down what the object might be. Would you recognise it if you saw it?"

"I have absolutely no idea."

"I wouldn't count on it," Melanie adds. "You didn't even recognise your own brother."

"If I can interrupt you both being *extremely creepy* for a minute," says Mike, "it's a moot point anyway. As far as the law is concerned, Dowlen's done nothing except go into a coma, so there's no way we'd get a warrant to search anything he has."

Casey frowns. "We can't link it to the brother?"

"They didn't live together, so, no."

"We could break in," I suggest.

"No," Casey says immediately and firmly, "we can't."

"*You* can't. You're a shining beacon of justice. But you can't really stop *me* from going wherever I want. You never know; I might recognise it. And if I see anything incriminating in there, like, I don't know, bloody clothes or something —"

"You'll what?" says Casey with a smile. "Testify in court that we have due course for a warrant?"

I subside with a grumble. "Fine, maybe not that."

"I could go with it," Melanie brightens. "Then, if we find anything, I can call in an anonymous tip."

Casey raises his brow. "You're going to break in?"

"Sure, why not? For all you know, I'm a criminal mastermind with *years* of breaking and entering experience under my belt."

"Who just preemptively confessed to a crime to two police officers."

"Maybe that's all part of my grand plan! You don't know me."

"Melanie, please don't break into

someone's home."

"Great! Consider me duly warned. Now, you can't get out of that bed, right? You can't actually stop me from leaving?"

"*Melanie.*"

She raises her hands. "Fine, fine, fine. I won't go and break into anyone's house. Scout's honour."

~~

"Of course, I was never actually a girl scout," Melanie tells me as the two of us stand in front of Dowlen's townhouse the next morning.

"I think Ara needs to be worried about you," I say.

"Really? *I* think Ara would be proud of me."

"I think you're projecting."

"Come on, you can't convince me that she's never broken into anywhere before."

"That's not a reason for it to suddenly be okay for *you* to do it. In fact, in general, I would say *don't* do what Ara does."

"Why not? Lavinder copied Ara with the hospital thing and it turned out fine for him." Melanie studies the front door, hands on her hips. "Ara's teaching me about supernatural stuff, and she's kept herself

311

safe for like 60 years, so why *wouldn't* I do what she does? I'm never going anywhere near voodoo, you know, as an example."

"So if Ara went and jumped off a cliff, you would too?"

"Oh, absolutely."

"Seriously?"

"Yep. Honestly, that expression's bollocks anyway. We're a social species, so of *course* we do things we see other people doing. If I saw everyone jumping off a bridge, you bet I'd jump off the bridge too, 'cause Godzilla's probably on it."

Melanie studies the door some more while I flounder, looking for a counterargument. Her phone buzzes in her pocket; she digs it out and checks it, then groans exasperatedly and puts it away again. "Fuck off, Dad, not now," she murmurs. "Okay, so I'm not going to be able to get that door open. *But*, I could probably jimmy one of the first floor windows open. No one ever thinks to secure those, especially since they stick all the time. Give me a minute."

"You've done this *before*?" I ask.

"Yes." Melanie hesitates. "No. Don't tell the police officers, okay?"

"*Why?*"

"Had to get back into my own house once when dad locked me out, and I got a taste for it, and I did a couple of stupid things after that. Are we here to lecture me, or are we here to break illegally into a comatose patient's house? Come *on*."

"I think I'm a bad influence on you," I mutter.

"I think it's insane that you think being a bad influence on a sixteen-year-old is worse than the fact you've *murdered* a whole bunch of people."

"Good point."

"Yeah! I have a lot of those. Give me a boost."

"Okay."

It takes both of us a good five seconds to realise I physically cannot do that, and we only realise it because when my hand goes right through Melanie's ankle, she gives a violent shudder and falls back against the porch railing with a start.

"Damn," she says, laughing at herself, her eyes wide and sparkling with adventure. "Books and movies aren't kidding. It really *does* feel like getting drenched with icy water."

"Sorry." I gesture at the window. "Will you still be able to get up there on your own?"

"Oh, yeah, I'll figure something out." Melanie laughs at herself again. "'*Give me a boost*', I said. Goddamn, Roy. Give me a *fucking* boost. Left my brain behind in bed this morning, that's what I did."

That makes me laugh too, which is a really strange feeling, because I haven't yet accidentally been inside anyone and felt like *laughing* about it. But Melanie's joy is infectious, and so is her complete disregard for rules and consequences, so I leave her to work out how to get up to the window and walk right through the door instead.

Ara's going to kill us for this later. We both know it. Melanie and I are hoping we can find something worthwhile to head off the worst of Ara's reaction. I'm a little more worried about Casey, who won't get *mad*, but will sure as heck get disappointed, and oddly, the thought of that feels worse.

Dowlen's living room looks exactly like I remember it, minus Dowlen. I stand in the middle of the room and look around, just to see if anything catches my eye or my attention immediately. Predictably, nothing does. I would probably have caught it the last time I was here.

My gaze falls on the wall where I almost killed Dowlen, and it lingers there. My feelings all clamour to be considered first, but I manage to ignore all of them. They can wait until later. I really don't want to run the risk of going *phoom* again.

I hear a crash against the panelling outside, and glance out the window. No sign of Melanie lying crumpled on the ground, so she's probably still okay.

I go upstairs next, and get a quick lay of the land, peeking through doors to figure out where the important rooms are. Two bedrooms, one bathroom. Why do you need two bedrooms in London if you live alone? Louis must stay here, at least semi-permanently, even if there's no official record of that. But there's one more door, and it's closed, and on the other side is an immaculate study, with displays that make me stop in my tracks.

They're all… *arcane*. There's really no other word for it. I don't recognise any of the objects, and I'm not drawn to any of them, but they strike an extremely worrying image all close together in one room like this. Dowlen must collect anything and *everything* that might have supernatural properties to them, because he has disparate collections from dozens of different cultures haphazardly organised and on display: Hannya masks on the wall, crystals and agates in a glass case, Buddhist prayer bells and drums on the shelves, embroidered velvet cloths and Havdalah candles on the shelves right below that.

I recognise nearly every object in the room, even ones I'm pretty sure I've never encountered before, but — I don't recognise any of them as *mine*, and I'm not drawn to any of them. It's an odd feeling, standing in the middle of the study and looking around; I can feel a hum in the air, as if all the different objects are vibrating ever so slightly against each other. I make a slow lap around the room, but the hum in the air doesn't grow any weaker or stronger. It permeates the air steadily no matter where I step.

"Roy!" I hear, muffled through a window. I glance up, and see Melanie balanced on the jamb outside the study window, gesturing pointedly. I grin in spite of myself, and walk over and poke my head out through the wall.

"Yes?"

"*Argh!* You — holy *shit,* Roy, don't *do* that!"

"Sorry. Do you need some help?"

"Yeah, I need some help! The window's stuck."

"And what, exactly, am *I* supposed to do about that?"

"I'm so glad you asked! Help me open it, you doofus."

"Do you need me to put my hand through your ankle again?"

"No, I'm serious. Give it a try. We *know* you can affect the world a little bit, so maybe just having your hands inside the window would, you know. Unstick it. Or make it easier to unstick."

I eye her dubiously.

"Look, what do we have to lose for trying? I'm kind of trapped out here, see?"

I eye the window just as dubiously as I eyed Melanie, then shrug to myself and pull my head back inside to try pushing it up from inside. Melanie balances herself, then uses her leverage to knock as much strength into the edge of the window as she safely can, and —

It pops open, and slides up with a screech of metal on wood.

"A-*ha*!" Melanie leans inside and tumbles down onto the carpeted floor. "Success!"

"We have no idea if I actually helped or not," I tell her, "but what the hell, I'll take the credit anyway. You're welcome."

"Nope, that was all me. That was *all me*. You did nothing."

"Oh, really?"

"Yep! I'm Superwoman. I'm She-Ra."

"Close the window on your own, then."

Melanie picks herself up, dusts herself off, and then hangs all her weight onto the window trying to close it. It doesn't budge an inch.

"I'll take my 'thank you' now," I say with a grin.

"Oh, buzz off. Where are we?"

"I think it's a study."

"Looks more like a personal museum."

"This is probably why Dowlen doesn't have an alarm system. Either he thinks something in here would take care of intruders for him, or the alarm system would interfere with whatever is going on in here."

"Interfere? What do you mean? Interfere

with what?"

I glance at her. "You don't feel that?"

"Feel what? No. What, should I feel a tingle or something?"

"Kind of, yeah. It's a bit like getting a massage."

"How do *you* know what getting a massage feels like?"

"Look," I say irritably, "Ara obviously thinks you have some kind of potential for this stuff, so will you just give it a try already? Stand in the middle of the room, right there. Shut your eyes. See if you can feel it."

Melanie rolls her eyes and does as I instruct, standing still with her arms out to her sides.

"Mm," she says, "nope. I'm not feeling a massage."

"Okay, well, maybe it won't feel like a massage if you're not — me. Just give it a try. Ignore everything else, listen to your gut. If someone asked you to do a reading on this room, what would you tell them?"

"I'd tell them they're stupid, probably a hoarder, maybe a kleptomaniac, *definitely* a colonialist."

"They'll pay you."

"Oh! Well, in *that* case..." Melanie takes a deep breath and lets it out slowly, rotating on the spot, wiggling her fingers. "Well," she says after a moment, "I'd probably tell them that someone died in this room."

"Really?"

"Nah, but that's usually what people want to hear when they pay for readings, right? Yeah. Someone died in this room, but it wasn't a *natural* death. They were poisoned. They died right there —" She points in the direction of the desk. "— in *that* chair, painfully, and now they've risen from the grave because they want justice."

I shake my head. "Ara would slap you for that."

"Yeah, I know. I'm not a great storyteller. I need to work on my creepy ambiance."

"You really don't feel anything?"

"Sorry, but no. Nothing weird. Like... it's a bit stuffy in here, and the open window isn't helping at all with that, and that's a little odd. But that's all I feel."

"Huh."

"Are you telling me all of this stuff is real?"

I shrug. "No idea. I'm just telling you what I feel."

"And you *feel* that all of this stuff is real?"

"I feel that they're all reacting to each other, yeah."

"So Dowlen actually knew what he was doing?"

"If he really is what made me kill people for ten years, I don't see how he *didn't* know what he was doing. Even if you just idly want a few people dead, when all those people drop dead of heart attacks, you'd at least do a little bit of *research*, right?"

"I like to think most people would care that their enemies are dropping dead mysteriously, yeah." Melanie walks over to one of the masks on the wall and squints at it. "What would happen if I move some of this stuff?"

"*Don't.*"

Melanie turns in surprise. "Why not?"

"I —" I blink, just as startled by the firmness of my reply as Melanie is. "I... don't know. But don't."

"Is that another one of those things you just know?"

"Melanie, I don't know, but I'm telling you, don't mess with anything in here. Remember what Ara said? If you don't know, don't go poking it with a stick."

"Respect the craft, blah blah blah, you got it. I just don't see how we're going to figure out which one is *yours* unless I can pick stuff up and fiddle with it."

"It might be out of view." I point to the cabinet of drawers. "Go open some of those."

"Go open some of what?"

"The — the drawers."

"Oh, right." Melanie steps over and pulls narrow drawers open one by one. "Look at this! It's like we're in some kind of jewelry store. What's the point of having plush velvet if you can't actually *see* the plush velvet? This cabinet could easily be made out of glass or something."

I lean around Melanie's shoulder so I can see what she's doing. "Maybe they don't like being seen," I say.

"Oh, so *all* possibly-supernatural objects are sentient now?"

"*I'm* sentient."

"Yeah, but you're at least partly human, and you want to be seen."

"Maybe other things don't."

Melanie rolls her eyes and opens the last drawer, just above the antique vases. "Aaand that's it," she says, and then stops. "Wait a minute, one of these is missing."

"Missing?"

Melanie points to an empty hole in the middle of the plush velvet. "See? That's a resting place for something small, and it's empty. Could that be it? Do you think Dowlen had it before the whole hospital thing?"

I take a step closer and run my fingers gingerly across the velvet. Now *this*, this feels familiar; this feels like the lingering remains of something I would have been drawn to. It's not so much a tingle as it is the *lack* of a tingle, a small space of dead air where my fingers contain the only atoms to exist.

Melanie *screams*. I jump back in surprise, lose my balance, fall against the display case in the corner, and send glass crashing into the wall behind it. The entire thing shatters. Two large agates fall heavily to the ground. Smaller crystals spill out onto the floor and bang into the nearby desk.

"*Ow*," I moan. I'm not on the floor — for one perceptually wild second I think I somehow managed to keep my feet, but then I realise I'm on the ceiling instead.

Melanie stands in the middle of the study, both fists over her mouth, elbows tucked right in close to her body making as small of a target of herself as she can. She stares at the broken display case, the glass shards on the floor, the scattered crystals, and visibly swallows her fear down. "Roy?"

"Yeah," I say. My voice feels wavy in the air. "I'm here."

"Roy?"

"I'm here, I'm — I'm right here."

"*Roy?*"

"I'm *right here*, Melanie, can you hear me?"

She doesn't answer. She stares at the crystals a few seconds longer, then swears loudly and pulls out her phone. I remain motionless up on the ceiling, paralysed by fear. I can't be invisible to her again. I *cannot* be *invisible* to her again.

"Ara?" Melanie paces up and down, holding her phone to her ear with two shaking fingers. "Okay, so — don't be mad, but I'm standing in Dowlen's house, and — yeah, yes, I'm fine, I'm safe, I — *Ara* —"

She stops. I can hear Ara's raised voice, even from my position on the ceiling.

"*Ara,*" Melanie finally cuts her off, "I'm sorry, okay, I won't do it again, but the fact is, I'm here, and I think we found where Roy's object is usually kept, only it's not here, and I think we did something incredibly stupid. There's a whole bunch of supernatural stuff in here, right, and Roy said they felt like a massage, like they were reacting to each other, and some were out of view, so I opened drawers for it to see, and there was an empty spot in one of the drawers, and... and then I *saw* Roy, like, tangible, solid, and fucking *terrifying*, Ara, I don't know what you see, but it sure as *fuck* wasn't what *I* saw, and I screamed and I startled it, and that broke one of the display cases, and — and now Roy's gone. It's not answering me."

There's utter silence for the next several seconds in the study. If Ara reacted to any of what Melanie described, I can't hear it. I can't even really *move*. It's not fear I'm paralysed with, I realise — I'm just *paralysed*. Something's holding me in place. I can't breathe. I don't even need to breathe, but the inability to breathe is making me panic.

"*Melanie,*" I gasp out.

She doesn't answer me. She doesn't say anything, just staring at the crystals, her phone hanging almost forgotten from her hand.

Then I hear Ara's matter-of-fact tone from the speaker, and in spite of everything that's just happened in the last five minutes, I can't help feeling a sense of relief. Ara's matter-of-fact tone is familiar, and comforting, and it usually directly precedes everything becoming alright again.

Melanie listens, nodding quietly to herself. "No," she says, "no pictures, but — I mean, I could probably put it back the way it was? But there needs to be an unbroken display case first. ... Yeah, but I won't be able to get the window shut without Roy, so if anyone knows the window shouldn't be open, then — yes. I used the window. Why *wouldn't* I have used the window. ... Could we maybe *not* tell the police officers? — I know, but Ara, it's a *crime* to — look, I almost didn't even call *you*, and I really super duper do not want to go to jail. Can it please just be the two of us? Please? ... Okay, yeah. I'll be right there."

She hangs up, stares at the crystals for one moment longer, then heaves out a sigh and heads for the window.

She's clambered all the way back down to the ground floor porch before I'm finally able to move, which, in this case, means crashing unceremoniously down to the carpet below me. It hurts, but I almost don't notice, because I can *breathe*, and I can *move*, and as long as those two things hold true I can make sure things end up okay. Or at least, not badly. Not *terribly*.

What if I get the urge to kill someone *now*, and I can't warn anyone?

That's not a helpful thought, and Melanie's getting further away.

I take a deep breath, close my eyes, and sink through the floor to the kitchen underneath it. Then I walk out through the front door, and hurry to catch up with Melanie several metres down the street.

CHAPTER TWENTY

Restock

I try assessing myself while I follow Melanie to the train station. Do I feel any different? My eventual, frustrating conclusion is: no, I really don't. I'm still putting one foot in front of the other, I'm still level and solid and whole, and the world still looks the same to me. My memory's still intact — at least as far as I can tell. Everything Melanie said has made sense.

So what changed? Why am I suddenly invisible again? Will I be invisible to Ara, too? Will I get to the hospital and have to watch her gaze pass sightlessly over me like I'm not even there?

I don't know if I could stand that.

328

What else can I try? I eye Melanie's shoulder just ahead of me. Can I still *affect* her, just enough for her to know that I'm still here? I take a moment to make absolutely sure I'm not feeling any compulsion to kill her, and then I take a deep breath and quickly tap her shoulder.

My finger goes right through her jumper, like I knew it would. Melanie gasps in surprise and spins on the spot. "*Roy?*"

"Yes," I answer desperately. "I'm here! Can you hear me?"

She doesn't answer. Seconds pass by in utter silence.

"Okay," Melanie says slowly. "If you *are* there, do that again."

I do it again, more quickly this time, just to be sure I'm not causing any damage. Melanie cringes, then abruptly grins. "You're still here! Oh thank *god*, you're still here. I'm so sorry, Roy, I didn't mean to do that, I thought we lost you just like last time —"

"It's fine," I try to interrupt her, but of course, she doesn't hear me.

"— and I really, *really* didn't mean to scream, you're really not that scary, I promise, it was just — *startling*, I guess,

329

you'd think years of watching horror movies would have actually *taught* me something —"

"*Melanie* —"

"— and, okay, fine, so it *was* scary, but I still knew it was you, I still should have —"

I tap Melanie's shoulder again. She cuts off with a pained grunt, then shakes her head and laughs. "Yeah, I'm getting hysterical again, aren't I?"

I smile. "Little bit."

"Okay. Okay. I… okay. What we need to do, right now, is go see Ara. They're letting her go, but only if someone comes to pick her up, so that's what I'm doing. I'll catch her up on you still being, you know, alive. And we can swing by Lavinder's room before we leave, 'cause maybe if Ara and I can't hear you anymore, Lavinder will still be able to… imagine-hear you, or whatever the hell he does."

It sounds like a good plan to me. It obviously sounds like a good plan to Melanie, too, because she nods to herself once and sets off again, looking far less lost and much more determined.

~~

It's weird, watching Ara rolled into the

waiting room on a wheelchair. I've never seen her looking that vulnerable, and I can't help feeling like it's my fault, whether Dowlen has some supernatural control of me or not.

It helps, though, that the moment all the paperwork is finalised and Ara is officially discharged, she *immediately* brightens and stands up easily with all the force of presence she's always had. "I could get *used* to that," she tells us cheerfully, gesturing at the wheelchair. "I'm gettin' on in years, you know. Being pushed everywhere makes me feel like a queen."

"You'd probably change your mind if it wasn't your choice anymore," says Melanie.

"Of course I'd change my mind if it wasn't my choice anymore. You think I'd let them do that to me if they were *forcing* it on me? Don't be ridiculous." Ara claps her hands. "Now, on to more important things. Roy's here, Melanie, right next to you. So you didn't break anything beyond repair, see?"

"Yeah, I know."

Ara pauses. "Really? How?"

"You know that thing you said Roy did to communicate with Lavinder and the Ouija board? It did that to me. It's still *here*, I just

331

can't hear it anymore."

Ara looks impressed. "Hey, nice job, Roy."

"Thanks," I say, even though neither of them hear it. I thought Ara might still be able to — or at least, *hoped* she might still be able to — but she doesn't look at me, doesn't nod, doesn't react. Seemingly all she has left is her gut feeling, that sixth sense of my presence.

I remember when that sixth sense of my presence was the only thing keeping me sane. I remember looking *forward* to it, to making long journeys across the globe all the way back to Ara's flat outside of London just so I could feel like someone wanted me there. Now, it rings hollow. It's so strange how much can change in just a couple of weeks, especially since I'm used to spending years and *years* experiencing no change at all.

"Now, I need to go home," Ara announces, "because I need to do some research. I got some books that might help us out here. Mel, you're comin' with me, because you saw the study and all the objects in it, and you might recognise something from the study if you saw it

again. Roy, you're stickin' like *glue* to
Lavinder. We all clear on that? Roy, stay for
yes, leave and come back for no."

I step into the emergency hallway, then
back in again. If they're going to be doing
research on who I am, then I bloody well
want to *be* there.

Ara shakes her head. "Roy, you're most
useful with someone who can actually
communicate with you, and if what
Lavinder said before is true, then he should
still be able to. He can warn us if you have
to kill again. I will call you both
immediately if and when we discover
something. Cross my heart."

"Actually, about that," Melanie pipes up.
"If Roy had to try and kill Lavinder — that
was *after* Dowlen got hospitalised, right? So
how did Dowlen control that?"

"Search me," Ara said with a shrug.
"Maybe the amulet's got a time-delay."

"Or maybe we're wrong, and someone
else has it."

Ara doesn't answer that. All three of us
are uncomfortably quiet for several seconds;
then Ara draws herself up with a deep
breath, and grins. "See, Roy? All the more
reason for you to stick to Lavinder. We need

a detective to track down who would possibly *benefit* from all the people you've tried to kill in the past two weeks. Make sense? Stay for yes, leave for no."

With a huge effort, I stay right where I am.

"Good! We've got a plan then. Come along, Melanie."

Melanie groans. "Sure, on the one condition that you don't make me feel like I'm some little kid growing up in the 50s."

"I told them you're my granddaughter, so *act* like it."

"Me? Your granddaughter? *Really?*"

"Stranger things have happened, and they bought it, so stop griping and let's *go*."

Ara links her arm with Melanie's as they head out of the hospital, and I stare after them, feeling more unbearably lonely than ever before.

CHAPTER TWENTY-ONE
Responsibility

The moment I step into Casey's room and see that he's awake, chatting amicably with Mike, I start speaking, because part of me is convinced that Casey will also completely fail to hear me in any way, shape, or form, and panic is starting to drive my every thought.

"Casey," I tell him quickly, "I went to go see Dowlen's townhouse, and I think I found where the object I'm bound to is kept, only it's missing, and I think I screwed things up somehow because now one of the display cases is broken and Melanie and Ara can't hear or see me anymore, and Ara suggested that —"

"Stop, stop, stop." Casey rests his head in

one hand. "Roy, stop. I can't understand you when you're going that fast. I can barely understand you when you're going nice and slow. Start again?"

He can understand me. My metaphorical heart might be racing, but the relief I feel is palpable. I take a long breath, and force myself to smile. "Promise me you're not going to get mad?"

"I don't ever get mad."

"Promise me you won't arrest anyone?"

Casey blinks. "Why?"

"Because someone might have done something a little bit illegal."

"Roy, even if I could prove you exist, I don't think I have the authority to arrest —" Casey pauses for a moment, and then sighs. "Melanie broke into the townhouse, didn't she?"

"You haven't promised not to arrest anyone yet."

"Melanie did *what!*?" Mike is on his feet now, eyes on Casey, gaze boring into his partner's like he's trying to see *me*. "Where is she?"

"Look," I say desperately, "I'm not confirming or denying that Melanie had anything to do with it, okay? But the

situation *right now* is that the object I'm
bound to is missing, I screwed up what I
think was a really delicate supernatural
balance of some kind, and now Melanie and
Ara can't hear or see me anymore."

Casey shakes his head. "One point at a
time, Roy. One thing at a time. The more
you bring up, the less sure I am that I'm not
just imagining it."

So we try again, and I take it slow, point
by point, with Casey repeating most of what
I say both for Mike's benefit and so I can
confirm that he's got it right. It takes longer
than I want, but I force myself to be patient,
because it's not like I have anywhere to *be*
anyway. I leave Melanie out of the
explanation as much as I possibly can,
which doesn't for a second fool Casey, but
thankfully he doesn't press the issue.

I get the feeling Mike *would*, if they had
any evidence beyond the word of a ghost.

When I finally finish, Casey pushes
himself up on his pillows to rearrange how
he's sitting, and takes a notepad and pencil
off the nightstand. "If Ara's doing the
supernatural detective work," he says, "we're
going to do the rest."

"The *real* detective work," Mike mutters.

"Sure. So we're looking for a killer. We're looking for a killer the same way we'd look for a killer if they hired a hitman to do the job for them. We have to prove intent and motive."

"Does the killer even know they're a killer?" Mike says. "For all we know, they don't believe in ghosts and shit either."

"And if everyone *you* idly wished was dead turned up dead over ten whole years, would you turn a blind eye?" I ask.

"Roy's pretty sure they know," Casey translates for me.

"Yeah, *Dowlen* knows, sure, I think we established that with all the shit in his study. But I thought the point of this is that if Dowlen had the object up until he went into a coma, then who tried to kill Casey? Do *they* believe in ghosts and shit? Do they have any idea what they're doing?"

I don't say anything.

Casey nods to himself. "You're right," he says. "I'm the one that doesn't fit. Who else doesn't fit?"

"Melanie," I say immediately. "That felt weird to me, even at the time. She's too young. She was *easily* the first person I've had to kill that young."

"The first kid?"

Maybe it's because my memories, when I
have them, only stretch eighteen years —
eight as a living human being and ten as a
vengeful ghost — but the word choice
makes me bristle. "The first *young person*,
yeah. *And* she survived. The only reason
you and Ara survived is that you were both
in the hospital. Melanie wasn't anywhere
near. She's the — she's the only person I
know of who didn't die."

Casey notes that down. "So let's assume
that's where things changed. Let's assume
that's where the object changed hands."

"Voluntarily?" asks Mike. "Did Dowlen
give it to someone, or did someone steal it?
Also, I know this isn't your forte, but you've
got to talk more, Casey. I can't hear the
bloody thing."

Casey smiles sheepishly. "Sorry. Melanie
didn't die, and that's unusual. It's also
unusual that she was so young. So Melanie
is probably where things changed. Maybe
when the amulet gets a new owner, it has
to... warm up, or something. Maybe it isn't
as potent as it usually is."

"Who else was there, past Melanie?" asks
Mike.

"Ara," I say, and Casey belatedly repeats. "There was Melanie, and then there was Ara, and then there was Casey."

"What about Dowlen's brother?" Mike makes an effort to look everywhere *but* at Casey, and the sight of it makes me laugh a little. "Louis, the guy who killed Andrea Relshaw? You tried to kill him. You tried to kill Dowlen, too."

"Yeah, but neither of those were compulsions. I went after Louis because he had a gun, and Dowlen —" I pause. "Dowlen wasn't —" I stop again. "*Huh.*"

Casey frowns. "Roy?"

"I just... I thought it was me, choosing to, both times, because it felt different, but — you said it yourself, Casey, Dowlen's the first person I actually *wanted* dead. Maybe the only reason it felt different was that it was personal. Maybe — maybe Dowlen was a compulsion too?"

Casey frowns, trying to process the words he doesn't hear. "So you think whoever has your amulet now, they tried to kill Dowlen's brother and Dowlen, too?"

"I don't know. Maybe. I can't tell. Maybe?"

Casey notes it down.

"So then the question is," Mike muses, "who wants to kill Dowlen and company, which would presumably make them a good guy, or at least a morally ambiguous guy, and *also* wants to kill a teenage girl, a cop, and a fortune-teller?"

"Someone without much ability to plan," Casey murmurs.

"Or someone who doesn't *know* that they're —"

"I think they wanted to hurt Melanie," I interject. "I think they meant to, but they didn't want to kill her. Maybe the object can do that."

Casey relays my theory, and Mike nods absentmindedly. "Okay. Question remains, though. Who would have reason to want all those people hurt or dead?"

No one says anything for several minutes.

"Maybe we're coming at it from the wrong angle," says Casey. "Roy, you said when you tried to kill Dowlen the same way you tried to kill his brother, there was some kind of wall or force surrounding his heart, right?"

Mike rolls his eyes. "Oh, sure, let's take the *magic* angle. Let's look at the one thing no one fucking understands."

"Yes," I answer, ignoring Mike.

"Have you felt anything like that before? With anyone else?"

"No." I pause. "Wait. Yes."

"Who?"

"Melanie's father. He was visiting her in the hospital, and Sam was there, and there was a heavy weight around him, and I didn't pay it any attention because I thought it was just a weight between him and Sam, people are like that sometimes when there's a lot of bad history, but — it was *really strong*, and I couldn't get through it, and —"

"One thing at a time, Roy, remember? Did you say Melanie's father?"

I swallow. "Yes."

"You tried to kill Melanie's father?"

"No. It was in the air around him. I couldn't get through it."

"Like Dowlen's heart?"

"Yeah."

Casey taps his pencil against the edge of his notepad. "Do you know his name?"

"Sorry, no."

"You said Melanie's with Ara?"

"Yep."

"Mike, my phone, please."

Mike makes absolutely no objections or

comments whatsoever, and passes Casey his phone, and the two of us stay quiet while Casey calls Ara and the phone rings out.

"Ara," he says, after what feels like much too long, "it's Lavinder. Can you ask Melanie what her father's name is? … Roy and I think there's a good chance he has the amulet."

Melanie's father. I don't know much about him, apart from what Melanie's told me. I haven't really *thought* much about him. He sounds vindictive enough to wish Ara dead for no reason other than disliking her, but Casey? And *Melanie* — why would he want to hurt his own daughter, if he's trying to make amends to her? Just to get back at Sam? Is Melanie's heart attack something he regrets, or *would* regret, if he knew it was his fault? If he stole the amulet from Dowlen, does he know what the amulet *does*?

Too many questions, and not nearly enough answers. I pace up and down the room while Casey talks, full of nervous energy, standing somewhere on the precipice between action and panic.

~~

Jason Foulk.

That's the name Melanie gives Casey over

343

the phone. Ara demands to know what Casey plans to do; Casey promises he'll get back to her, and before he even hangs up, Mike has his own phone out, asking a colleague to do a background check on Jason Foulk.

"Still with us, Roy?" Casey asks quietly while Mike talks.

I nod. "Yeah. I'm still here."

"You okay?"

"Kind of." I hesitate. "Mostly, I'm just trying to convince myself that going into Dowlen's head like I did with you is a very bad idea."

Casey's head jerks, his eyes wide. "You *what*?"

"I know, I know, I'm not going anywhere. I don't even know what room he's in."

"Do you even know how you did it with me?"

"No."

"Do you know how you'd get out again?"

"Just — the same way I did with you."

"You know Dowlen would wake up and remember it —" Casey pauses. "And — just to check, you *did* say you're thinking about diving into Dowlen's head, didn't you? I'm not imagining that?"

"I said I'm trying to convince myself not to."

Casey sighs and pushes both hands through his hair. "For my sake, please don't."

I can't help smiling. "Well, as a favour to *you...*"

Mike thanks the colleague he's talking to and hangs up. "I knew it," he says with an air of finality. "Jason Foulk's a criminal. He's been booked before."

Casey looks at him. "For what?"

"Possession with intent to distribute, assault and battery, lots of small-time stuff. You know, relatively speaking, compared to *murder.* Divorced, lost custody of his kids, unemployed. Blames his ex and son for pretty much everything. Ticks nearly every single box for branching out into attempted murder, don't you think?"

"What about opportunity?" Casey asks. "We don't know if he had any way of finding out I'm investigating Andrea Relshaw's murder, and even if he did, why would he be trying to protect Dowlen's brother?"

"Melanie said he's always been into shady stuff," I point out. "Maybe he works for

Dowlen."

Mike, who still can't hear or perceive me in any way, says: "We don't know for sure he *cares* about Relshaw. He might not even know what he's got his hands on. He might be idly wishing for things, and have no idea that's hurting anybody, 'cause no one's actually *died* yet. And — why would he deliberately want to hurt his daughter, anyway?"

"Leverage?" Casey suggests. "He might have been planning to blackmail her or her brother with it."

"Blackmail his own *daughter*?"

"She doesn't live with him, Mike. Hasn't for a while. Blackmail, or a guilt trip, or a chance to reconnect, or even to threaten her brother. Not all parents care about what's best for their children."

Mike opens his mouth, snaps it shut, and nods grimly. "Okay. Fine. What's the motive for Ara?"

"He was angry at her," I say immediately. "The second time I went to see Melanie, Ara was with me, and Melanie had to send him out of the room because he was so angry about her visiting."

Casey relays this to Mike, who frowns

and shakes his head. "That won't fly in court."

"We're not talking about court, we're talking about magic."

"*Magic*, for fuck's sake — I was angry at the woman, too, remember, and I sure wasn't planning on killing her."

"It didn't need to be a plan. Just a wish."

"Jesus *Christ*, Casey —"

Casey waits, but Mike doesn't finish the thought. Instead, he blows out a breath, hands hooked together behind his head, and closes his eyes. "Okay. Angry dude, anger management issues, wishing that someone was dead. Why *you*?"

"If Roy's right, and he works for Dowlen, maybe Dowlen told him to. Maybe he was there, when we paid Dowlen a visit, hiding upstairs."

"*All* of that assumes he knows exactly what the fuck he's got, and exactly how the fuck it works."

"Let's ask him."

"Not *now*, you idiot, you're recovering from a goddamn *heart attack*."

"Mike, if he knows what he's got, how much longer do you think we have before —?"

Almost as if the universe was just waiting for the right moment to play an ironically cruel joke, my head starts to swim, and the urge to kill pulls me in the direction of the door.

I go to stand on the opposite side of the bed from the door, straining against the pain it sets right behind my eyes, and press my palm to my forehead. "Casey?"

He stops immediately. "Roy?"

"It's happening. Right now."

"Who?"

"I don't know," I answer. I feel the pull getting stronger, the pain behind my eyes getting worse, and I have to lean heavily against the bed as though some wind might drag me out of the room otherwise. "I don't know, but whoever it is, it's — it's *bad*, it feels like Jason Foulk's going to try to take matters into his own hands —"

I can't *possibly* know for sure, I can't possibly *prove* that someone will die even if I manage to stay here and do nothing, but for once that doesn't seem to matter. Casey looks directly at Mike, wearing the sort of expression he'd never worn when he was a kid — determination, drive, purpose. "Roy says we've got one, and Foulk might be there in person. Are you going to help me get dressed so we can go stop a murder, or tell the doctors to lock me in here instead?"

Mike hesitates. "I can stop a murder without you."

"You can't talk to Roy."

Painful seconds stretch out while Mike struggles furiously with his answer; then he swears loudly and goes to toss Casey's clothes at him. "If you drop dead while we're out," he says, "I'm making Roy and Ara do the paperwork, and I'm kicking your ass three ways from Sunday."

Casey gives him a light smile. "Sounds good to me."

CHAPTER TWENTY-TWO

Retribution

Casey tries to call Ara as we walk quickly outside, but the call goes straight to voicemail. He asks me if, by any chance, I know Melanie's number. I tell him I don't. Casey doesn't express any concern about why Ara didn't answer, but I can see that concern written plainly all over his face, and the only reason neither of us mention it is that murder *needs* to be higher on the priority list.

Mike laughs, and doesn't stop laughing for several minutes, gesturing ambiguously in front of us. "It's like in Hollywood," he explains, once he has some breath back. "Seances, and all that shit. It's never just 'sure, here's who killed me, here's exactly what I want, here's the exact phone number you need to call, here's the exact place you need to go'. It's always vague. Always the bloody rotten hand pointing in the vague direction of a mass burial. Why the fuck would a ghost know a phone number? It can't even tell us who it's meant to kill."

"Nope," I agree, keeping stubbornly cheerful. "That would be too easy."

"And remind me again why we can't take the bloody car?"

"Roy doesn't know where to go in the car," Casey answers, quickly and with only the slightest hint of exasperation colouring the edge of his words.

"We could be going halfway across London!"

"We could also be going to Africa," I say absently.

"Does that happen?" Casey asks, startled. "Do you get pulled halfway across the *globe*?"

"Sure. It doesn't matter how long it takes me to get there, just that I keep moving in the right direction."

Casey translates, and Mike scoffs. "That's a bit of a useless kill switch, isn't it? You want someone dead, and it takes them months to actually die. What's the point of that?"

"Learning patience," says Casey.

"So it wouldn't suit *me* at all, then."

"But if the cold-blooded murder was instantaneous, *that* would suit you?"

"Look — shut up."

I laugh, in spite of everything. Casey gives that small smile that I know means he's laughing, too.

I can't help but be a little bit excited. I don't know where we're going, or what's going to happen when we get there, or how we're possibly going to stop me from killing whoever the latest victim is, but for the first time in ten years, I almost don't care. It feels like I'm going on an adventure with friends, and with two *police* officers to boot. It feels like I have backup. Unconditional support. I don't need the memories of an abusive upbringing to recognise that unconditional support is something I have never, *ever* had in my life before. In *any* version of my life.

Whenever we're not on the move — like, for instance, when we're on the train — Mike shifts uncomfortably on the spot, full of adrenaline, anxious and eagle-eyed. He points to the overhead map several times

and swears to Casey that we're on a route
headed for the airport, and need he remind
us they don't have jurisdiction in any
African country, and also how come I know
exactly where to go on public transport but
not in the car or at the very least in a taxi?
Neither Casey nor I have answers for him,
and although he couldn't possibly have been
expecting any answers, he looks sullen and
bitter all the same.

We don't end up at the airport. We end up
on the other side of a large park, nearly
twenty minutes away from the hospital,
where a row of dilapidated apartment
buildings greets us across from the bus stop.

"Straight down here," I tell Casey, as we
pass one of the looming council estate
buildings. "And a left at the end, I think."

"You know," Mike says conversationally,
"I don't think we have jurisdiction here,
either."

Casey shrugs lightly. "We're just visiting a
friend."

"We can't exactly say we've prevented a
murder when we have absolutely no
evidence a murder's going to occur."

"Right. So we're just visiting a friend.
Maybe taking that friend to the hospital, if

they look ill enough."

Mike subsides with an unsatisfied grumble, and we keep walking.

"We're getting close," I say, several minutes later, as we stand outside a run-down apartment block. "Whoever it is, they're in there."

"See?" Casey tells Mike. "Not Africa. We're fine."

"We're most definitely *not* fine, but sure, you're right. Things could always be worse."

A few seconds pass, during which nothing worse happens. Mike and Casey both breathe audible sighs of relief, and I direct Casey up the stairs to one of the doors in particular.

He pauses right at the foot of the steps. "Roy, should you stay out here?"

I stop. I didn't think of that. How on *earth* didn't I think of that? I felt nothing while we were moving, but now that I've stopped, I can feel the pain settling in again, and it is *boggling* to me that I forgot about it for even a minute. "Yes. Definitely."

"Can you tell me which apartment it is?"

I look up at the windows, but nothing more specific drifts into my mind. I squeeze my eyes shut. "No."

"Can you come far enough to tell me which apartment it is, then go back outside?"

I grimace. "Maybe. It'll hurt."

"I've got a better idea," says Mike. "Let's get everyone to come out here, and have ambulances already on the way."

"How on earth are we going to do that?" asks Casey.

"Fire alarm."

Casey blinks, smiles, and looks into the distance past Mike. "Would that work, Roy?"

"It wouldn't be any *worse*," I decide.

"I'm making the executive decision," says Mike. "Wait here, I'll be back in a sec."

He vanishes into the building, and less than a minute later, the sound of a fire alarm pierces the quiet sunny afternoon.

~~

"What the fuck do you *mean*, it's not any of them?"

Mike stares furiously at Casey, like Casey is the one telling him none of the apartment dwellers milling around on the pavement across the street are the next victim, which — technically he is, but Mike really needs to learn not to shoot the messenger.

"It's not," I repeat. "Whoever it is, they're

still inside."

Casey translates. Mike does not look any less furious. "*Why*?"

"Why would I know?" I demand. Pain is starting to make it hard for me to think.

"Alright," Casey says, quietly and reasonably, "so it's back to Plan A. Roy?"

I stare at the building's windows. Something isn't sitting right with me, but I can't tell what it is.

"Roy?"

It feels almost like *deceit*. Like something has happened here that should *not* have happened, and if it were my choice, I'd break the contract right here. That's weird; is that me, or is that the big scary thing I argued with yesterday, the ancient formless *thing*? How on earth am I supposed to be able to tell?

"*Roy*."

I start. "What? Yes. Sorry. What?"

Casey's eyes narrow with concern. "You okay?"

"Yeah, I'm fine. Just — something's wrong."

"Something's wrong?"

"I don't know what. Something happened that shouldn't have happened."

"Like what?"

"If I knew, I would have *led* with that, Casey."

"Can you tell if Jason Foulk is in there?"

"No."

Casey nods and looks at Mike. "Roy says something's wrong, but doesn't know what. We're going in."

Mike nods. "Right behind you."

Casey and Mike follow me into the building. I could let the tether pull me where I need to go with my eyes closed, but this time, I keep them *wide* open. The fire alarm is still going, still boring into my awareness, and I can see the silver handle on the wall where Mike must have pulled it. It's the staircase we need, though, and I narrate that out loud to Casey, so he can follow me where I'm going.

It's slower than I like. Directions are hard, with Casey. The way he explained it on the way here, when there are two alternatives and I'm directing him towards one, it's far too easy for him to imagine I'm also directing him towards the other one. He has to repeat what I say out loud, so I can confirm or deny for him. Up one flight of stairs, and then it takes precious minutes to coax him up the *second* flight of stairs instead of down the corridor, and then he wants to continue going up the stairs when I'm being tugged down the hall instead. Still, we get there in the end, and then we're standing outside a door with a silver seven painted into the peeling wood.

"Here?" says Casey.

I nod. "Here."

Casey beckons to Mike. "Can you still go outside, Roy?"

Once again, I didn't think of that, but this time — "No."

"Can you stay here?"

I test the idea in my mind, like testing a little bit of chocolate on the tip of your tongue to make sure it tastes as good as everyone says it does. "Yes."

"Good."

With a nod, Mike knocks hard on the door. "Police, open up."

The alarm continues to ring, and there's no sound of anyone moving on the other side of the door.

Mike raises his voice again. "We have reason to believe someone's still in here. There's a fire, and you need to evacuate right *now*. If you don't open this door, we'll

358

need to force our way in."

I know who it is, on the other side of the door, even before he opens it. I can tell because an intangible force pushes me back against the opposite wall, like a gentle but inexorable wave in the ocean. I struggle to move through it, and utterly fail, and then he opens the door and meets Mike's gaze without a flicker of recognition. "What?" he says. "What do you want?"

It's Jason Foulk, Melanie and Sam's father.

"Sir," says Mike, with the sort of patience that only comes with long years of practice dealing with stubborn members of the public, "as you can hear, there's a *fire*. Are you the only one in the apartment?"

"He's not," I say. I'm being pulled *past* him, into the flat. "His victim's in there. Casey, *his victim's in there.*"

"Yeah," Jason says, oblivious to me. "Just me here —"

His gaze falls on Casey, and *there's* a flicker of recognition. Also some fear, if I'm not very much mistaken. He cuts off, swallows visibly, and tries again. "Look, officers, the alarm goes off all the goddamn time, it's nothing. I'm not leaving."

Mike glances at Casey. Casey carefully and subtly shakes his head, then tilts it past Melanie's father. Mike gets the message immediately, and when he turns on the man again, it's with far less self-possession and a lot more anger. "Sir," he says, "step aside."

"What?"

"We're coming in." With that brief warning, Mike shoulders his way through into the apartment; he's a big man considerably taller than Jason, so even when Jason tries to grip Mike's upper arm to stop him, it works about as well as trying to stem a spurting water leak with only a fingertip.

Casey follows after; he doesn't have the force of presence Mike does, but he knows exactly how to use his natural humility to slip past someone who doesn't want him there. By the time Jason turns back to the doorway, Casey's already inside, and Jason's gaze passes sightlessly over me before he grows an expression of absolute rage and slams the door shut.

I wait for the invisible force surrounding him to subside, and then I follow its edge as far as it'll let me, through the door and into the tiny sitting room.

Right away, I can tell this isn't *his* flat. For

one thing, it has too much personality in it; posters of bands and games on the wall, motivational cat pictures, hanging lights, bookshelves filled with actual books, video game consoles by the TV. For another thing, there's Sam, Melanie's brother, standing extremely carefully in one of the doorways, hands spread to his sides, breathing sharply and looking like nothing so much as a coiled spring ready to jump out the nearest window.

He looks *scared*. He didn't look scared of his father back in the hospital. Why is he scared now?

"Sam, isn't it?" says Mike, who, standing in the centre of the room, seems to take up at least half of the small space. "Melanie's brother?"

Sam looks at him, shock and confusion written plainly all over his face, and he doesn't say anything.

It's Sam, I realise with a start, *Sam* I'm drawn to, and I take several steps back towards the front door, wincing through the pain it presses into my head. But it's oddly *possible* for me to step back, where it's never been possible before; and again I get that feeling that something is *wrong*, that I'd break the contract if it were my choice, because *I'm* authorised for this and *no one else* is.

"I want you to get out of my flat," Jason snaps. "Right the hell *now*."

"*Your* flat?" Mike raises a sceptical eyebrow. "That's weird. This isn't the address we have on file for you. Breach of parole not to update that, right?"

"It's mine," Sam speaks up, his voice hoarse with fear, but quietly defiant. "It's my flat."

"Do you want this man here, Sam?" asks Mike.

"No."

"I don't blame you. Let's all go outside until the fire department gets here, sound good?"

"You're supposed to be *dead*."

Jason's voice, by contrast to his son's, is flat and shaking with barely constrained malice. Casey and Mike both look at him — and then they both go abruptly, worryingly still, which probably has something to do with the gun I belatedly notice Jason's got levelled right at Casey.

My breathing stops. Everything about me seems to stop. The last time this happened, I had to dive into the aggressor's heart to stop him, and I lost a week to that. I can't dive anywhere close to Jason now; not while that invisible wall surrounds him. There's nothing I can do, and the thought of that is killing me.

Metaphorically speaking. I think. I *hope*.

"Okay, mate," Mike says slowly. "You're about to make the dumbest mistake of your life. Put the gun down."

"Someone tell me where in the hell my daughter is!"

"Your daughter's fine," says Casey quietly. "I spoke to her less than an hour ago. What do you mean, I'm supposed to be dead?"

"You — it — you know *exactly* what I mean."

"I can make a good guess, but that's it." Casey holds his palms out in a supplicating gesture, and doesn't otherwise move a muscle. "What's the object you're using? Do you have it on you?"

"*Fuck* you."

"Why do you want to kill your own son?"

Silence falls heavy in the flat, broken only by Jason Foulk's panicked breathing.

"Jason," Casey goes on, still quiet, still perfectly calm, like they're all family having

363

a slightly heated argument rather than two police officers facing a man with a gun. "I understand most of what's going on, but I don't understand how or why you fit into things. Can you tell me what's been going on for you? Tell me how I can help."

"*Fuck you.*" Jason gestures angrily with the gun, aggressive enough to make everyone stiffen. "I'm just — I'm here to — I need to find Melanie, and this brat here is — *get the hell out of my flat.*"

"Jason, you know I can't do that. Not while you still have that gun. You have a decision to make here, and none of the rest of us are going to be able to make it for you. Either you shoot us, and you end up behind bars for the rest of your life, or you talk to me, and tell me what's going on. Why do you need to find your daughter?"

The next few seconds stretch into a ringing eternity. Everyone's feelings are so loud that I can almost *hear* them, threading into the cacophony of the fire alarm in the hallway outside. I swear if I put my hand to my chest, I'll feel a pounding heartbeat.

Then, incredibly, Jason actually *does* lower the gun. "It's this thing," he says, nearly all of the anger gone from his voice. "It's this fucking —" He pulls a chain around his neck out from under his shirt, and there's an amulet on it twinkling silver and gold in the light from the window.

"This thing makes you do it," Jason goes on desperately. "Spencer didn't tell me it *makes* you do it. You don't understand. I'm — shit, I'm a lot of things, but I'm no killer, I don't want to *have* it, but I can't give it up, you don't understand, *I can't get rid of it.*"

I thought I'd feel something, seeing the object for the first time. I thought my awareness would narrow to a laser point, like it did when Dowlen's brother showed up at Ara's flat with a gun, or that I'd get all tingly, or — *something.* Instead, it just looks like a normal amulet, dangling from a thin chain. It's an oval with four small holes in its centre, simple and unadorned. Completely unremarkable. If I didn't *know* I was bound to it, I wouldn't have given it a second glance. Maybe that'll be different if I touch it.

"Can you give it to me now?" Casey asks. "You can end this, right here."

Jason violently shakes his head and drops the amulet back under his shirt. "No."

"You're not a killer, Jason — you haven't

killed anyone. Not Melanie, not Ara, not me. It's not too late for you to turn this around."

It is too late. It's *far* too late. I look at Sam standing in the doorway, a kid who definitely doesn't see *family* holding that gun, definitely doesn't see someone he feels any obligation or responsibility or even pity towards. It's far too late, for Sam. It's probably too late for Melanie. Jason screwed them both up permanently, and I don't understand why Casey is lying to him when he's holding a *gun*.

I try inching towards him, but that same inexorable force holds me back.

"I *can't*," Jason says desperately.

"You didn't have to show it to me," says Casey. "But you did. You're stronger than that amulet is. You *want* to get rid of it, Jason. You can do it. I promise, you can do it."

For a moment, I'm overcome by how quiet and calm Casey has been this whole time. Casey's been through exactly the same thing Sam has, the same thing Melanie has, the same thing *I* did. And yet, here he is, offering someone who perpetuated that sort of abuse hope, offering someone like that

redemption, and I can't tell if that's strength
forged from inner fire or if it's simply a con,
to try and get everyone out safe. I can't tell if
I'm proud of him, or angry and betrayed.
Probably I'm some of both.

For a moment, Jason falters, and I can
almost see him taking Casey up on his offer.
He bites his lip, looks from Casey to Mike to
Sam, puts his hand over the amulet like he's
about to take it off. Then something
changes, and his fury returns, and then both
of his hands are on the gun again. "You just
want it for *yourself*," he snaps, "you *bastard!*"

If I had to describe what happened next, I
would not have been able to find the words.

In a timeline that never happens, but
which I can still see in slow, stark, and vivid
detail, Jason pulls the trigger with two
fingers. A bullet explodes out of the barrel
and sinks right into Casey's collarbone.
Casey staggers, blinks, and falls against the
wall. Sam goes straight for the window,
which doesn't have any kind of fire escape
on the other side, but he must have thought
his chances were better outside scaling the
face of the building than in here with his
father. Jason turns the gun on him, on his
own *son*, and pulls the trigger again, and a

second bullet explodes out of the barrel to graze Sam's arm just before he makes it out the window. If he still has the strength to hold on and climb safely down to street level, I don't see it. Jason doesn't move after that, because he's in too much pale-faced shock, and so Mike easily moves in, disarms him in one swift movement, and unloads the gun. Then he steps over to kneel next to Casey, calling for backup and EMTs right *now*.

None of that happens in the split instant I have to make a decision. But it's *about* to. I know that with all the surety that I know my own name. Jason made the decision to take matters into his own hands, to personally kill the person he ordered *me* to kill, and he followed through on that decision, which unequivocally breaks whatever contract he has with me and the amulet. The force surrounding him is gone. I can move. I could dive into his heart, I could stop him from *ever* pulling the trigger, kill him right here so he doesn't hurt anyone else ever again.

But I'm sick of killing.

What I do instead, I do immediately, with the absolute certainty it'll work. I step up, I put my hand over the amulet where it sits under Jason's shirt, grab his gun with my other hand, and force it up towards the ceiling, so that when Jason pulls the trigger, the bullet goes through the ceiling instead of Casey's neck.

Jason stares right at me, eyes wide with terror. Someone behind me calls my name — probably Casey — but for the moment, I ignore it. I don't think I have the solidity to disarm Jason like Mike did, so I force Jason's fingers down on the trigger again; bullet after bullet puts a small hole into the ceiling, until, after six shots, the gun clicks empty.

Then I move back into the doorway.

Mike takes my place in an instant to disarm and pin Jason against the wall. Casey takes the gun, checks it, and puts it down on the bureau. Sam, over by the window, does nothing; he just stares.

"Roy?" Casey looks wildly around. "Roy, are you still here?"

"Yeah," I say. "Yeah. I'm here. Right here."

"How did you do that?"

"Uh, which part?"

Casey gestures. "*All* the parts."

I think about it for a moment, and then

shrug. "The amulet?"

With Jason pinned against the wall, Mike snaps the amulet right off the chain, and tosses it to Casey. "There you go," he says. "I'll pretend I never saw it. Go nuts."

"Thanks."

"Except don't, you know, *actually* go nuts. Don't wear it around your neck. If you start murdering people, I *am* going to find a way to book you for it."

In spite of everything, Casey smiles. "Duly noted."

"What," Sam says, quietly and with feeling, "the *fuck*, was that?"

"Kid," says Mike as he snaps handcuffs onto Jason's wrists, "I have no goddamn clue. Ask my partner."

"Probably best to wait for your sister to join us," Casey says. "I get the feeling you'll believe her before you believe any of the rest of us. Are you okay?"

Sam rubs his shoulder absently. "Yeah. Fine."

"You're shaking."

"I'm *fine*."

"Humour me, and come get yourself checked out."

"I'm *fine!*"

"If you come get yourself checked out, I'll tell you everything you want to know about what just happened."

Sam pulls up short, glares for a minute, and then sighs. "Sure. Okay. Whatever."

I stay behind for a few seconds as the others file out of the flat and over to the staircase. I look up at the bullet holes in the ceiling, where some tiny bits of plaster and dust are still dancing in the sunbeams through the window.

I just saved three lives without killing a single person.

I grin, and I can't stop grinning. I just *saved three people* without hurting *anyone else.*

Take *that*, any and all goddamn ambiguous spirits of vengeance!

~~

There's a lot of confusion outside the building for the next couple of hours.

Obviously, there was no actual fire, and it transpires that the fire alarm *does* go off every now and then for no reason, so the fire truck that arrives is prepared for a false alarm — except then there's six gunshots, and two police officers already on the scene, which, as you can probably imagine, results in a little bit of a mass panic. It takes a while for authorities to confirm that no one has been shot or injured, that the suspect is already in custody, and that those involved are being debriefed and assessed for any signs of shock.

That includes Casey. For as much as he called Sam out on being more affected than he claimed, the moment one of the EMTs lays eyes on Casey, one of those red emergency blankets is instantly on his shoulders and his vitals are being checked in the back of one of the ambulances on scene.

When he has a few moments to himself again, I sit down beside him. "Hey."

His head rises a little. "Roy?"

"Yep, it's me. I'm here. Sitting right next to you."

"Don't worry, I have the amulet." He takes his hand from his pocket to show me, where it's wrapped in a handkerchief so he doesn't touch it with his bare skin any more than he has to. "See? Safe and sound."

"You *are* going to give it to Ara, right?"

"Absolutely. I love you, but I'm not willing to risk whatever murderous possession Jason was under."

"You what?"

"Mike reckons you need to be wearing it,

but I'm not taking any chances."

"No, not that bit, I mean — you said you —"

For some reason, I can't repeat it, but Casey seems to understand anyway. He smiles sadly down at the amulet in his hand. "Of course. You're my brother, aren't you?"

Neither of us say anything for the next minute, as bustle and confusion continues to swirl around us.

"Can we go back to the house?" I ask quickly, before I lose the nerve. "Where we lived? Would you take me there?"

"Why?"

"I still don't remember much. I think it would help to walk around where it — where it happened."

Casey doesn't answer at first; then he sighs. "Well, I was planning to take some time off after this. I don't see why not." He pauses. "No, I see *exactly* why not, but — for you, yes."

For you, yes. Warmth seeps through every bit of my conscious awareness. "Thank you."

"You're welcome."

It takes a while longer for me to build up the nerve to ask my next question. "So — Jason saw me, at the end there."

"Did he?"

"He did. He looked right at me. Did you — see anything?"

All I can think of is Melanie's scream, back in Dowlen's study. Her hurried explanation later, to Ara and to me, that she'd been startled by my appearance — that I'd appeared as something terrifying to her.

Casey doesn't answer. I wait, because not immediately answering 'no' is basically my answer already and Casey might be willing to elaborate on that, but the seconds stretch on and he says nothing.

"Casey?"

"Here." He holds the amulet out in front of him. "Do what you did back there."

"I'm sitting next to you, remember?"

"Oh." Casey shifts and holds the amulet out to his side instead.

"Other side."

He laughs a little, and shifts again. "Here?"

"Yep." I stare down at the amulet nestled in its handkerchief. "Why?"

"Trust me."

"Oh, if *that's* all..." I reach out, slowly, half expecting to bump up against that guardian force again, but nothing happens

until I put my fingers over the small oval.
Like a switch was flipped, Casey's gaze
snaps right to mine, and for a moment time
stands still as we stare at each other.

Then Casey smiles, and it lights up his
whole face, and I wish I could hold onto it
forever. "It's like looking in a mirror," he
says, and puts one hand gingerly on my
shoulder, where it rests solidly like I'm a
real person with real substance.

I can see my own shoulder, I realise with
a start. I can see it. I can *see* it.

"How?" I ask weakly — and my free hand
goes straight to my mouth, because for the
first time, I can hear my own voice, I can
hear my own voice, and it almost *hurts*, and it
highlights just how much I didn't *exist*
before this, just how much my imagined
idea of who I was clashes with who I
actually am right here and right now.

"*How?*" I repeat through clenched fingers.

"We'll ask Ara when she gets here," Casey
answers. "Right now, I don't care." Then he
pulls me, gently but firmly, into a hug.

I don't go through him. He doesn't go
through me. He's warm, and solid, and
comforting. There's a memory that wraps
around my mind, a wish that a terrified

younger me made, certain Casey was in danger and wishing that either he or I could teleport to where the other one was so we could cling to each other and never let go again.

Until an EMT walks up several minutes later, neither of us let go.

"Mr Lavinder, I just need to —" The woman cuts off with a start. "Sorry, I didn't mean to interrupt."

Casey pulls back and looks over at her. "It's fine. What do you need?"

"Your vitals check out, so you're free to go, I just need you to sign something quickly. Was your brother in the building as well?"

"My — what?"

The woman looks directly at me. "Your — I'm sorry, I just assumed..."

I stare at her. My heart hammers in my chest. "You're — are you talking about *me*?"

"You look so alike, I just thought —"

"*Roy!?*"

I look past the EMT, to where Ara and Melanie are running over, and before I can even begin to try to think of anything to say, Ara's gripped me by the shoulders and crushed me into her arms. Melanie joins us, and then Casey is *forced* to join us because his hand is on top of mine over the amulet, and I finally understand what people mean when they say a good hug can leave you feeling breathless.

Reality waits on the other side of this moment, peppered with questions and mysteries and explanations and decisions, but this time, the moment isn't over until I say it's over. I stretch it out, encased in warmth and friendship and family, and for the first time in my ten years of existence — for the first time in *either* of my lives — I don't want to be anywhere except exactly where I am, with exactly the people I'm with.

CHAPTER TWENTY-THREE

Restrictions

It's extremely hard to say no to Ara when she decides you're going to be at her apartment later that evening for, in her own words, a big family Sunday dinner. Mike *tries* to say no, and eventually withers under her hard stare. Sam tries to say no, and Ara wins him over with the promise of answers and also chocolate cake for dessert.

It's not just dinner. It's also to work out, in relative privacy, how the amulet actually *works*. I have the presence of mind to wait until the EMT is out of sight before taking my hand off the amulet, and Ara, who still had a hand on my shoulder at the time, leaped back with a startled cry when I vanished and her hand sank through me

378

without warning. Ara unilaterally decides that it's in everyone's best interest to know exactly what the amulet's rules are, and no one dares argue with her.

Whatever Melanie and I did in Dowlen's study, for the moment it seems to be permanent. No one can hear me, and no one can see me. The only evidences I exist are Casey's vague awarenesses of the things I say, and Ara's sixth sense of my presence. When I speak, I can't hear my own voice anymore, and it takes everything I have to remember not to stand or sit near anyone else. It feels especially cruel, now that I've been so immersed in what having family could be like, to have to isolate myself again. Distance hurts, in a way it never used to hurt.

But, back in Ara's flat, we make several very important discoveries.

The first important discovery is that I can hold the amulet. It's painful for me, like holding a hot fire poker and a block of ice at the same time, but bearable for short periods. And when I'm holding the amulet, properly holding it, then *everyone* can hear me, and I can hear myself.

"You know all that 'guess what number

I'm thinking of' crap isn't *nearly* as impressive anymore, right?" Sam tells Melanie.

Melanie laughs. "Speak for yourself, you prick, I am going to *forever* treasure the memory of your face when you saw me doing that."

"Isn't it *creepy*, though?" asks Mike. "I still think it's thoroughly creepy. If anything, I think it's even *more* creepy now."

Sam shrugs. "I think it was creepier when a demon appeared out of nowhere and saved our lives, but sure, whatever floats your boat."

"Oh, yeah, speaking of that, we're all agreed that's what happened, right? I don't know where this whole 'it looks exactly like Casey' thing comes from, 'cause what I saw looked like a bat straight out of hell. It's going to haunt my goddamn *nightmares*."

That was the second important discovery we made. If someone else touches the amulet at the same time I do, then I become *visible* to everyone, and what I look like changes depending on who it is. When Casey's hand closes over mine, I look exactly like him. When Melanie does it, I look like —

"You know," Melanie says thoughtfully as she stares at me, "I think I could get used to it."

I blink. "You screamed and shoved me into a display case."

"Well, excuse *me* for having some very healthy self-preservation reflexes the first time I see a monster-ghost. Now? I'm into it."

"You're insane," says Sam. He's also staring at me, and there's not a hint of morbid fascination in *his* expression, like there is in Melanie's. Just disgust.

Melanie grins. "Nah, I just play a lot of video games. Demonic appearance is relative. Hey, someone get me a mirror! Roy can see what they look like!"

"Nope," I say immediately. "I'm good, thanks."

"You sure?"

"I had a nightmare once already, I *really* don't want any more."

Melanie shrugs. "Suit yourself."

When Ara puts her hand on the amulet, the general consensus is that I look much more like a proper ghost. "And not a cheap knockoff costume either," Melanie says speculatively, studying me intently. "Like, the white sheet with the black holes for eyes? No, this is proper black mist. You're *vaguely* humanoid, but then the rest is just... blurry."

Mike points at me. "I like this one the best."

"*Seriously?*"

"It looks the closest to what some murderous spirit *should* look like, in my opinion, but with the added bonus of not giving me nightmares for the rest of my life."

Ara rolls her eyes and grins at me. "Men are cowards," she announces.

"So how come Lavinder gets the reflection, you get the ghost, and I get a demon?" Melanie asks.

"I haven't the foggiest," Ara tells her. "I can make some educated guesses, though. Here's my first educated guess: they're all Roy, in some form or other. Lavinder's related by blood, so he gets that side. I see the dead, and I see the truth of things, so I get the mix. Anyone else sees what the *amulet* does."

Melanie's eyes widen. "So we're seeing *death?*"

"Vengeance."

"Remind me never to hold a grudge

against anyone *ever again*." Melanie hesitates. "Also, don't let Sam touch the amulet. Ever."

Sam, who has stayed far away from it the entire afternoon, scoffs. "No arguments here."

"I'm keeping it," Ara decides.

"Why?" Casey asks. "We don't know if enough contact with it would make you... vengeful. It might make more sense to rotate it through a few of us instead."

"Anyone know who Rhamnousia is?"

No one answers. A few people exchange confused looks.

"That's why," Ara says smugly. "She's an ancient Greek goddess of retribution. Some people still worship her. Keeping vengeance in check means knowing the *history* of vengeance. Here are some more, see who can guess them: Thanatus? Letum? What about an Onryō? Anyone? No? Poena? Invidia? How about a glaistig? Petbe? Takhar? Váli? Víðarr? Ne —"

"You are *definitely* just making up words now," says Mike.

"I didn't make up a single goddamn word, you uneducated cockalorum. My point is, I know how to keep things like this safe, and

383

how to keep other people safe from *them*. And what I don't know, I'm in a much better position to find out than any of *you*. Besides — Dowlen found a way to make its effects more permanent, whether knowingly or completely by accident, and he's a complete buffoon, so I should be able to recreate it easily. With some research, I might even be able to put it under Roy's control, so it can reveal itself to whoever it wants."

I stare at her. "*Really?*"

"Sure. Dowlen's an idiot, and if *he* worked some shit out, you can bet your arse I'll work out *more*."

I could hug her. I almost do, before remembering that only Casey's touch on the amulet lets me do that. But whatever my smile looks like on the blurred form of a ghost, Ara can definitely see it, because she smiles back, beaming all warm and fond.

On the other side of the temporary dinner table, Mike clears his throat, drawing all eyes to him. "So," he says, awkwardly and clearly uncomfortable. "I — and bearing in mind, I haven't run this by Casey at all — and bearing in mind also that this stuff is terrifying and I don't want anything to do with any of it — I was thinking, it would be... really useful, having someone on the force who can walk through walls and eavesdrop on suspects. You know, on a... consulting basis. Unofficially. Case-by-case. You know, once in a while, when we get stuck. If you — if that's something you'd be. Interested in."

"Yes," I say instantly. "Yes. Please. *Yes*."

"Oh. Good. It's not — insane, then?"

"It's *very* insane, and I would *love* to help out."

Mike doesn't like looking at me no matter what, and he hasn't used my name once so far, so it's Casey he turns to for confirmation that it's not an insane idea. Casey just looks levelly back at him with his mouth quirked and head tilted slightly to the side. "I agree," he says simply.

"Great. I already regret making the offer, so we're off to a great start."

"Also," says Ara, raising her voice over the conversation, "*everyone* is coming to dinner here every single Sunday from now on. No exceptions, no excuses."

"What?" says Mike.

"*What*?" Sam echoes.

"Ara, I don't really think that's —"

Melanie starts.

Ara cuts them all off with a dramatic wave of one hand. "You two," she says, pointing at Melanie and Sam, "are kids. Mature kids, sure, but kids nonetheless. One night of free food a week. I ain't taking no for an answer. And *you* two," she points at Mike and Casey, "are married to your infernal jobs and probably don't cook for yourselves *nearly* often enough, so one night of free, good, healthy, nutritious food once a week."

Mike puffs up. "I am *not* married to my —"

"We have a spirit of vengeance here, concrete proof of ghosts and supernatural weirdness, and your first thought, your *very* first thought, was how you can use that to *solve your cases.*"

"What else are you supposed to do with it?" he demands defensively.

"Ara," I interrupt, "if it's all the same to you, I'm going to take my hand off the amulet now. It's starting to hurt."

Ara lifts her hand without a word, freeing mine, and then wraps the handkerchief back over the top of the amulet again. "What you're *supposed* to do," she says, having not taken her eyes off Mike once, "is have a mental breakdown —"

"Yep, did that —"

"— then examine and rearrange your religious beliefs and your ideas about spirituality and the afterlife —"

"Nope, not a chance —"

"— then have a good long cuddle with folks you love and want to protect —"

"I can't have a good long cuddle with everyone in my jurisdiction —"

"— and *then* you reaffirm your place in your family and you arrange to have a good full dinner with them once a week so you can all support each other and make the spirit of vengeance feel like it has just as much of a right to existence and family as everyone else."

"Lady Arabetta, this is *insane*."

"Family *is* insane! Doesn't stop most of 'em. It's not gonna stop us either. Now pipe down and eat your chocolate cake, cockalorum."

Mike opens his mouth, closes it again, and subsides. "Yes, ma'am."

"So we don't actually get a choice in this?" Sam demands sullenly.

"In getting unconditional love and

acceptance? Hell no. Want more dessert, Sam?"

Ara set me a place at the table, and that's where I've been sitting until now, but with the amulet hidden I stand up and retreat over to the sofa where I can see everyone. It's familiar, having some distance, and now that I know I can have that warmth and closeness and friendship whenever I want, I have to take a distant moment to bask in the whole picture.

Sam's arguing with Ara. It's a sign of respect, for him, which is not in the least bit obvious, because he's more likely to dismiss and ignore someone than to argue with them. Mike's arguing with Casey, or *trying* to argue with Casey, and failing because Casey is just watching him with a smile rather than engaging back. Melanie's offering comments in both discussions as she feels are warranted, and in the middle of them all, nestled in a handkerchief on top of the table, me.

I have a family.

I'm excited about the future.

My world has grown bigger than I *ever* could have imagined, and I can't wait to experience every single new thing it has to offer.

THE END

Thanks for reading! If you want to be the first to hear news about the sequel, please sign up for my newsletter emails at http://www.amariamson.com.

www.ingramcontent.com/pod-product-compliance
Lightning Source LLC
Chambersburg PA
CBHW030221120726
47903CB00005B/1321